IN THE KING'S NAME

The Bolitho Novels by Alexander Kent

Alexander Kent

In the King's name

the Bolitho novels: 28

McBooks Press, Inc.

www.mcbooks.com

ITHACA, NY

Published by McBooks Press 2012
Copyright © 2011 Highseas Authors Limited
First published in the United Kingdom by Century, Random House, 2011

Cover Painting: Geoffrey Huband
Cover and Text Design: Panda Musgrove

ISBN: 978-1-59013-481-8

Library of Congress Control Number: 2010917810

Visit the McBooks Press website at www.mcbooks.com.

Printed in the United States of America
9 8 7 6 5 4 3 2 1

*To my Tiger, with all my love
and with thanks for your love and support.*

Was I to die this moment, 'Want of Frigates'
would be found stamped on my heart.

—HORATIO NELSON

1 "Us and Them"

"Captain, sir?"

Quietly spoken and almost lost in the creak and murmur of shipboard sounds, but Adam Bolitho was instantly awake. If he had managed to sleep at all. A few hours, three at the most since he had slumped into the old chair, to prepare himself and be ready.

The great cabin was still dark but for the same small, shuttered lantern burning.

He looked up into the face above his chair. The white collar patches seemed almost bright against the darkness. The midshipman removed his hand immediately; he must have touched his captain's shoulder.

"The first lieutenant's respects, sir." He faltered as feet thudded across the deck overhead, slithering to a halt as a voice snapped a warning. Probably some of the newly joined men who had not realised the skylight was directly above this cabin.

He made another attempt. "He sent me, sir. The morning watch is mustered."

He gazed fixedly at his captain as Adam swung his feet onto the deck and sat upright.

"Thank you." Now he could see the moisture on the midshipman's coat, reflecting the lantern light. "Still raining?" He had not even pulled off his shoes when he had come down here to be alone with his thoughts. He could feel *Onward* moving steadily beneath and around him, still sheltered by the land. Plymouth, but not for much longer.

The thought gave him time. "Have you settled into life aboard yet, Mr. Radcliffe?"

He sensed the boy's surprise that he had remembered his name; he had only joined *Onward* a few days ago. His first ship, and such small details mattered. Today of all days.

"Yessir." The boy was animated now, nodding and smiling. "Mr. Huxley has made things much easier for me."

Radcliffe was a replacement for Deacon, the senior midshipman, who had left the ship to prepare for the Board, the vital examination which would decide his future, that step from midshipman's berth to wardroom and a career as a King's officer. They all joked about it, and poured scorn on the grim-faced senior captains who usually comprised each Board. But only afterwards. Adam had never forgotten. And neither did any one else, if he had any sense.

They would miss Deacon. Keen and quick-witted, he had been in charge of *Onward*'s signals crew, the "eyes" of the ship. Adam remembered him when *Onward* had been beginning her approach to Gibraltar, or on their way home from the Mediterranean, and after their savage clash with, and capture of, the renegade frigate *Nautilus*. Men had been killed, others wounded, and the ship still bore the scars and reminders. And he recalled pride, too. On that morning with the Rock looming against a clear, empty sky, Deacon had written down Adam's signal in full before having it run up to the yards. *His Britannic Majesty's Ship Nautilus is rejoining the Fleet. God Save the King.*

The midshipman was still waiting beside the old bergère where Adam was seated, body swaying to *Onward*'s movement as another offshore gust hissed against the hull.

"My compliments to Mr. Vincent. I shall be joining him on deck directly."

Vincent would understand. But when *Onward* had first commissioned and Adam had been appointed in command, they had remained strangers until . . . *Until when?*

He heard the screen door close, voices: Midshipman Radcliffe on his way back to the quarterdeck with his captain's message.

Of one company. This was not the time to think of the missing faces, the dead men and the ones who had been put ashore badly wounded. Some would be over there in Plymouth today, watching and remembering as the anchor broke free of the land.

Even when he thought he was immune to it, the pain could still take him unawares, like a wound. Those seamen might become like the aimless groups that waited on the waterfront at Falmouth, criticising the ships coming and going with the tide, sometimes not a whole man among them.

And in Falmouth when they had moved aside to let him pass with Lowenna. *The captain with his lovely bride, who wanted for nothing.*

He walked across to his sleeping cabin, which was still closed. It was the morning watch, four o'clock, when most honest folk would be safely tucked up in bed, some recovering from Christmas, or preparing for the new year: 1819. He was still unaccustomed to it, despite having seen it on the official document, with the familiar wording which had left no room for doubt. *Being in all respects ready for sea . . .* And his signature.

He knew there were many who would envy him today. There were nine hundred captains on the Navy List, some without hope of getting a command. Even here in the naval port of Plymouth there were plenty of empty hulls, whose only destination was the breaker's yard. And it was said that there was not an admiral flying his flag who was under the age of sixty.

The older seamen still yarned about the great sea battles, when there had never been enough ships. At Trafalgar, when "Our Nel" had been only forty-seven years old.

Adam Bolitho was thirty-eight, newly married, and now, after only the briefest time together, he was leaving her again. *Lowenna . . .*

His hand was on the cabin door, but he stopped himself from opening it. Her portrait was hanging just beneath the deckhead, where it could be reached easily and stowed away if the ship cleared for action, even if only a drill. Where was she now? Lying in that same bed and waiting for the first hint of dawn, or some movement in the old grey house? Remembering? Accepting, or regretting the inevitable?

The sea is a widow-maker . . .

He swung away from the door, thankful for the sound of voices beyond the screen. The Royal Marine sentry at his post, probably half-asleep on his booted feet, but always ready to challenge or announce any one who might attempt to intrude on the captain's privacy.

Not this time. It was Luke Jago, his coxswain and a law unto himself. And Adam was suddenly grateful.

Mark Vincent was the first lieutenant, and a good one despite their initial differences, and he had to be ready to assume immediate command should death or injury befall his captain. Only a fool would ignore that very real possibility. Adam touched the small desk as he passed, without truly seeing it. In one of its drawers was the broken epaulette which had been severed by a musket ball during the fight with *Nautilus*. It had felt no more dangerous than a hand brushing against his shoulder, or a fragment of falling rope; he had not even noticed it until Jago had told him. A few more inches, and Vincent would have been called to take Adam's place. He would have died like his beloved uncle, Sir Richard Bolitho, who had been marked down by a French sharpshooter during Napoleon's escape from Elba. Almost four years ago, but when you walked the streets or along the waterfront in Falmouth, it could have been yesterday.

Unconsciously Adam had reached up to touch his shoulder, reliving it, remembering Jago's words, the obvious concern.

"Best to keep on the move, Cap'n." Jago had tried to make light of it. "It's *me* they're after!" But the familiar wry grin had deserted him.

He wondered what Jago thought about leaving England again, after only a brief respite in harbour while the necessary repairs were carried out. Jago had spent most of his life at sea in one ship or another, and mostly in time of war. For him there was nothing else. He had seen the idlers watching from the jetties, and others pulling past the anchored frigate as if unable to stay away, and had said with feeling, "Better to be stitched up in a hammock right now than end up on the beach like that lot!"

Jago had been there in church as their guest when Lowenna had married his captain, sitting with John Allday and his wife, Unis. There must have been more than a few yarns after the ceremony. And a lot of memories.

"Mornin', Cap'n! Up an' about already, I see!" Jago was putting down a steaming mug and turning up the solitary lantern, apparently indifferent to *Onward*'s motion as the deck tilted again. "Wind's steady enough—nor'east. We'll need a few extra hands on the capstan." He flicked open the razor until the blade caught the light and glanced at the old chair. "Ready when you are, Cap'n."

He watched as the faded seagoing coat was tossed onto a bench and Adam lay back in "the chair with a frog-sounding name," as Hugh Morgan, the cabin servant, had been heard to describe it. *So many times* . . . Jago could shave his captain in a storm without effort, and the razor was very sharp; he always made sure of that. Adam glanced at the stern windows. He must be mistaken, but they seemed paler already.

"'Ere we go, sir!" Jago steadied Adam's chin with his thick fingers. He could think of a few throats that wouldn't have risked being in this position. One in particular.

He heard the sound of voices, feet scurrying across the deck: the morning watchkeepers preparing the way for all hands when the moment came.

He dabbed Adam's face with a towel still hot from the galley fire. The first lieutenant was making certain that nothing would go wrong, with every naval telescope trained on *Onward*, ready to find fault if there was any misjudgment or error. And this man under the blade would be the target.

The captain was unusually quiet, Jago thought. Getting under way: a thousand things to remember. Maybe you never got used to it. He recalled the lovely woman in the church, the way she and Bolitho had looked together, surrounded by all those people and yet apart. He couldn't imagine what it was like. He thought of the painting in the sleeping cabin behind him. And she had posed for it.

He wiped the blade and grinned. "Close shave, sir."

Adam stood up and looked at him directly. "Steady as a rock, Luke!"

He heard a muffled clink from the little pantry. So Morgan could not sleep, either.

"I have a letter to finish." *The hardest one to write.* "I want it to go ashore in good time."

Jago nodded. "The guardboat will take it, sir. I'll make sure of that." He hesitated by the screen door, but there was nothing more. "I'll leave you in peace, sir."

Adam called after him, "Thanks, Luke."

"Sir?"

But Adam had walked to the quarter windows and was standing there, a slim figure of medium height, eyes as dark as his hair, pale shirt framed against the outer darkness like a spectre. As if he could see the nearest land.

He heard the door shut, the sentry clearing his throat while Jago told him the captain mustn't be disturbed. He moved to the little desk and pulled open another drawer. The letter was there, half-written.

The ship was suddenly quiet, and he could hear the repetitive squeak of the hook where his best uniform coat hung from the deck-head, complete with the new epaulettes. He had worn it at his wedding in Falmouth. Adam touched his skin, and the slight scrape left by the razor when Jago's concentration had wavered, a rare thing for him.

He dipped the pen and wrote slowly, as if to hear the words.

It was not tomorrow. It was now.

Lieutenant Mark Vincent stood by the quarterdeck rail and stared along *Onward*'s full length, making sure he had missed nothing. It was almost physical, this relaxing muscle by muscle, like a gun captain who has made the final decision before opening fire. He had been appointed to *Onward* just over a year ago when she had been commissioned here in Plymouth, and he thought he knew every inch of her one hundred and fifty feet, above and below deck; how she behaved at sea, even how she looked to any passing vessel. Or to an enemy. She was a frigate which had more than proved herself during her short life, and one any man would be proud and, these days, lucky, to command.

He pushed the envy to the back of his mind, until the next time.

It was rare to see the deck so crowded. The lower deck had been cleared, hammocks smartly stowed in the nettings with a minimum of fuss. He glanced up at the sky, shreds of ragged cloud scudding ahead of the cold north-easterly, with only a few pale streaks of blue, like ice.

"Guardboat's casting off, sir!"

Vincent said curtly, "As ordered." He did not know the seaman's face, one of the replacements for somebody killed or injured in their brief, bitter fight with *Nautilus*, but a few drills or an Atlantic gale would soon change that. And most of the new hands were volunteers, a far cry from his first days at sea when they had been pressed men or worse, "scrovies" as the worthless were termed—picked up by local crimps when they were too drunk to know what was happening.

He thought of the idlers he had seen on the waterfront when he had been ashore on some mission or other, doubtless some of the same Jacks who had once cursed every minute they had served aboard a King's ship.

The guardboat was pulling away from the chains, the officer waving to someone by the entry port, the oars reflecting in the choppy water as they angled to take the first pull. Vincent unslung the telescope from his shoulder and trained it across the slow-moving boat. A two-decker of seventy-four guns was anchored between *Onward* and the inshore moorings and catching the first gleam of sunlight on her high poop and gilded "gingerbread," and the rear-admiral's flag at her mizzen. He closed the glass with a snap. Like a warning, or perhaps it was instinct. There were several figures on deck with telescopes pointing toward *Onward*. Officers, despite the early hour; the greasy smell of breakfast still lingered on the cold air.

He looked over at the companion and saw the captain's coxswain climbing into view and pausing to touch his hat to the Royal Marine officers ranged beside a squad of scarlet coats.

As if it were a signal, Vincent crossed the deck, which had been cleared to allow space for the capstan bars to be slotted into place. Jago walked past the big double wheel and took up his station at the rail.

Another quick glance, and Vincent saw the signals crew standing by the flag locker, Midshipman Hotham in charge, his narrow face set in a frown, and very aware of the moment. A clergyman's son, but, as he was always quick to point out, "so was Our Nel!"

The Royal Marines' boots clicked together and someone saluted. The captain touched his hat, and Vincent thought he might have nodded slightly to his coxswain. He faced Vincent and smiled.

"It'll be lively when we clear the Sound." He was looking along the deck and gangways at the groups of seamen at their stations, most of them staring aft at their captain.

Vincent swallowed: his mouth felt bone-dry. *How does it feel? His decision. I might never know.*

Young Hotham's voice scattered his thoughts. "Signal from Flag, sir!" A pause, and a telescope squeaked as somebody else focused on the flags breaking to the wind. *"Proceed when ready!"*

Adam saw the acknowledgment running up the halliards, Hotham peering eagerly forward as the bell chimed out as if to mark the moment.

Vincent shouted, "Man the capstan! Fo'c'sle party stand by!"

"Heave, m'lads, *heave!*"

Adam turned, momentarily caught unawares. It would take time to become used to another new voice. Harry Drummond, the bosun, was a professional seaman to the tips of his iron-hard fingers, but it was impossible to forget the massive Guthrie, around which the ship's company had seemed to revolve like hands obeying the capstan. He had fallen like a great tree, his men stepping over him to obey his last order.

The pawls of the capstan were moving, clicking into place as more men added their weight to the bars. Someone slipped and fell sprawling; the deck was still treacherous with rain.

But he heard a voice trying to raise a cheer as a fiddle scraped, and squealed into a familiar sailor's shanty.

> *There was a lass in Bristol town—*
> *heave, me bullies, heave!*

It was Lynch, the senior cook, eyes shut and one foot beating time to every clink of the capstan.

Adam stared up at the yards, the topmen strung out like puppets against the hurrying clouds. The long masthead pendant gave some hint of the wind's strength, and he could picture *Onward*'s outline like a lithe shadow edging slowly toward the embedded anchor.

"Heave, me bullies, heave!"

He heard Julyan, the sailing master, speaking to the quartermaster and his extra helmsman. Calm, unhurried, just loud enough to carry above the chorus of wind and rigging. One eye on the compass, another on his captain, whose ultimate responsibility this was.

Adam remained by the quarterdeck rail, the ship and her company moving around him, but as if he were quite alone. Did you ever become so accustomed to this moment, or so confident, that it became merely routine?

The capstan was moving more slowly, but steadily, and no more hands were called to add their weight to the bars. He could see their breath like steam blown away on the wind, and feel the air on his spray-wet cheek like ice rime.

He glanced forward again, and across the larboard bow. The two-decker was anchored apart from the other ships, her sealed gunports a chequered pattern shining in the strengthening light. There were lighters moored alongside, empty, like undertakers waiting for the last rites. How did the ship feel? *How would I feel?*

He looked away, but not before he had seen the powerful shape of Lieutenant James Squire at his station in the eyes of the ship, watching the incoming cable. A born seaman and navigator, and one of the most senior men aboard. He had come up from the lower deck, and had won respect and popularity the hard way. Two midshipmen stood nearby: David Napier and the latest addition to the berth, John Radcliffe, who was about to begin a day, good or bad, which would live in his memory—his first at sea in a King's ship.

Adam could recall his own. Only the faces seemed blurred or merged by time, save for a few.

Jago murmured, "Morgan brought yer boatcloak, Cap'n." He was standing by the packed hammock nettings, but hardly raised his voice.

"Still got a lot to learn!" Then the familiar chuckle.

The cabin servant had thought of everything that his captain, any captain, might require under any circumstances. *But he doesn't know me yet. That I would freeze or be soaked to the skin rather than take cover on this day.*

Adam glanced down and saw that Maddock, the gunner, had paused by one of the upper deck eighteen-pounders as if to speak with its gun captain. A careful man, perhaps still puzzled by the latest order from the admiral's headquarters ashore.

There will be no salutes fired today, until . . .

Adam saw him look up, his hand resting on the gun's wet breech, head half-turned. He was deaf in one ear, common enough in his trade, but quick enough to acknowledge Adam's private signal from the quarterdeck.

He had heard the first lieutenant brushing Maddock's question aside, his mind too full of the business of getting *Onward* under way: "Sir John Grenville, Admiralty. Today's his funeral. That's why!" And Vincent had turned away to deal with another problem.

Adam had last seen and shaken hands with Grenville in the very cabin beneath his feet. Both of them had known they would not meet again. *He gave me hope, when he gave me Onward.* And in his way, Grenville was sharing it today.

Adam saw Squire move toward the cathead and gesture behind him, as if he could feel the anchor like a physical force.

"Stand by on deck!" That was Drummond, the new bosun. An unhurried but sharp, almost metallic voice which carried easily above other sounds around him. He seemed to be blessed with a good memory for faces, even names: in his brief time aboard, Adam had never seen him consult a book or slate.

Faster again, the capstan bars turning like a human wheel.

"Anchor's hove short, sir!" They faced one another along the ship's length. Squire did not even cup his hands.

"Loose the heads'ls!"

Always a testing moment. Maybe too soon? *Onward* thrusting over her own anchor, at the mercy of wind and tide.

Adam stared at the masthead; the rain was heavier and the long pendant was moving only sluggishly in the wind. He was soaked and his neckcloth felt tight around his throat, like a sodden bandage. He could feel the tension on deck, sharing it. Small things stood out: a leadsman hurrying to the chains, ready to call out the soundings instantly if they moved into shallows before *Onward* was under way. Vincent would take no chances today. Beyond the revolving capstan he saw Jago piling muskets to allow some marines to add their weight for the last few fathoms.

"Anchor's aweigh, sir!"

Shouts, running feet, a few curses as the sails broke free and more water cascaded from the flapping canvas. Adam felt the deck tilt more steeply as the topsails filled and hardened, the quartermaster and an extra helmsman straddle-legged at the big double wheel to keep their balance.

Julyan was close by, outwardly untroubled as bowsprit and tapering jib-boom began to answer the helm, so that the anchored flagship appeared to be moving as if to cross *Onward*'s bows.

"Steady—meet her." Julyan peered at the compass, rain dripping from his hat. "Steady as you go." Adam saw him look over at the quartermaster, perhaps still surprised. His predecessor had been Julyan's friend. He had been killed there at the helm during the fight with *Nautilus*.

Adam shielded his eyes to gaze up at the topmen spread out along the yards, no doubt breathless after fisting and kicking the canvas into submission. A fall to the deck, or into the sea alongside as the hull submitted to the wind, must never be far from their minds.

Lieutenant Squire was watching the anchor until it reached and was secured to the cathead, the mud and weed of the seabed still clinging to the stock and flukes. His forecastle party was already lashing it firmly into place. He wiped spray from his face with his fist. *Until the next time* . . .

He gazed aft and waited until he knew the captain had seen him before crossing his hands to signal that the anchor had been made secure.

The remaining cable was still being hauled inboard, where it was seized by the nippers, ship's boys who would scrub and scrape it before stowing it below. No more than children, he thought, and what a filthy job: it reminded him of the mudlarks, naked youths who dived for coins in the shallows at some seaports. It had cost a few of them their lives.

Squire glanced at the two midshipmen, Napier and the new arrival, Radcliffe. Both good lads, although it was hard to judge either of them without experiencing a pang of envy. Napier's background was vague; he had close ties to the captain's family and was a ward of some kind, and Radcliffe was always full of questions and completely untrained. It was said that his father had an important position in banking. A different world.

"Bosun's Mate! Pipe those waisters to be ready to add their weight to the braces!"

Squire swung round, still waiting for the voice, even though he knew he was mistaken.

The bosun's mate in question was newly rated, and had been one of *Onward*'s best topmen and a fine seaman until his promotion. He replaced Fowler, a man Squire had known for years; they had been on the lower deck together. A bully and a petty tyrant, he had become a real enemy.

I wanted him dead. Him or me.

Now Fowler was missing, having gone ashore in Plymouth, and they had marked him in the muster book as *RUN*. Deserted. But nobody really knew. Maybe he was dead; maybe someone else had had a score to settle. But until Squire knew for certain, he would remain a threat.

He gestured to the new midshipman, who responded instantly.

"My respects to the first lieutenant, and tell him we are all secured here." He raised his voice as Radcliffe turned to run toward the gangway. "Easy does it! I think we've earned our pay today!"

He waited until Radcliffe had dropped out of sight. It was always too easy to take it out of those who could not answer back. He should have known that better than most. He watched some of his seamen mopping the stained deck and dismantling their tackle. Dull, necessary routine, but it gave him time to calm himself. It was over.

Someone had called his name and he tugged his hat lower over his eyes, peering into the rain. They were under way, the flagship lying across the quarter with only her flags moving, her decks deserted. He stared ahead again, the blue-grey water reaching away on either bow, the jib-boom pointing the way, like the naked figurehead of the youth with outstretched trident and dolphin beneath it.

He looked toward the land; a church or slender tower was visible despite the downpour. People might still be there, watching the solitary frigate as she headed for the open sea. There would be mixed feelings among the civilians. Pride, perhaps sadness, but certainly not envy. It was still too soon after the long years of war, the fear of invasion and, not least, the hated press gangs.

Lieutenant James Squire gripped a stay and felt it quivering as if the whole ship were straining forward, eager to leave.

And he was free.

He heard Napier's voice, and saw him stoop beside one of the anchor party with a spare block and tackle in his hands. "Like this—it'll run free next time." He smiled. "Wet *or* dry!"

The seaman was new, and Squire could not remember his name, but he appeared not much older than Napier. He saw him reach out with an answering grin to help the midshipman to his feet. It was a small thing, but Squire knew that it mattered, more than he could explain.

Napier was pleasant if slightly shy, and had already proved himself reliable and quick to learn. Squire gazed along the shining deck where men and boys had died. Brave, too. *One day, maybe soon . . .* He turned and said abruptly, "You were at the wedding, I'm told."

Napier wiped his hands on a piece of waste. He was still not used to Squire's sharpness and swift changes of mood. A man you would never really know, unless he himself allowed it.

"Yes, sir. There were a lot of people . . ."

"And the bride?"

Napier recalled the church, the ceremony, the light on the uniforms. And the girl, Elizabeth, Adam Bolitho's cousin, dressed as a midshipman, carrying the flowers. She would soon forget. He would not.

"They looked so *right* together."

Squire laughed. "Well said! And so they should." For some reason, he knew Napier would say no more. *Like me, he has nobody to leave behind.*

"Message from the captain, sir." Radcliffe was back, breathless, cheeks glowing from the cold wind. He held out a folded piece of signal pad and grinned at Napier. "Rain's stopped!"

Squire unfolded it deliberately. "I told you to *walk*, Mr. Radcliffe. You're puffing like an old Jack!" It gave him another few seconds, and as he opened the message he realised that the rain had indeed stopped, and the sea surging away from the stem was beginning to shimmer, although any real sun was still hidden beyond the clouds.

"Hands take station for leaving harbour. It'll be lively when we reach open water. Officers' conference aft, at noon." He looked at the two midshipmen. "That includes *you*, for some reason."

Both boys turned to watch a small schooner, sails in momentary confusion as she altered course toward the anchorage. Napier would be used to it, having served with Captain Bolitho before, but Radcliffe had not been long enough afloat to get his feet wet. But in all his years at sea Squire had never known a captain who made a point of sharing his immediate plan with his chain of command.

His men were separating to join others on deck, directed by the master's mate and other senior hands; the wind was strong enough to require more weight on the braces as *Onward* made more sail. Squire shivered. It never failed to excite him, even now. And he thought enviously of the youngster Radcliffe. So many years to make his own.

He saw Napier going aft and pausing as he met the newly rated bosun's mate, Tucker, heading in the opposite direction. Their hands touched, not by accident, and Tucker grinned as Napier spoke. Some good had been done. Tucker had been promoted because of Fowler's disappearance.

He stared at the foretop and waited for a face and a name to form in his mind.

"*You*, Willis! Move yourself! We've not got all day!"

He knew his men. It was his strength.

Napier heard the shout but ignored it and ducked beneath the larboard gangway between two of the eighteen-pounders. The sky had become clearer, but they must have been too busy to notice. The sea bursting from the stem where he had just been standing was glittering in hard sunlight, but the touch of the drifting spray on his skin was still like ice.

He looked at Tucker, also called David, and gripped his arm. "Haven't had the time to tell you properly. I'm so glad for you—well deserved, too!"

Tucker glanced down self-consciously at his blue jacket and the telltale silver call hanging around his neck. "It'll take some wearing to get used to it!" He said it strongly enough, but when he looked up at the braced topsail yards and the small figures spaced at intervals against the sky he seemed less confident. "I know every man-jack up there, and what I was doing with them only a few weeks back. The same risks, the same laughs when we had all canvas doing what we wanted."

Napier nodded. "I think I understand, David. I'm still getting used to it myself."

Tucker showed his teeth in another grin. "It's *us* and *them*, remember?"

"Nothing to do, *Mister* Napier? I'd have thought that by now . . ." It was Monteith, the third lieutenant, hands behind his back, head on one side, and angry. He looked past them. "The boats need securing for sea, as you may recall."

"I've already detailed hands for that, sir!" Another voice: Drummond, the new bosun, very erect, but casually picking a piece of oakum from his sleeve as if the bustle and shouted commands around him were beneath his notice. He did not drop his gaze as the lieutenant glared at him. "But if *you* are taking over, sir, I am needed elsewhere."

Napier thought Monteith would explode, or give vent to the usual sarcasm. Instead, he shaded his eyes as if to peer abeam and snapped, "I can't do everything!" and stamped away.

To Tucker the bosun said, "I'll need you at four bells, right?" and walked aft unhurriedly, calling out an occasional name, or pausing by the various working parties as he went.

Tucker shrugged. "Sorry, David. I didn't see him." He turned sharply as one of the foretopmen slithered down a backstay and landed as lightly as a cat at his feet. "Hey, Ted, why'n't you warn me he was coming?"

Napier recognised the seaman called Ted. He had often seen him together with Tucker, working aloft like the others they had been watching, repairing rigging, and tending the wounded after battle. Sharing a lively hornpipe during a dog watch when *Onward* had first commissioned. Friends.

Now the same man turned his back, remarking over his shoulder, "Didn't know it was an *order!*"

Tucker stared after him as if he had been struck. Then he said quietly, "It's become a different ship."

Napier gripped his arm again and waited until their eyes met, seeing the pain.

He smiled. "So, welcome aboard!"

Adam Bolitho stepped into the great cabin and heard the screen door close behind him. He had not recognised the Royal Marine on guard duty: another stranger. But he had noticed that Sergeant Fairfax was nearby, as if by coincidence.

He put his hand out to steady himself; the motion was more pronounced now that *Onward* was in open sea. But he knew it was not simply that. His entire body ached with tiredness and strain. He had been on his feet since Midshipman Radcliffe had roused him when the morning watch was called—he stifled a yawn—about ten hours ago.

He walked aft, angled to the deck, eyes on the hard light from the stern windows, sloping now to the thrust of wind and sea. He glanced briefly at the old chair, where his day had begun. To sit in it now would be fatal. Even when he had called the meeting here at noon he had remained standing. Some might have thought he was impatient to get it over and let routine take charge. Maybe the newcomers thought so, anyway.

There had been two lieutenants, the Royal Marine officer, all the warrant officers, and the six midshipmen together in a tight group. Vincent had remained on watch. The tallest present was the new carpenter, Chris Hall, who had served at sea in several men-of-war, but had also been attached to the dockyard on maintenance and even involved in the building of various types of vessel. Like other lofty visitors to the great cabin, he had taken his place under the skylight, but even there he had been stooping slightly. How did he manage between decks, or working in the lower confines of the hull?

He watched the occasional dash of salt spray, drying across the stern and quarter windows. At least the rain had stopped.

There was still a smell of rum lingering between decks. He had heard a few cheers when the order to "Up Spirits" was piped. It was the least he could do for men who had been hard at work since first light on a bitter morning.

There had been the usual comments after the meeting. Lieutenant Squire clapping Vicary, the purser, on the shoulder and grinning. "Cheer up! It's not coming out of *your* purse!"

Vicary was always complaining about stores and wastage; it did not help matters.

Murray, the Scottish surgeon, had added, "Won't need so much grog anyway, where we're bound for!"

Adam stared at two gulls which were riding the wind, drifting from side to side below the taffrail. The galley must have thrown some scraps over the side.

But the surgeon's words were still with him. *Where we're bound for.* It was Freetown, on what had been the slave coast of Africa. And it still was, for those who carried out their endless patrols there. But why all the secrecy and apparent urgency? And why *Onward,* so soon after the Mediterranean, and that bloody action with *Nautilus?*

But he had discovered nothing more when he had gone ashore for the last time to sign for the sealed despatches which were now locked in his strongbox. Even that had been unusually formal: his signature had been witnessed by one of the admiral's aides, a senior captain, another unfamiliar face. Courteous but unhelpful.

"*Onward* is a fast frigate, Bolitho, as you will know better than any one." He had paused as one of his clerks sealed the despatches and stamped the wax. "Repairs completed to your satisfaction. Fully manned and stored." He had walked to the familiar window and said after another silence, "And . . . available."

Reminding him that another captain could be appointed within a day. Less. Adam had not forgotten the Admiralty waiting-room when he had been called to London. The jealousy and the hostility. Nor would he.

He walked across the cabin and heard muffled voices beyond the pantry door. Morgan and a much younger servant, a boy sent to help him during the conference. Morgan seemed to be waiting, judging the moment. Was it so obvious?

More voices, the sound of a musket being tapped on the grating. A dispute of some kind, then the door opened and closed and Jago said, "Not much to see, Cap'n. More rain on th' way."

Adam reached for his boatcloak and changed his mind. "Trouble just now?"

Jago glanced at the door. "Yer sentry's new. Just needs to be told, that's all, Cap'n."

He stepped aside as Adam left the cabin. The sentry was ready, and snapped smartly to attention as he passed, but he noticed Sergeant Fairfax's burly shadow lurking by the companion ladder.

On deck it seemed almost dark, although the bell had only just chimed for the first dog watch.

Vincent touched his hat. "Standing by to alter course, sir."

Adam looked past and beyond him into the murk. Low cloud again, vague figures mustered and waiting by the braces and halliards, but strangely silent, so that the shipboard noises and the surge of water alongside predominated.

One of the midshipmen was waiting to offer him a telescope, his collar patches very bright, like those in the cabin before dawn.

He felt the air quiver, and then the vibration of the rail under his hand.

Someone said, "Thunder!"

Vincent looked toward him but did not speak.

All those miles astern, and yet the salute was with them. Personal. Sir John Grenville's farewell, or a last gesture of remembrance. *His old ship.*

Adam heard an older voice say, "Thass th' Lizard over to starboard, my son. Last you'll see of England for a while, so make th' most of it!"

Jago had handed him his boatcloak; it was raining again, but he had not felt it. The same rain must be falling in Falmouth, on Lowenna's garden . . . As close as they could be.

And she would know.

2 CHAIN OF COMMAND

LIEUTENANT MARK VINCENT hesitated at the top of the ladder beneath the companion to give his eyes time to meet the glare on deck. After the sheltered chartroom, it was almost blinding.

The helmsman called, "Sou' by west, sir! Steady as she goes!" Probably to warn Squire, who had just taken over the forenoon watch, that the first lieutenant had reappeared.

Squire was talking to a midshipman, Walker, who was writing on a slate, tongue protruding from one corner of his mouth in concentration.

Vincent waved and said, "Carry on." He was merely a visitor.

He walked to the lee side of the quarterdeck and stared at the gleaming expanse of sea, empty as a desert, the horizon unbroken by cloud or shadow. He considered himself an experienced sailor, and never took the sea and its moods for granted. The last few days had tested those beliefs to the extreme. The weather had worsened as soon as they had cleared the Western Approaches and left the land astern. The wind had stayed in their favour, but had often been too strong to spread more canvas and run before it.

Four days of it: this was the fifth since *Onward* had weighed at Plymouth. He felt the planking beneath his shoes, quite dry now—on the quarterdeck at least. Some of the newly joined hands must have been wondering what had made them quit their homes in the first place. And not just the inexperienced. He had heard Julyan, the master, admit,

"More than once on the fringe of Biscay, I thought we were going to lose our sticks!"

Vincent shaded his eyes and stared along the upper deck. Repairs were still being carried out. The sailmaker's crew huddled below the starboard gangway, busily cutting and stitching a torn sail, while a gunner's mate was testing the breeching on one of the eighteen-pounders. Splicing where necessary; then it would be checked again before another drill. Trust and blame went hand in hand.

He looked up at the taut spread of canvas; the captain had hinted that they would get the topgallant sails on her soon, probably during this watch. It was Bolitho's decision. The nagging thought was always there. *Suppose it was mine?*

And how did Bolitho really feel about leaving the land so soon after the *Nautilus* mission, and, more importantly, his bride?

Vincent had remained with *Onward* while her repairs were being completed, in command, and so unable to attend the wedding at Falmouth. But he had heard enough about it, and the rest he could imagine. Lowenna was not someone you could easily forget.

"Ah, I thought I would find you here, Mark. Always busy, keeping us all afloat, eh?"

It was Murray, the surgeon, so light on his feet, like a dancer or a swordsman, although he was neither, as far as Vincent knew. Outwardly easy-going, and popular with most of the ship's company, which was rare enough in his profession. For the most part surgeons were feared, even hated. *Butchers* . . .

Murray was smiling quizzically. "And if it's not too late to say it, a very Happy New Year to *you!*" They solemnly shook hands. He had a grip like steel, Vincent thought.

Murray turned to gaze abeam, apparently untroubled by the hard sunlight. He had pale blue eyes, which seemed almost colourless in the glare, and his profile was narrow-featured with a prominent hooked nose.

"Where are we, Mark? I'm damned if I know."

Vincent had to smile. Rapier-straight, that was Murray's way. In the wardroom, and amidst the casual chatter and banter between various duties and watches, he would always come directly to the point.

But his attention had been diverted as a seaman hurried by, and the moment was past.

"How's the knee, Slater?"

The man stopped as if startled, then he grinned. "Good as new, an' thankee, sir!"

Murray walked to the companion. He had some notes to make, and in any case Vincent was already pointing out something to another working party, the first lieutenant once more.

He thought of the seaman to whom he had just spoken—Slater. Murray had always had a good memory for names, and was grateful for it. Some never seemed to acquire the ability, never bothered or did not care, but he knew from experience that it was often the only link they had. Slater had injured his knee in a fall during one of the sudden squalls off Biscay. It might have been a lot worse, and he might not have recovered.

Just a name. Even if you had to take off his leg.

Midshipman Huxley scuttled past him with a folded chart, doubtless on some mission to see the captain. Another two weeks before landfall, maybe more. Bolitho left nothing to chance.

Murray paused at the ladder and looked up as he heard feet thudding across the deck above. Probably a marine, he thought. Then someone shouted, "He's just gone below!"

He waited, suddenly tense, and a pair of legs appeared on the ladder, blotting out the glare.

"Beg pardon, sir, there's bin an accident in the galley! I was told—" He fell silent as Murray waved his hand.

"I'll fetch my bag."

It would only be a bruise or a burn. *But just in case* . . . He found that it amused him. He was more like the captain than he had believed.

Tobias Julyan, the sailing master, watched as the captain, who had been leaning over the chart table, straightened his back and jabbed his brass dividers into a piece of cork. It would prevent them sliding away into some hidden corner if *Onward* was hit by another fierce squall.

Adam said, "If the weather holds we should be able to fix our position." A quick, impetuous grin. "And our progress, with more certainty."

Julyan glanced around the small chartroom. A world apart. Without it, all the sweat and tears expended elsewhere would amount to nothing. No matter what the old Jacks liked to think. "This *is* the Atlantic, sir. I think she's done us proud."

"And so have you." Adam dragged the heavy log book into a shaft of sunlight and did not see Julyan's pleasure. He turned a page. The first day of the new year of 1819. It was a Friday. Strange that so many sailors, and not just the older ones, regarded Fridays as unlucky. He had never discovered why.

Luke Jago had reminded him this morning as he had been finishing his shave. "They said I was born on a Friday, so that should tell us somethin'!"

Jago seemed to live one day at a time. Always ready. Perhaps because he had no one and nothing to leave behind, or come home to. The sea and the navy were his life, until the next horizon.

Like the severed epaulette. *Always ready.*

Adam heard a tap, and the chartroom door opened a few inches. He thought it would be Vincent, impatient to begin making more sail. But Julyan said, "Your cox'n, sir." He picked up some notes and pulled the door wide. "I shall be standing by, sir."

The door closed behind him and Jago stood with his back against it. Their eyes met, and Adam said quietly, "Trouble, Luke?"

"A short fuse if you asks me, Cap'n." He scowled. "Someone a bit too handy with a blade. In the galley, of all places!"

Adam reached for his hat. "I'm going on deck."

Jago watched him leave and swore silently.

Bloody Fridays!

Hugh Morgan, the cabin servant, heard the screen door slam shut and waited warily as the captain strode aft to the quarter. Morgan had served several captains, and Bolitho was the best so far. Old enough to have borne the full weight of responsibility, young enough to consider those less fortunate and still finding their way. But there were bad days, too. This was likely to be one of them, New Year or not.

"Can I fetch you something to eat, sir? You've touched nothing since they called all hands."

Adam pushed himself away from the bench beneath the stern windows with their gleaming panorama of water, greyer now than blue.

He said, "I apologise. There was no need to bite *your* head off!" Then, "I'm expecting the first lieutenant directly. Maybe the surgeon, too. The meal can wait." He tossed his hat onto a chair and asked abruptly, "How well d'you know Lord, one of the cook's mates?"

"The one who was stabbed, sir?"

Adam sat down as if something had been cut. If Morgan knew, the whole ship would know.

Morgan watched the signs. It was bad all right. "Brian Lord. Good lad to all accounts. The cook speaks well of him. Not *too* well, of course!"

Adam smiled and felt his jaw crack. "You should be a politician."

Morgan relaxed a little. "Too honest, sir!"

Adam looked astern again, at the regular array of a following sea, marked by the shiver and thud of the rudder. At any other time he would have been satisfied. Proud. Instead, he kept remembering the anger on Jago's face; he knew the course of events better than any one. The man could have died but for Murray's prompt action, and could still die. There had been blood everywhere.

The deck tilted suddenly and he saw Morgan pivot round to stare at the pantry door behind him. Someone must have lost his balance; there was an audible gasp and a sound of breaking glass.

Morgan waited for a few more seconds, and said, "Not one of my best goblets, I hope?"

The door swung open. The new mess boy was getting to his feet, some shards of glass in his hands.

Morgan said reprovingly, "There's clumsy you are, boy, like an ox in a chapel!" He was dangerously calm, and his Welsh accent was more pronounced.

Adam reached out and took the boy's arm. "Watch your step, my lad. The surgeon has enough to do just now."

Morgan shook his head. "This is my new helper, sir. Chose him myself, too!" He nudged the broken glass delicately with his shoe. "I am not usually so mistaken."

Adam said to the boy, "What's your name?"

The boy looked from him to Morgan, who repeated, "Chose him myself, sir. From your own part of the world, see."

The boy seemed to find his voice. "Tregenza, zur. Arthur Tregenza. From Truro, zur."

His round, open face was a mass of freckles, which matched his ginger hair.

It was a small thing, Adam thought, not even worth his attention. Morgan would deal with it. But for some reason it was important. The boy's first ship . . . And from Truro, only a dozen miles from the old grey house in Falmouth. Where she would be waiting, wondering . . .

Adam said, "You must tell me about yourself when we have more time. But take care until you know *Onward*'s moods a little better. She can be a lively ship when she chooses!"

Morgan was looking meaningly at the screen door, and the boy retreated.

"We'll leave you in peace, sir. Maybe you'll care to eat later?"

"Thank you. I would appreciate that."

Morgan was opening the door even as the Royal Marine sentry was lifting his musket to rap on the grating. Interrupted, he said awkwardly, "The first lieutenant, *sir!*"

Morgan stood aside for Vincent to pass and shut the door behind him.

Vincent said, "I just left the surgeon, sir." He touched a stain on his sleeve. "Lord has lost a deal of blood. Even now . . ." He broke off, and added bitterly, "After all we've been through!"

Adam sat down again. "Tell me, Mark. In your own time."

Vincent stared unblinkingly up at the skylight. "Lord had been sent to the galley to fetch something—he doesn't remember what. Instead, he found the man—Lamont—stealing meat, putting large pieces into a bag. He was using one of the cook's own knives." He looked across the cabin for the first time. "You could shave with one of them."

Adam pictured the cook, Lynch, who had played his fiddle as *Onward* weighed anchor. *Sharp knives meant less waste.*

Vincent held up his right forearm and ran a finger down it. "He cut Lord from wrist to elbow. Somebody wrapped a shirt round it. Then the surgeon came."

"And the one responsible—this man Lamont?"

"Joined us at Plymouth, just before we left. Transfer from a ship awaiting overhaul. Or demolition. Able seaman, ten years' service. It was all rather vague."

Adam watched the sea catching the sun again. A hard light, with no hint of warmth. "Lamont? Did you see him?"

Vincent looked past him as spray spattered across the glass. "I was off watch at the time, sir. But someone heard Lord scream. The bosun was the first to reach the galley, and he called the surgeon. Otherwise . . ." A pause, then, as if to emphasise it, "*Aye,* I questioned Lamont. The master-at-arms was also present. Lamont claimed it was self-defense. I cautioned him. I knew you would want to know all the details."

"You did right, Mark. You can carry on with your routine until we learn something useful."

Vincent picked up his hat. "I feel it was partly my fault, sir. I had no time to test Lamont's worth when he was signed on."

The door closed and Adam stood watching the sea once more. Prepared, or resigned, and with an overriding sense of disappointment. He gazed around the cabin where he still sometimes relived the last fight, the thunder and crash of cannon and the crack of muskets. Men calling out in pain or in rage, helping one another. Dying. All that, and yet the barrier between himself and Vincent remained, an unseen enemy.

He thought of Thomas Herrick, his uncle's oldest and dearest friend, and his words on one occasion. *Command is complete or worthless.*

The door creaked. It was Morgan. "I thought you called, sir?"

Adam let his arms fall to his sides. Perhaps he had spoken aloud.

But he was ready.

The two midshipmen sat facing one another across the table. Around them their mess was quiet and deserted, although not for much longer: there had been a shrill of calls on deck, and a smell of food if they needed reminding. Midshipmen never did.

David Napier touched the bruise on the back of his hand, left by a rope clumsily dragged when they had been shifting one of the boats on deck. The salt air had made it sting like a burn. One of the new men had been too eager, or preoccupied.

Midshipman Huxley gestured with a spoon. "Put some grease on it."

Napier smiled. "Won't get any sympathy, will I?"

"If we lower the jolly-boat later, you'd better stand clear! You might lose the other one!"

Just words, but they were friends, and had been since they had joined *Onward* together on the same day, Napier recovering from injuries and the loss in action of his last ship, and Simon Huxley struggling to accept the suicide of his father following a court-martial, although he had been found not guilty and cleared of all blame. It was a quiet, unquestioning friendship neither ever tried to explain. They only knew that it mattered.

Dishes clattered nearby and somebody laughed. Huxley said, "I wonder if young Lord is going to come through it?"

It was on both their minds, and probably everybody else's, maybe even on the man's who had let the rope run out of control.

"Never saw a lot of him. But I know he went out of his way to make a cake for Jamie Walker's thirteenth birthday!"

Huxley smiled. "On the day of the battle with *Nautilus!* I forget if we ever even tasted it!"

"What d'you think will happen about Lord?"

Huxley lowered his voice confidentially. "I've been looking it up. If the worst happens, there will be a court-martial. There was one at Portsmouth a few months ago. Someone was hanged."

A chair scraped back and Midshipman Charles Hotham, the senior of the six-strong mess, sat down noisily and glared at the empty plates. "I should damned well think so, too! Don't know what the fleet's coming to, especially where meals are concerned!"

They laughed. It was the only way. Hotham was a clergyman's son. So was Nelson, he always proclaimed.

John Radcliffe, the newest member of the mess, sat down muttering apologies for lateness. The others were on duty.

Hotham made a grand gesture to the hovering messman. "Glasses today, Peter! Today of all days, I think. Some of *my* wine." He watched critically as it was being poured. "To our unfortunate shipmate!"

Napier hardly noticed the taste. It was suddenly easy to see Hotham like his father. All in black, even to the collar.

He glanced across at the scarred and sturdy desk they all shared when making their notes on navigation and seamanship, in anticipation of the day of the Board. And when composing letters that might eventually reach England. Cornwall, in his case. Would she even remember him, or care? She was an admiral's daughter. *The* admiral's daughter.

He reached for his glass, but Peter, the messman, was already refilling it. A dream, then. So be it. *Elizabeth.*

There were voices, very low, just outside the door, and a moment later the messman was back. "Surgeon's still workin', sir."

Radcliffe stared at his wine, untouched, and the steaming tray. "Suppose . . ." Then he lurched to his feet and left the mess.

Huxley looked over at Napier with concern. There was no answer.

Adam Bolitho paused as though to regain his balance, although that was merely an excuse. It was pitch dark after the gloom of the quarterdeck, and strangely silent, so that the ship's own sounds seemed unnaturally loud and intrusive. He had waited deliberately until after midnight when the watch had changed, and most of *Onward*'s company were swinging in their hammocks and asleep. If they were lucky.

He touched the timber: it felt like ice, and the white paint looked very fresh in the faint glare of a light. This was pointless. Murray would be asleep too, after what he had been struggling to do all day, or still preparing his report. Despite all his brutal experience, the Scot was not the kind of man to dismiss it simply as his duty.

Here, even the smells were different. The hemp and tar, salt and canvas seemed miles away, and clean. Adam's foot brushed against something and he heard someone gulp and mutter. It was a fold of the loose smock worn by one of Murray's assistants, his "crew" as he called them, slumped in a trestle chair and already snoring again.

Even in the feeble glow, Adam could see the tell-tale stains. Too many memories. Even the confined smells. Oils of thyme and lavender and mint, and others less medicinal, more sinister. Alcohol, blood, sickness. And always the pain. The fear.

The door was not completely shut, in case of an emergency, and it swung easily under his hand, so that the light of a shuttered lantern seemed almost blinding. Nobody moved. One man was slouched in a canvas seat, a partly folded bandage in his lap, his splinted leg propped on a chest: one of the seamen who had been injured off Biscay.

Murray was beside the cot, his back to the door, stooped, unmoving, the inert body lying in his shadow. He could have been asleep or dead. Adam looked down into the still face, younger than he remembered, eyes shut, skin as white as the sheet that partly covered his bare shoulders.

Then Murray spoke softly, without turning his head. "I knew you'd come. I felt it." He moved his head slightly and Adam saw that he was dabbing Lord's mouth with a rag, and with his other hand was gripping Lord's free hand. The right arm was stiff with linen bandages and protected by what appeared to be weighted pillows. There were stained dressings on the deck, and more piled in a keg nearby.

Murray half-turned his hawkish profile and said quietly, "Pass me that jug, will you?" He bobbed his head with a little sarcastic smile. "If you please, *sir?*" He released the hand he had been holding and lowered it to the cot, and waited, motionless. Then he said, "Come on, laddie. Once again, eh?"

Adam almost held his breath. It was over. *If I had kept away . . .*

But the hand was moving. Hesitantly, slowly, then decisively toward Murray's hairy, outthrust one. He grasped it and dabbed the man's mouth again. "I am here, Brian. We are here."

The voice was very faint. "Arm hurts."

Murray's tousled hair fell over his forehead. "At least you can *feel* it, thank God." He lifted the sheet and listened to the heart before moistening the dry lips again. Adam could smell the brandy.

The surgeon was staring now at the glittering array of instruments nearby. *"Not this time!"*

As if he were speaking to himself, or to death.

Lieutenant Hector Monteith stood at the foot of the mizzen mast, and glared around at the seamen already mustered by the quarter-davits to lower the jolly-boat for towing astern.

"Take the strain! Turns for lowering!" His foot tapped impatiently as one man broke into a fit of coughing. "We don't have the rest of the forenoon, Scully!" Then, *"Lower away!"*

The jolly-boat, maid of all work, gave a jerk and began to move, empty but for a man fore and aft to check the tackles. Always a lonely task at sea.

Monteith bawled, *"Handsomely!"* He moved to the side. "This is not a contest!" He saw the man in the boat's bows hold up his fist. "Avast lowering!" The boat had settled on the water, lifting and falling easily on the frigate's wash. "Recall those men." He glanced along the rank of seamen on the quarterdeck and knew the first lieutenant was on the opposite gangway. Watching him. "And don't forget! A boat towing astern could save a life!"

The seaman named Scully, who had coughed, muttered, "So long as it's not yours!"

Luke Jago turned away from the boat tier where he had been changing the lashings on the gig. *His* gig. When they finally reached Freetown the captain would want the gig, no excuses. Jago had no complaints about that. A man-of-war was always judged by her boats. And that was how it should be.

He saw Monteith, hands on hips, overseeing the men mustered by the sloping davits. The watch had almost run its course, but Monteith would not dismiss them until the stroke of eight bells. He was the third lieutenant, and a junior one at that, with a face so youthful he might still have been a midshipman, but he had all the makings of a "hard-horse." Suppose he ever gained a command of his own?

God help his ship's company, Jago thought. He gripped the hammock nettings as the deck sloped suddenly and some loose tackle clattered against a hatch coaming.

On cue, Monteith snapped, "Stow that properly and in a seamanlike manner, Logan!"

The seaman answered just as sharply, "It's Lawrence, *sir*," but he hurried to obey.

Jago thought of Falmouth and the big grey house, and the girl on the captain's arm at the church. All those people . . . *an' I was a guest. An' more than that.*

He had been recalling all the stories, yarns he had shared with John Allday, Sir Richard Bolitho's old coxswain, who had been with the admiral when he had been shot down aboard his flagship, *Frobisher*, in 1815. Allday was landlord of the Old Hyperion inn and had a charming wife to warm his bed, and a daughter, too. Everything. But in many ways he was still the admiral's coxswain, and his heart was aboard *Frobisher*. Even the fine model Allday had been making of their old ship remained unfinished, as if he was unwilling to break something between them, some link to the past.

Jago heard the shrill of a call and the cry, echoed below deck: *"Up Spirits!"* and murmured, "But stand fast, the Holy Ghost!" He had already caught the whiff of rum, even in this keen Atlantic air.

There were voices and he saw the first lieutenant stride across the quarterdeck, not to speak with Monteith but to attract the attention of an untidy figure in a linen smock, one of the surgeon's crew. The man looked utterly drained and unsteady on his feet, and had doubtless been working in the sick-bay without sleep since the previous morning. "Jock" Murray, as he was known behind his back, never seemed to spare himself, nor those who shared his trade.

Jago was too far away to hear what was being said, but words were not necessary. He saw Vincent gesture to his right arm, and the other man's drawn face clearing and breaking into a wan smile. Then his astonishment as Vincent reached out and clapped him across the shoulder. Some seamen were stopping nearby as if to share it, and one of them shouted to the working party near the quarter-davits, who were still waiting to be dismissed.

Only Monteith remained alone, and unaware that a man's life had been saved.

Jago jumped down to the deck and took a couple of deep breaths. But the pain was still there, like a knot in his stomach. *A tot of grog might help.* Why did he always think that? It never had.

"Ah, here you are, Luke!"

It was Sergeant Fairfax, his uniform a vivid scarlet amidst the shrouds and canvas. They were friends and had served together in the past, although Jago could barely recall when or where.

Fairfax rubbed his chin, having reached a decision. "Thought you might drop into the barracks directly. I owe you a tot, I seem to remember. Maybe a couple?"

Jago touched his arm and saw the fresh pipeclay drift from his belt. "Later, mebbee, Tom. I'll be with the cap'n."

Fairfax knew him better than most. Except, maybe, Bolitho. He glanced over toward the cabin skylight. "So be it, matey!"

Below in the great cabin Adam Bolitho sat, his body at one with the motion of the ship, a following sea weaving reflections across the deckhead like lively serpents. Astern, and as far as any lookout could see, the ocean was theirs. Empty, not even a bird to give any hint of life but their own.

In the tall glass Morgan had placed by his elbow, the dark red wine was rising and falling so slowly, hardly at all. Morgan had retreated to his pantry again, and the door was partly closed, with not a clink or a rattle to disturb his captain; he had even sent his new recruit, Tregenza, to another part of the ship for the same reason.

Adam glanced at the chair which had been moved directly oppo-site this old bergère, where Gordon Murray had almost fallen asleep after painstakingly taking his captain through the procedure by which he had saved Lord's life. It had been a very close thing. The blade had just missed severing the major artery and vein, both of which branched through the inside arm, and, had that happened, stitching the wound would have been impossible even in a hospital ashore.

Murray had stifled another yawn and apologised. "Even now, one cannot be certain. There is always the danger of infection . . ." But he had suddenly smiled. "However, I am confident that, given time, he'll be back in his galley wielding those knives. He's a strong lad. Courageous, too. I'm quite proud of him."

Adam had watched him swallow wine. Some of it had dripped over his chin like blood.

"And we're proud of *you*. When I first saw the wound . . ." Adam shook his head. "I'll see that it goes in your report. We're privileged to have you among us."

He sipped his own wine now, but it seemed metallic on his tongue. He looked up, taken off guard as feet thudded across the deck overhead. In step. Marching. Marines.

Morgan had materialised like a ghost and was picking up the empty glass. "Later, sir, I shall—" He did not continue.

The door was open. It was Jago, wearing his best jacket, and with his hat squeezed under his arm. He looked at Adam's uniform and then at the old sword which was lying across the table. "Ready when you are, Cap'n."

Adam picked up the sword. Jago was waiting to fasten it to his belt, like others before him.

"You'll never know . . ."

But the shrill of calls and hurrying feet stifled the rest.

"Clear lower deck! All hands! All hands lay aft to witness punishment!"

It was now.

3 THE WITNESS

LIEUTENANT JAMES SQUIRE leaned on the quarterdeck rail to ease his stiff shoulders. Four bells, and still two more hours of the forenoon watch to complete. He glanced at young Midshipman Walker, who was sharing the watch, and wondered what would have changed in the navy *by the time he's my age.*

He smiled. Probably nothing.

He saw some of the new hands clustered around the forward eighteen-pounders while the gun captains took them through the drill, loading and running out. They were on the weather side, and with *Onward* leaning slightly to the wind they would find the guns needed all their strength. Maddock, the gunner, never spared any one where his broadside was concerned.

Men working on or above deck had paused and were looking on, some of them perhaps remembering their fight with *Nautilus,* and others, like Drummond, the bosun, further back still. He had served at Trafalgar aboard the *Mars,* in the thick of the action.

"Stand by! *Together,* this time!" Maddock had just taken over, head on one side, the deafness his only weakness after too many broadsides in the past. But woe betide any one who tried to take advantage of that disability. Maddock could lip-read from one end of the gun deck to the other.

Several of the seamen working on deck were barefoot, either to save shoe leather, or to harden their soles for shrouds and ratlines. A few would regret it.

But they must all feel the difference, even the last to join at Plymouth. There was a suggestion of warmth under a clear sky, and the bite had gone from the wind. Squire's face cracked into a wry smile. *Almost.*

He knew that the midshipman had moved closer. A bright lad, eager to learn and not afraid to ask questions. But it was not that. If he leaned further over the rail he would see the large grating inboard of the nearest gun, scrubbed almost white again, and dried by the wind and sun. Where a man had been seized up in the presence of all the ship's company and flogged.

Midshipman Walker was not yet fourteen, but soon would be, the same age as Squire when he had joined his first ship. In his two years aboard Squire had witnessed two hundred floggings. His captain had believed in discipline of the most ferocious kind. He and others like him had contributed to the great fleet mutinies at the Nore and Spithead, even as England had been living in daily fear of a French invasion.

Since he had joined *Onward* there had been only one flogging, suspended halfway through, before the punishment of the seaman Lamont two days ago. And Lamont was lucky he would not be doing the Tyburn Jig when he reached port and higher authority.

You might become hardened to it, but you never forgot. Squire thought of Jago, the captain's coxswain, a strong man, and a loyal one. But Squire had seen him being washed down one day, twisting his muscular body under a pump. The scars of the cat were unmistakable. Jago had received a written pardon from an admiral, and a sum of money in compensation amounting to a year's pay, and the officer who had ordered the unjustified punishment had paid for it with a court-martial. But Jago would carry the scars to his grave. Squire had glimpsed his face as Lamont was being flogged, and wondered how he could remain so faithful to any captain after his own experience.

Midshipman Walker exclaimed suddenly, "I think he deserved it!"

Squire sighed. *Out of the mouths of babes . . .*

"Deck there!"

Every one, even the helmsman, looked up as the cry came from the foretopmast. It seemed ages since the lookouts had sighted anything, and this was certainly not land. Squire stared at the small silhouette who was signalling with his arm, but he already knew the face and the name. Always reliable. But he would need more than the naked eye.

He saw the midshipman reach for a telescope, but took it from him and shook his head. "Not this time . . . Bosun's Mate! Aloft with you! You'll feel at ease up there!"

It was Tucker. He took the telescope and held it to his eye briefly before slinging it across his shoulder. "Starboard bow," was all he said.

Squire replied, "Aye, probably nothing, or out of sight by now. But . . ."

Tucker was already striding along the gangway, as he must have done countless times in his service as a foretopman. Squire watched him until he had reached the shrouds and began to climb. *Keep busy, mind and body*. It helped. Squire had learned that for himself.

David Tucker climbed steadily, his eyes fixed on the foretop and the hard, bellying curve of canvas. He was conscious of the men by the guns, heard Maddock's voice as he repeated some instructions; a few faces might have turned in the direction of the figure on the ratlines, or maybe not. What did he expect? Anger? Hostility? Certainly not sympathy.

He reached the foretop and pulled himself out and over the barricade, his body hanging momentarily over the creaming water below. *Don't look down*, they used to shout up at him in those early days. Now it was something he told others.

A seaman was splicing nearby, and glanced at him only briefly as he passed. As if he were a stranger.

Only two days ago, but he had relived every moment. He should have been prepared. Harry Drummond, the bosun, must have been warning him.

"You've got your feet firmly on the first step of the ladder, Dave. Obey orders smartly an' without question, an' you might go higher!" He had grinned. "Like me!"

Tucker had witnessed more than a few floggings since he had joined his first ship as a mere boy. The Articles of War were read aloud by every captain; no individual could plead ignorance of them.

But he could still feel the shock.

When the pipe had called all hands to witness punishment, Rowlatt, the master-at-arms, had pulled him aside and handed him the familiar red baize bag containing the "cat." He could even have been smiling. "First time for everything, my lad!"

Tucker realised he had reached the crosstrees almost without noticing the dangerous part of the climb. He knew the lookout well; they had often shared this precarious perch. He came from York, and Tucker had always wanted to know how he had found his way into a King's ship.

He said now, "I remember when the cap'n gave you his own glass when you came aloft!" He nudged Tucker's arm. "Been a bad lad, have you?" And laughed.

Tucker trained the telescope on the rough bearing, the sun lancing from the sea, stinging and blurring his vision. He knew the sun was not to blame. And he was grateful beyond any words.

He focused the lens slowly, his body timed to the movement of the mast, which swayed as if completely separate from the hull beneath. Perhaps the lookout was mistaken, or his eyes were dazzled from hours of staring at the empty sea in its ever-changing moods. Tucker tensed and murmured, "*Got* you!"

But for the man from Yorkshire's keen eyesight, they would have missed it altogether. A small vessel, possibly a schooner but now mastless and low in the water, the only sign of movement the torn remnants of her sails.

He handed the telescope to the lookout. "There she is. What's left of her."

"Abandoned." The lookout passed the telescope back. "No boats on board."

Tucker leaned over and looked at the deck below. Nobody appeared to be gazing up at the foremast now, but Squire would want to know. And the captain . . . He remembered the emotionless voice. *One dozen lashes.* How had *he* felt about it, if he had felt anything?

He slung the telescope across his shoulder and dug his foot into the first ratline.

The lookout said, "Thanks," and lifted his hand. "Don't lose any sleep." Something in his voice made Tucker turn back. "The bastard deserved it!"

Lieutenant Squire was waiting and listened to his report and the description of the abandoned vessel without interruption, then said, "Nothing we can do. But the captain will need to know about it. I'll take you to him."

Midshipman Walker piped up, "He's coming now, sir!"

Adam waited without comment until Tucker had repeated his description, and said, "We'll alter course and intercept. It might tell us something."

Squire bit his lip, a habit only others noticed. "Could be dark when we find her, sir." He glanced up at the masthead pendant. "If she's still afloat."

Bolitho stared across the open sea, and then back at him. "At least we will have tried." He turned toward the companion. "Chartroom. Tell the first lieutenant."

Squire touched his hat, and beckoned to Midshipman Walker. "You heard what the captain said, boy. So go to it!"

He heard Bolitho's voice on the companion ladder, speaking with the surgeon, either about the wounded man or the one who had stabbed him. All the same to a sawbones . . .

But only one man made the real decisions, and he was doing it now.

Adam Bolitho walked across the quarterdeck and saw Vincent lower his telescope and turn toward him. Beyond him and deceptively close was the disabled schooner, stern-on for the first time since the lookout had signalled for assistance.

Vincent said, "She's called *Moonstone*, sir," and grimaced. "What's left of her."

Adam leaned his hip against the rail and steadied the telescope as he adjusted to the deck's uneven motion, and the plunging of the other vessel. He could calm himself, as he had often done, just by touching the engraving. His uncle's telescope, like the old sword in the great cabin below. Strength or envy? Maybe both.

"*Moonstone*. By God, she's been fired on."

Vincent said, "You know her, sir?"

Adam shifted the glass carefully. Faces and groups of sailors, staring at the drifting schooner, as many had been doing for most of the day. Some waiting for the bell to chime from the forecastle for the first dog watch. And beyond them the sea, without the bluster and occasional whitecaps, but sullen, almost breathing.

He glanced at the sky and at the trailing masthead pendant. They could not delay much longer. He thought of the sealed orders in the strongbox below, the scarlet lettering: WITH ALL DESPATCH.

He looked directly at Vincent but he knew Monteith was hovering by the gangway, waiting to take over the watch, and already peering around as if to find something neglected and demanding his attention. He was aware of Jago too, arms folded, and staring not at the schooner but astern, outwardly relaxed; but to Adam it was like a warning. Like the stabbing in the galley. Or the epaulette sliced away by the invisible marksman's shot.

He recalled Vincent's question.

"*Moonstone?* Yes. Three years ago when I was with *Unrivalled* . . . in these same waters, or near enough." He raised the telescope again, more slowly, focusing on the broken spars and splintered bulwark. Feeling it. "Freetown, the anti-slavery patrols. *Moonstone* was under Admiralty warrant, liaison between our flag officer and the shore authorities."

Vincent was listening, but his eyes never left the schooner. Perhaps knowing her name had given her an identity, and made it personal.

"She's going under."

Adam looked at the sky. The wind was dropping, and there was a ridge of cloud now on a horizon which had been as sharp as steel. He said, "We'll board her."

He heard eight bells ring out, and the slow response of feet and voices as the watch was relieved.

Vincent did not move, even when Monteith strode across the deck

and touched his hat to him, but with his eyes on his captain. Vincent
looked toward the starboard gangway where Squire was pointing at
something aboard the drifting schooner, shaping it with his strong
hands.

"Mr. Squire, sir?" It sounded so formal that at any other time . . .

Adam beckoned to Jago, whose response was immediate. "No. You
go, Mark. I need to *know* . . ."

"But it's my watch, sir."

Adam touched his arm. "Take the gig and a few extra hands. The
jolly-boat has shipped some water, by the look of it."

Jago was beside him. "Standin' by, Cap'n."

Adam looked up at the sky, and the loosely flapping topsails. *With
all despatch* . . . The wind was dropping and had already backed a little.
Onward might easily lose the time she had gained after her rough passage from Biscay, and they would get no thanks from the admiral when
they eventually reached Freetown. Least of all for boarding a crippled
vessel which would likely capsize and founder at any moment.

He gazed across the water. The schooner was rolling steeply in each
trough, showing her copper and the splintered holes where shots had
smashed into the hull. Others had brought down most of her spars and
rigging. *Moonstone* must have been a fast sailer, like most of her breed.
Then why had she not spread her canvas and run?

He said, "At the first sign of trouble, Mark—"

Vincent looked at him and nodded slowly. "I know, sir. One hand
for the King."

The falls were manned and the gig was already at deck level as
Vincent turned and said, "I'm taking Napier," then climbed down the
quarter as the call came to lower away.

The gig veered away, and Adam heard Jago order the bowman to
cast off.

Unsteadily at first but more strongly as the oarsmen lay back on their
looms, the gig was already pulling toward *Moonstone,* and was soon
out of sight as Jago steered around *Onward*'s stern to take advantage
of her lee. But not before Adam had seen Vincent half-standing in the

sternsheets, and the white midshipman's patches on the thwart below him. David Napier had proved his worth and courage before this, and had paid for it. But was that the only reason for Vincent's choice?

Lieutenant Squire had joined Adam by the compass box, and asked, "How long, sir?"

"We will reef tops'ls directly." He looked again at the listing schooner. "An hour. No longer." He had seen the clouds, closer now. "Tell the bosun to have the jolly-boat hauled alongside and bailed out."

Squire touched his hat and strode heavily away.

In the gig, Vincent reached out and gripped Napier's shoulder to steady himself as the tiller went over for the final approach, and felt him tense as if waiting for the impact. Or a challenge.

The bowmen were ready with two grapnels, in case one fell short.

"Back water, starboard." Jago's voice broke the silence as the gig nudged alongside the schooner's hull, and another grapnel was hurled from aft.

Vincent had boarded a good many vessels on one mission or another, especially in the early days leading up to the Battle of Lissa. But someone else had been giving the orders. Now, with the *Moonstone*'s side looming over him, small things stood out. Her gunports were closed, and had been newly painted. Carronades, eight or ten of them, enough to deter other small craft or would-be boarders, were unmarked, strangely at odds with the battering on the opposite side which must have dismasted her.

And now the silence. Only the occasional creak of the hulls, and the sluice of water between them. He could even hear the oarsmen's heavy breathing after their pull away from *Onward*'s side.

Jago said loudly, "Standin' by, sir."

Vincent looked at the bulwark and wanted to lick his lips; they felt like sand. But he reached out and seized a fistful of the broken rigging that trailed above the sealed ports and called, "Be ready!" They all knew what to do. *If not . . .* He felt his knee grate on something metal, and the breeze on his face, and he was standing on the other vessel's deck. In seconds the boarding party had fanned out on either side of him, forward and aft, but it had seemed an age while he was standing here alone.

And *Onward* was in sight again, unmoving above her own reflection. Vincent examined the schooner's guns: all secured for sea. Even a solitary swivel gun, mounted near the wheel, was still covered, and the flag locker was tidily packed with bunting.

Someone said, "Must have taken 'em by surprise."

Napier had come across the deck, a long splinter of wood in his hand. "Blood, sir."

Vincent took it from him. "It's blood, right enough. Must have been a lot of it, too."

Jago was on his knees by the shattered bulwark. "Fired up from a boat alongside." He frowned as the abandoned wheel jerked slightly, as if to invisible hands, and indicated the deck. "Or from 'ere, as th' bastard stepped aboard."

Vincent joined him, then reached out and touched Jago's sinewy arm. "It makes sense . . . That was well said, Cox'n. No signals made, no attempt to attack or repel boarders."

Jago was still looking at Vincent's hand on his sleeve. "Means they must have known each other." He scowled. "They was friends!"

Napier looked back at *Onward*. She had turned slightly, her sails aback and flapping. Napier could see the gilded figurehead of the boy with his trident and the dolphin. Where he had sat and yarned with Midshipman Huxley, who had joined the ship with him, and who had shared so much of the elation and the pain.

"Do we return to *Onward*, sir?"

Vincent was also looking toward the frigate. "We'll carry out a search as ordered. But I don't like the look of those clouds." He added sharply, "We can't take *Moonstone* in tow. She's sinking anyway, or soon will if a squall blows up."

He tugged out his watch. Napier had seen it lying on the chart table several times, but had never been able to read the inscription inside the guard.

"One hour, less if possible. I'll go aft—you check the crew's quarters."

He looked at Jago. "First sign of bad weather, sound the alarm and we'll clear the ship." Something came into his mind and he smiled. "No heroics, eh?"

Jago said, "What about the galley, sir?"

Vincent turned, with his hands on the fallen foremast. *"No."* Then, more quietly, "I shall go there now. Might tell us something." He tugged open a small hatchway. "You keep an eye on the deck and the boat." There was no response. *"Your* gig, remember?"

Jago breathed out noisily, waiting for two seamen to accompany the first lieutenant. *Bloody officers.* But he said aloud, "Watch yer step. Yell out if you need 'elp." He tapped Napier's arm as he had seen Vincent do and grinned. "An' don't make a meal of it."

Two of the gig's crew, one carrying an axe, the other with a shuttered lantern, followed Napier past a gaping hold. It must have been opened to search for something, or to remove it. It was unreal, hard to believe. The vessel was dead, and yet at each step . . . Napier leaned over the coaming and peered down, only to see his own reflection in the trapped water beneath him, head and shoulders framed against the sky.

The water was swilling back and forth with each uneven roll. Not deep, anyway. He saw a narrow ladder and climbed onto it, and called to the two seamen, "Take a look at that other hatch! Keep together!"

One of them waved, the other bared his teeth in a grin.

Then Napier felt the deck under his shoes, slippery, gritty with dirt from some previous cargo. He winced as the hull swayed over again and the trapped water swept around his ankles. It shocked him, like an icy touch. He waited for his nerves to settle.

He heard another hatch cover being dragged aside, then slammed shut again.

There were piles of canvas propped against one side of the hold, shining faintly, soaked through. They appeared to have been properly stacked—spare sails or awnings—but had been tossed aside as the schooner was dismasted and began to submit to the ocean.

More thuds, further away now. Not that far, he reassured himself. *Moonstone* was less than half the frigate's length. Must have been a fine little ship under sail. To command. Probably a twin of the one named *Pickle* which had been sent by Vice-Admiral Collingwood to carry the vital and terrible news to England after Trafalgar, the great victory over-shadowed by Nelson's death. He must ask Drummond, the bosun, about it some time . . . It was strange, but he still saw Joshua Guthrie in his mind, *Onward*'s old bosun, who had been killed.

He flinched as something fell and scraped across the deck above, perhaps a broken spar or part of the foremast. It was only a matter of time before she foundered, but how much of that time did they have? He saw some of the canvas lurch over, heard somebody shout and his companion answer, glass breaking as it fell to the deck. Then silence.

The hull swayed again and Napier moved carefully along the side of the hold and waited for the deck to right itself. It did not.

He shouted, "Anything, Lucas?" and heard the muffled reply. "Nuthin' yet!" Anxious, even scared.

"Join the others!" and he heard the thud of feet, a hatch slamming. People had died, and they might never discover how or why. It was pointless to risk any more.

Vincent would be ready to leave, for his own reasons. One of the carelessly tied bundles of canvas thudded against his legs. He told him-self to remain calm, but it was like a shouted warning. The time was now.

He turned to look for the ladder. It was in shadow, or perhaps the light was going anyway. He recalled what Vincent had said about the clouds. One squall bursting over *Moonstone*'s deck, and she would be on her way to the bottom.

The fabric of his breeches caught on the edge of something that must have been shielded by the canvas and other debris, a small door or screen where tools or tackle might be stowed for unloading cargo.

He called, "Wait, Lucas!" but there was no answer. What was the point, anyway? He felt the water swilling across his feet again. It seemed deeper. *Go now.*

He had known fear in the past. This was different. He simply could not move.

The deck lurched again; perhaps he cried out, but there was only silence. Any second now . . . And then he heard it.

At first he thought it was only in his mind, the last cry, like when *Audacity* had gone down, but then he heard it again. A tapping, a scraping, hesitant but close. Human? He was scrabbling against the little door now, tugging at the rough clip, leaving blood on the frame but feeling nothing, only a wild desperation. Water was surging around his legs; this could be the final plunge, but it was all out of reach, unreal. Only the faint sound was vital.

Another coaming, and he almost fell. He tried to wedge the door open; otherwise he would be in complete darkness. There was very little light anyway. More fallen canvas and coils of rope, sodden papers floating like leaves, clinging to his hands as he steadied himself. The furtive scrabbling had stopped, if it had ever existed. Maybe it was in an adjoining space or hold. There was a muffled echo, as if something had reverberated against the hull, and he knew it was a shot. From *Onward*, from another world. The pre-arranged recall.

He pushed his shoulder against the door but it did not shift. *If only.* Then he froze, unable to think or breathe as something groped at his thigh and fastened to his wet clothing. Like a claw, and it was alive.

He saw the face for the first time, only the eyes catching the feeble light when the door moved slightly.

Napier struggled to move closer until their faces were almost touching, felt the shocked gasp of pain as he tried to push the debris away from the twisted limbs, heard the ragged breathing. The coat was torn and matted, not only with water but with blood, and Napier could see the faint shine of gilt buttons. When his hands fumbled against the ice-cold fingers, he felt the pistol they still gripped. It would never fire again.

Napier leaned closer, overwhelmed by the man's pain and the smell of the filth in which he had been sprawled. How could he have hoped and lived so long after all he had seen and suffered?

The other hand fell against Napier's wrist, clutched it, and for a few more seconds clung like iron.

"Knew . . . you'd . . . come." He coughed and swallowed, then was silent again. Only the eyes seemed alive. Wild.

Napier thought he heard a shout. Maybe the gig was about to cast off. Leave him . . . He felt no fear.

He asked quietly, "How long have you—" and got no further, feeling the hand move to his throat, his face, limp now, but determined.

"Tell them, matey, an' don't forget, see?" He coughed blood, but his fingers had tightened. "Knew you'd come, see?"

Napier heard another spar slither across the deck, but he did not move. *"Tell me!"*

The eyes were closed now, but the voice seemed stronger. How could that be? "I should have known . . . but too late."

"Who did this?" Napier felt the hand try to respond, but it was still. Only the eyes were alive, and the lips.

"No quarter. One by one. But I knew you'd come."

Napier knew it was too late, for both of them. This was all they had left. And he could not move. Soon now . . .

He felt the fingers tighten again. "Remember the name! *Tell them.*"

There was silence, and Napier heard another sound: the trickle of water over the coaming, lapping against their legs.

The face moved, almost touching his; he could feel the cold, rasping breath. *"Ball—an—tyne."* He was trying to squeeze his hand. *"Say it!"*

Napier repeated, "Ballantyne." He felt the hand relax, and knew that he was now alone.

There was a crash, more loose gear falling in the hold, and he stood, waiting numbly for the end. Then he was gasping, his mind reeling as the door was wrenched aside, and he was being dragged clear of the floating debris.

Luke Jago exclaimed, "This is no place for you! So out of it, my lad!"

Napier was on his feet, staring back: Jago was bending over the body, the gilt buttons moving as he thrust his hand between them, the eyes fixed and gazing across his shoulders.

"Gone, poor devil." He took Napier's arm sharply and together they headed toward the ladder. Only then did Napier realise that the water was around his knees.

"What can I do?"

Jago stared up at the sky and the thickening layers of cloud and took a deep breath. "Pray, if you believes in it!"

They were both on deck, swaying together like two drunks recovering from a lively run ashore.

Vincent was leaning against the bulwark, alone, with his back to the sea. He snapped, "We'd almost given you up!" and gestured briskly. "Into the boat with you!"

Jago waited for them to climb down into the gig and followed. The grapnels had already been removed, and the bowmen were ready to cast off.

Napier stared at the schooner's side, trying to marshal his thoughts. "Shove off forrard! *Out oars!*"

He could sense Jago's nearness and rock-like calm as he took control of men and oars.

Someone shouted, "She's goin', lads!"

Napier saw *Moonstone* start to turn on her side, showing her scarred deck, and the open hold where he would still be trapped but for Jago's timely arrival. One of the broken masts slid down the deck, and he heard it crash against that same bulwark, dragging tangled rigging and canvas after it.

He gripped his wrist and could still feel the dying man's desperation, hear his voice. The urgency and the despair. The rudder squeaked and he twisted round to see Jago swing the tiller bar, eyes steady as he gauged the moment.

There was a rumble like distant thunder, and sharper sounds as the hull continued to heel over toward them: carronades which had not been fired in *Moonstone*'s defense crashing free, their great weight uncontrolled and speeding her last moments. And suddenly she was gone, the gig pitching only briefly as the wash subsided.

Napier rubbed his eyes with the back of his hand. When he looked again he saw *Onward*, her sails aback and livid against the low clouds, waiting.

The ocean was deep here, and in his mind he could see the schooner still on her way down into eternal darkness. He gripped his wrist again and knew the memory would never leave him. Nor would he allow himself to forget.

It was a pledge.

4 Dangerous Rendezvous

In Cornwall it had been a hard winter so far, but on this February morning the sky above Falmouth was clear and sunlit, at odds with further inland where the trees were still etched white with frost.

Not much wind, but what there was felt like a honed blade. There were plenty of people about, muffled up against the cold, and the hardier types behaving as if it were a spring day. A few, all women, waited by the fishermen's wharf, but most of the boats were at sea or empty alongside. All the usual idlers waited on the waterfront, passing the time of day or waiting to share a drink with friends. A servant from the nearby inn had just been seen rolling an empty barrel across the courtyard, a welcome signal to the onlookers.

There had not been much movement in the harbour or Carrick Roads, but this day was different, and they were discussing the newcomer critically: a King's ship, something of a rarity of late, with the exception of revenue cutters and naval supply vessels.

Many of the idlers were old sailors themselves, discharged, or thrown on the beach for a dozen different reasons. Many of them loudly proclaimed they were glad to be free of the navy and its harsh discipline, or various officers they had served in the past. Bad food and poor pay, and the constant risk of injury or death. But they were usually the first on the waterfront whenever a sail was sighted.

She was a brig, one of the navy's maids of all work, busier than ever now with so many of the heavier vessels being paid off or scrapped. She was shortening sail as she turned slightly toward her anchorage, tiny figures spread out along the upper yards of her two masts, the canvas not even flapping as it caught the sunlight. Like her hull, the sails shone like glass and were hardened with salt and ice. A fine sight, but to some of the old hands watching from the shore she meant hazards as well as beauty. Fisting and kicking the frozen canvas into submission so that it could be furled and reefed was dangerous enough, but one slip and you would fall headlong onto the deck below, or into the sea alongside, where even if you could swim . . .

She was still turning, her sails almost aback, soon to be hidden by the old battery wall above the harbour. Only her masthead pendant showed to mark her anchorage. One man, who had brought a telescope, had seen the new arrival's name and called out, *"Merlin!"*

But he was alone. His friends had drifted away.

Commander Francis Troubridge turned his back to the sun and stared at the land, the nearness of it. With the wind dropping to a light breeze, the approach had seemed endless. He would become used to it, with time and more experience. He had a good ship's company; some had served aboard *Merlin* since she had first commissioned. One hundred and thirty all told. Hard to believe, he thought, when you considered she was only one hundred and five feet in length. Teamwork and companionship were vital. He looked at the houses, one above another on the steep hillside, but he could not see the church as he had the last time he had been in Falmouth. Only three months ago.

So much had happened since.

He glanced forward where men were stowing away loose gear, sliding down backstays, racing one another to the deck. A few were slower, quietly cursing the scrapes and grazes inflicted by the frozen canvas, which could tear out a man's fingernails no matter how experienced a sailor he was.

Troubridge had come to know the names of most and remembered them, something he had learned as a flag lieutenant, when the admiral had always expected him to know everything. That was over. He was

Merlin's captain now. And she was his first command. And to most of these men he was still a stranger. It was up to him.

"Standin' by, sir!"

He raised his hand above his head and heard the cry from the forecastle.

"Let go!"

The splash of the anchor and the immediate response as the cable followed it, men hastening it on its way and ready for any stoppages. There were none.

He had been in command for almost a year, and with previous experience, mostly at sea, he should have been used to it and prepared for anything. But at moments like this it was always new. Different. Beyond pride. If anything, what Troubridge felt was excitement.

"All secure, sir." Turpin, his first lieutenant, was a square, muscular man who could move quickly when it suited him, from watching the anchor drop from the cathead, alert for any mishap, then aft again just minutes later. He was a born sailor with a strong, weathered face, and clear blue eyes that seemed to belong to someone else looking out through a mask at everything around him. And now at his captain.

Turpin had always served in small ships, and had originally been promoted from the lower deck. When Troubridge had first stepped aboard, Turpin had conducted him over every inch of the ship, pointing out every store and cabin space, messdeck, magazine, even the galley. Proud, even possessive. He was about ten years older than his captain, but if he cherished any resentment he had not revealed it.

Merlin's previous commanding officer had been put ashore, taken suddenly ill with a fever he had picked up on the anti-slavery patrols. He had since died. But as is the way in the navy, nobody now mentioned his name.

Her second lieutenant, John Fairbrother, was younger than Troubridge and seemed to look upon *Merlin* merely as a stepping-stone to promotion. The brig also carried a sailing master, who, like Turpin, was very experienced with smaller vessels and had served on three oceans. And, surprisingly for her size, *Merlin* boasted a surgeon,

Edwin O'Brien, although now, with peace and the brig assigned to the Channel Fleet, his might remain a minor role. It might have been different on the slavery patrols, or hunting pirates in the Mediterranean, where in a ship often sailing alone a surgeon's skill was paramount.

The four of them made up *Merlin*'s little wardroom. She carried no midshipmen or Royal Marines and ceremonial was kept to a minimum.

Turpin said, "We are here to await orders, sir?" It sounded like a statement, but Troubridge had come to accept that. The lieutenant hardly ever seemed to write anything down; he carried everything in his head.

Troubridge stared across the water and saw the church for the first time since that day. The Church of King Charles the Martyr, where he had had the honour of taking the lovely Lowenna up the aisle to become Adam Bolitho's wife.

Turpin broke into his dream-like reminiscence with a blunt, "Memories, sir?" The blue eyes gave nothing away, but no doubt he was remembering that the admiral had granted special leave so Troubridge could attend the wedding.

He nodded. "Yes. Good ones."

"Will you be going ashore, sir?"

"We're to remain here for five days, as you know. If nothing changes we'll take on board two Admiralty officials. Like our last mission, I'm afraid. Not very exciting."

Turpin said sharply, "Better 'n being laid up." The slightest pause. "Sir."

It was the first hint of envy, and Troubridge was surprised by it. If only . . .

Someone yelled, "Boat headin' our way, sir!"

Turpin grunted, "Mail boat. See to it, Parker!"

Troubridge walked across the deck, past the big double wheel and polished compass box, and reached the side in time to see the mail boat already pulling away from the entry port, somebody waving his arm and calling back to *Merlin*'s side party.

A seaman was coiling some rope and avoided his eyes when Troubridge moved past him. Maybe it was always like this. Adam Bolitho had mentioned the loneliness of command, trying to prepare him.

Turpin's shadow was beside him again. "Only two letters, sir. Don't know we're here yet, I reckon." He thrust one out. "For you, sir."

"Thank you." Troubridge walked into the shadow of the mast, knowing Turpin was watching him. He broke the seal. Not a letter but a card, undated. He had never seen her handwriting, so how could he have known it was from her?

> *I saw you anchor this morning. Welcome back.*
> *Visit us if you can.*
> *Lowenna.*

He walked back across the deck and gazed at the houses and the church tower.

She must have heard from someone, maybe the coastguard, that *Merlin* was arriving in Falmouth today and had made a visit to the headland, or here to the waterfront to watch them anchor. She might even be over there now. He felt for the card again. She was just being courteous, and was probably always surrounded by friends.

Troubridge replaced the card in its torn envelope and slid it into his pocket.

Visit us. What else could she have said? If she only knew . . .

"Everything all right, sir?"

He waved and said something insignificant and Turpin turned away to deal with a supply boat which was about to come alongside.

What he had hoped for, even dreamed about; and apparently she had thought about him, too. They were good friends, for all sorts of reasons . . . Troubridge recalled exactly when he had wanted to tell her that he would always be ready to come to her, if she were ever in need. In the church that day before the ceremony. He had got no further than *if ever* . . . and she had touched his lips with her fingers, scented with autumnal flowers. *I know, and I thank you, Francis.*

He had never forgotten the time he and Adam Bolitho had broken down the door of a studio and found Lowenna standing over the man who had tried to rape her, the gown ripped from her shoulders, a brass candlestick poised over him. *I would have killed him!* And he had felt his own finger on the trigger of the pistol he was carrying.

He touched the card in his pocket. Like hearing her voice.

Turpin had rejoined him. "Can I do anything, sir?"

"I'll need a boat in half an hour. I'm going ashore. Back before sunset. Send word to the revenue pier if you need me beforehand."

Turpin glanced around conspiratorially, as if someone might be listening. "Somethin' wrong, sir?"

Troubridge was staring after the mail boat, still pulling steadily toward the waterfront. "Something personal. I must leave a message. And thank you, Mathias, for your help."

Turpin's leathery face revealed surprise as well as concern. At having been allowed to share something he sensed was private, and also at the casual use of his first name. Then his face broke into a grin. "Leave it with me, sir." He gestured to a bosun's mate and added quietly, "Watch your back, eh?"

It was perhaps as close as they had ever been. But it was a beginning.

He would go below and write a short note to have taken up to the big grey house. After the flagship, *Merlin's* cabin seemed small. But it was a refuge, and it was his. Turpin had probably used it himself while he was waiting for the new commanding officer, or hoping for his own promotion.

Watch your back. But the immediate enemy was guilt.

Troubridge wedged his elbow against the seat as the vehicle lurched into another deep rut, hidden by one of the countless puddles left by heavy overnight rain.

Everything seemed to have happened so quickly that his mind was still reluctant to cope. A message, in a strong scholarly hand which he guessed belonged to Dan Yovell, the Bolitho steward, whom he had met several times, had been brought out to *Merlin;* the boatman had departed without waiting for any response. *A carriage will be sent.* And despite the weather and the roads, it was waiting for him on time.

Another face he remembered: Young Matthew, the coachman, who had driven them to the church that day. "Young" Matthew because his father, also Matthew, had been coachman at the estate before him. His father had died long since, but the nickname remained, although he was probably the oldest man there.

The carriage was a landau, new and beautifully sprung. Troubridge had seen some of them in London, and his admiral and Lady Bethune had used one while in residence there. The landau had twin hoods which folded right back and allowed the occupant to see and be seen, if the weather was kind enough. The hoods were made of greasy harness-leather, which had a strong smell when wet. Like now.

Once again he tried to grapple with his thoughts, but events were now out of his hands. There had also been a curt letter from the two Admiralty officials: their arrival would be a day later than expected. Sunday at noon. Equally curtly, it had stressed: *No ceremonial.* He had expected Turpin to be pleased about that, but if anything he had taken it as an insult. "Be different if we were a ship of the line, with a guard of honour, I suppose!"

Troubridge thought of it when he was leaving the ship: the trill of calls, Turpin doffing his hat and the boat alongside, oars tossed, ready to carry him ashore. Would he ever become used to it? Take it for granted as his right? He had heard Adam Bolitho say that if you did, you were ready for the beach. Or burial.

Once he had looked back at the brig, rolling easily in the offshore wind. Small, but able to give a good account of herself if challenged. She carried sixteen big thirty-two pounders, eight of them carronades. He had studied her figurehead, oblivious to the stroke oarsman watching him. The carver had produced a fine example of a merlin falcon, wings spread beneath the bowsprit, beak open, and ready to pounce, like a young eagle.

Troubridge could understand, and share, Turpin's reaction to the message.

He saw two farm workers grin and wave mockingly as the landau splashed past them. The same two had overtaken them earlier when the deeply rutted track had slowed the horses to a walking pace.

There were a few cottages now, and he noticed that most of the frost had been melted by the rain. Two cows by a gate, breath smoking, and someone tying up dead branches, squinting at the vehicle clattering past. Then, around the side of a low hill, the sea, like water against a dam. Never far away, and in the blood of the people who lived here.

The landau stopped and he heard Young Matthew speaking to his horses, calming them as a heavy farm wagon splashed by, wheels almost touching theirs; greetings were exchanged, but even here he had noticed that Young Matthew kept a musket close to hand. He had said matter-of-factly, "This is called Hanger Lane, zur. Didn't get that name for nothin'."

Troubridge was unarmed. This was Cornwall.

He saw an inn lying back from the road. The Spaniards. Someone had mentioned it to him. It had been Thomas Herrick, Sir Richard Bolitho's oldest friend; he was now rear-admiral, retired. He had shared the carriage too, en route to the wedding. Herrick had stayed at the inn and had spoken well of it. Just as well: it was the only accommodation around.

They were turning now, and Young Matthew leaned over from his box and peered through the window. "I have to stop and pick up somethin', zur." His eyes crinkled. "Bit too early when I came by this mornin'!"

Two figures had already hurried from somewhere, and Young Matthew waved to them. He was no stranger here, apparently.

He jumped down and stamped his boots on the cobbles. "Horses can do with a drink, too." He opened the door and waited as Troubridge stepped down, wincing as the feeling returned to his legs and buttocks. "They roads do make a lot of folk seasick, zur."

Troubridge noticed his arm was near enough to assist if required, and was reminded of his discreet understanding when the one-armed Herrick had arrived at the church. And the exchange of glances between the aging rear-admiral and the coachman. Appreciation, maybe more than that.

"I think you should step inside, zur. They always has a good blaze goin' on days like this." He looked at the sky and some rain spilled from his hat. "Wind do have changed. Us've seen the worst of it."

He stumped beside Troubridge to the door and called to someone else. "Won't be long, zur. I hope."

Troubridge paused inside the dark entrance to get his bearings. The inn was old and had been added to and altered over the years. Perhaps Bolithos had paused here over the centuries on their way to join a ship, or return to one.

Like me.

"Can I fetch 'ee somethin', zur?"

"Thank you, no. I'll be going directly."

The inn servant wore an apron that touched the floor and had a feather duster protruding from his pocket, like a tail. "Then sit over 'ere, and get yer blood movin' again!"

It was a high-backed seat, almost opposite one of the fires. Young Matthew was right. And there was probably more than one "good blaze" going today. He was aware of voices coming from a larger room close by. Maybe they were waiting for a local coach, or had horses stabled here.

He realised that the man in the apron was hovering nearby and said, "Perhaps I will have a drink. Something warm . . ."

"Taken care of, zur. Here in a trice!"

Troubridge relaxed slowly; the heat was doing its work. He felt as if he had just ended a watch on deck. Young Matthew had thought of everything. It was brandy with a measure of hot water. He felt it sting his tongue and knew there was not much of the latter. He would have to reward him in some way, and yet not offend . . .

Someone said, "That was the Bolitho carriage just drove in. Homeward bound, too. Must have been up an' about bloody early."

"I hear Cap'n Bolitho is at sea again." A different voice, but Troubridge was now fully alert.

"Just got wed, too. What does *she* do with 'erself while 'e's away?"

There was a harsh laugh. "Well, you know what they say. While the cat's away, the mice will play! I could tell you things about that lady."

The speaker must have shaken his head. "No, but not for much longer. I'll have her beggin' for it!"

Two things happened at once. Troubridge was on his feet and across to the connecting doorway, his eyes blazing. "Shut your filthy mouth, you drunken bastard, or I'll do it for you!" At the same instant a door from the kitchen opened unhurriedly and Young Matthew paused to put a covered basket on the floor by his feet.

"Ready when you are, zur." But he was looking at the loudmouth. "Surprised to find you here, *Mister* Flinders. With all that work goin' on at your estate?" He looked directly at Troubridge and stooped to pick up his hat, which had fallen when he had jumped to his feet. "Finish your drink first, zur."

Troubridge stared at the other man. Flinders. It meant nothing. And quite suddenly he was icily calm, as if he were watching the flash of gunfire and waiting for the fall of shot. He picked up the glass and said, "I'll share it!" and threw the contents in the other man's face.

Then he unfastened his boatcloak and folded it over his arm, replaced his hat and tugged it down over his forehead. He could hear deep breathing, and somebody retching in another part of the inn. But still nobody uttered a word.

Outside the rain appeared to have stopped, so that the puddles in the innyard seemed to glitter like fragments of broken glass. They walked to the landau without looking back, and Troubridge said abruptly, "Thank you. I'm sorry about the drink."

One of the horses shook its head and rattled its harness, recognition or impatience. Young Matthew patted its neck and ears as he passed and said, "Easy, Trooper, we'm goin' home now!" Then he opened the door and looked at Troubridge with only the hint of a smile. "What drink was that, zur?"

The road seemed in better condition hereabouts, and the horses were soon trotting briskly and, Troubridge noted gratefully, avoiding the ruts. There were several people about, and they overtook two farm workers plodding in the same direction. *Surely not the same two?* When so much had happened, and might have happened?

They had arrived, the curved driveway and the imposing grey house exactly as he remembered them. Even the old weathervane with the silhouette of Father Time against the sky.

Young Matthew's boots hit the ground as he jumped down from his box, and others were appearing to hold the horses and take the basket from The Spaniards, or merely out of curiosity. There was another vehicle on the driveway, coachman and groom standing beside it, obviously waiting to depart.

Troubridge breathed out slowly. For a moment . . . But the doors had opened and he saw Nancy, Lady Roxby, waiting to greet him, her arms outstretched as he took off his hat and bowed over her hand. She was smiling, perhaps a little emotional as he stooped to kiss the hand, and clasped him around the shoulders.

"Francis, my dear! Welcome back!" She offered her cheek, and added, "Command suits you!" He must have glanced at the other carriage, and she shrugged. "Unexpected visitor. Just leaving—at last!"

Then she took his arm and together they walked into the spacious hallway. Some features he did not remember. Most of it was like yesterday.

And Nancy you could never forget. No longer young, she was Sir Richard Bolitho's sister, but she had a beauty that never dimmed, and a wit to match it. She would deny both, but as Troubridge had seen for himself, heads always turned when she passed.

"Come and talk to me, Francis. The lady of the house will not be much longer." She guided him into a large room that overlooked a garden and a line of leafless trees. It was well furnished, but his eyes were immediately drawn to a gilded harp, which stood with a stool beside it. He had heard about the harp and imagined it often.

When he turned, Nancy was seated on a couch, looking up at him.

"Sit down, Francis." She gestured to a chair. "Get the chill out of your bones. I know too well what that road is like."

He had not noticed how discreetly she had steered him toward the fire.

She was suddenly serious, even angry, one hand clenched into a small fist. "I heard you had words with our Mr. Flinders this morn-ing." She did not wait for confirmation. "This is Cornwall, remember? Bad news rides a fast horse!" She pushed some hair from her forehead; the gesture made her look even younger.

"I was told that he works on the estate, ma'am?"

"*Did* work! He was my steward." She smiled thinly. "I gave him his marching orders this morning. I came here to tell Lowenna, but the carriage had already gone to collect you. Otherwise . . ." She glanced at the windows. "Well, the gentleman is leaving. About time, too!" There was a tartness in her voice that reminded him strangely of her nephew, Adam Bolitho.

Troubridge heard the wheels on the driveway and someone calling out to the coachman.

"I shall leave you both alone—you must have so much to talk about. I shall see you again presently, I hope, Francis?" She broke off as the door swung open.

It was Lowenna. She exclaimed, "I'm so sorry to keep you waiting like this! Jenna told me you had arrived, and in all that foul weather, too! And look at *me!*"

Troubridge took her hand and kissed it. She was wearing a long in-formal gown tied about her waist with a ribbon sash. Oddly, her feet were bare.

"He simply wouldn't go. So many questions!" She turned her eyes from Nancy to Troubridge. "How lovely to see you, Francis. How long will you be in Falmouth?" He felt he was the only one in the room. She smiled again and touched her lips with her finger. "Ssh! I know, you're not supposed to tell any one!"

Nancy looked at Lowenna's robe with what Troubridge thought was disapproval. "Did he . . . ?"

Lowenna laughed. "No, he only wanted to see my shoulders, to make a sketch or something." She walked to the open fire and shivered. "Come into the study, Francis. There's a proper blaze there."

Nervous, excited, shy; he did not know her well enough to tell. *You don't know her at all.*

She said, "I *hated* keeping you waiting." She walked across the entrance hall, her bare feet soundless on the cold floor, and opened the library door. "That was Samuel Proctor. *Sir* Samuel, as he is now."

Troubridge looked curiously around the big panelled room, at dark portraits and paintings of ships, men-of-war in action. He said, "I've seen some of his work. Fine pictures."

She turned and stood with her back to the fire, smiling. "You are full of surprises, Francis. He was a friend of my guardian's . . . or claims he was!"

She bent down to pick up a piece of cloth before using it to cover another painting, which stood against the bookcase that lined one wall. He had already seen it: the perfect body, her long hair across one shoulder. And the harp.

She was saying, "He painted Lady Hamilton. Poor Emma. She never lived to see it."

She looked up and into his eyes, her chin lifted. Like that moment in the church. Pride or defiance? "He wants me to sit for him."

"Are you pleased?"

"Honoured." She touched his arm. "I want to hear about *you*, Francis. Your new ship, everything." And then she looked away, just as suddenly. "I didn't want it to be like this. I was told about this morning."

"Lady Roxby?"

She did not answer. "I had told Young Matthew to stop at The Spaniards to collect some cheese. They make their own, and I remembered how you enjoyed it when you were last here." She faced him again, and he could see her breathing. "It was some filth about me, wasn't it?" She reached out and touched his lips, that intoxicating gesture. "I know. Elizabeth saw it before I did. She said he was 'always watching.'"

She shuddered.

He said quietly, "I would have killed him."

She gazed at him, her expression exactly as it had been captured in the painting. She repeated slowly, "Lovely to see you, Francis . . ." and drew in her breath as he put his arms around her. "Don't. I'm not made of stone!"

But she could feel his hands on her back, her spine, and knew the gown had slipped from her left shoulder; she tensed as he kissed it.

Like a fantasy or a fever. Not the heat from the fire, but their own.

She heard herself say, "Stop," and then in the next breath, *"Kiss me."* She was pressed against him, their mouths making words impossible, their tongues sealing their embrace. He was kissing her shoulder again, and she had felt his hand against her skin. Her breast.

They stood quite still, their bodies a solitary shadow against the books. Somewhere a bell was ringing, and there was a sound of hooves. She buried her face against his shoulder. A single horse. But she could not move.

Now a man's voice she did not recognise, and a woman's: young Jenna.

She stood back and covered her bare shoulder. Her gown was dishevelled, and the ribbon sash unfastened.

He said, "Let me . . ."

But she could not look at him. She opened the door and saw Jenna standing with a man in uniform, his boots and spurs caked with mud.

"Who is it, Jenna?" How could she sound so calm?

The girl bobbed her head. "Courier—for the commander, ma'am."

Troubridge walked past her, seeing the courier's eyes flick over his uniform before he handed him a sealed envelope. He did not know the handwriting: the seal was enough.

He said quietly, "I must return to the ship." He did not even say *my ship.*

Nancy was here now, glancing from one to the other. She had seen Lowenna's gown; he hoped she could not imagine the rest.

Troubridge said, "A change of plan. My passengers are arriving a day earlier after all!"

Nancy said easily to the courier, "Something hot to drink before you go?"

"Why, thankee, m'lady!" He clumped away.

Lowenna said, "I'll tell Young Matthew. If I sent you with any one else, he'd never forgive me."

It was over. And she thought she could hear Harry Flinders laughing.

5 FLAGSHIP

CAPTAIN ADAM BOLITHO climbed from the companion and paused to prepare his eyes for the glare. The morning watch was only an hour old but the sun, reflected from the sea, was almost blinding after the chartroom. But for the angle, it could have been noon.

A glance aloft to the masthead pendant, no longer limp or curling above the canvas but streaming its full length, pointing the way ahead. The topsails, too, were responding again, not full or straining like other times, but answering well to wind and rudder. *Will it last?*

For four days the wind had been their enemy. Veering and backing, or falling away altogether, a mockery rather than a challenge. Hardly a watch passed without all hands being called as *Onward* changed tack. Even during the night, when even an experienced sailor is never at his best.

Adam stared along the length of the ship and felt the wind, slight as it was, pressing the shirt against his back. Like the air, his skin was already warm and clammy. As Jago had remarked over his razor, "Best to keep dressed down while you can, Cap'n."

Most of the men working on or above deck were stripped to the waist, some badly burned by sun and wind, and despite the early hour there were several of them loitering on the gangways, peering ahead, or pointing at the vast span of land that reached out on either bow as far as the eye could see. At first only a long unwavering shadow, unmoving, beyond reach, but now, after two days of doubt and uncertainty, it was reality. Measureless. Not merely land, but a continent.

Adam glanced at the sails again, and thought he saw one of the topmen pointing at something, grinning or swearing, he could not tell. But he felt it. Shared it. *At moments like this, we are one company.*

He knew that Vincent was standing with his arms folded, observing the men around the wheel and compass box. It was his watch, although he and his captain had met a few times when every one had been mustered for another alteration of course. Like strangers in the night. This was different. As first lieutenant, Vincent would be on his feet and dealing with everything from mooring the ship to any ceremonial required.

Vincent turned now as someone gave a quiet cheer, but seemed to visibly relax as men moved aside to let another find a place at the nettings. It was the young assistant cook, Lord, with one of the surgeon's crew hovering at his side. The bandages gleamed in the hot sunlight, and Adam could sense his surprise, even confusion, as the way was cleared for him. There were grins and jokes, too. Lord looked steadily at the land, unable to respond. Perhaps the emotion was too much. It was his first day on deck since the stabbing.

It gave Vincent time to cross the quarterdeck and touch his hat to Adam. "Holding steady, sir. West nor' west. We'll anchor in the forenoon if this holds." He glanced at the thin plume of greasy smoke from the galley funnel. "Good thing we piped all hands an hour early!"

Adam smiled. "They've done well." He saw some of the first to be called appearing on deck, yawning and looking curiously at the land as they began to stack their rolled hammocks in the nettings, a bosun's mate making sure that there were no errors to spoil the array. He added quietly, "And so have you, Mark."

Vincent walked to the compass box and back, and said only, "D' you know the admiral at Freetown, sir?"

Adam saw a fish leap in the ship's shadow, not a shark this time. He was still thinking of the stricken schooner *Moonstone*. Maybe Vincent was, too.

"Rear-Admiral Langley? Only by name, I'm afraid. There have

been several changes since I was last here, to all accounts."

Vincent nodded slowly. "They'll all be hungry for news. Wanting to know what's happening at home."

Adam looked toward the spreading panorama of green and felt the sun on his neck, like a hot breath. And this was early. *News from home.*

The admiral might be watching *Onward* right now through his telescope, if he allowed himself to appear so eager. He thought of the sealed orders. *With all despatch* . . . And after their delivery, what next? Take on supplies and fresh water, and then back to Plymouth?

He saw the cook's assistant looking at the galley funnel, and the surgeon's mate shaking his head. *Not yet.* You didn't have to hear them speak. He looked again: most of the hammocks had been lashed and stowed, and one of the last men to stand away from the nettings was throwing his head back and giving a huge yawn. He froze as he realised that he was eye to eye with his captain.

Adam raised a casual hand and smiled, and saw the seaman abruptly bob his head before hurrying away.

The calls shrilled: *"Hands to breakfast and clean!"*

Adam shaded his eyes and said, "You go below too, Mark. We'll all be busy enough soon."

He saw Vincent rub his chin and then nod. "Thank you, sir. I'll not take a moment. If you're sure."

Adam heard the companion close, and walked to the quarterdeck rail, gazing toward the shore. Even without a telescope he could see some small local vessels, far away, like dried leaves floating against the unmoving backdrop. One day, Vincent would understand that at a moment like this a captain needed to be alone. With his ship.

The two midshipmen stood side by side on the forecastle as the land, now alive with detail, continued to reach out and embrace the ship. Despite the sounds of spars and rigging, which most sailors took for granted as part of their daily lives, the silence was unnerving, and a moment before, someone had gasped with alarm as the first strokes of eight bells had sounded from the nearby belfry.

David Napier nudged his friend's arm with his elbow and felt him respond.

Lieutenant Squire stood stolidly with his hands clasped behind him, big feet apart, watching the guardboat which had pulled out to greet *Onward* on her final approach and had taken station directly ahead. The wind had held after all, but the pace seemed painfully slow under the lee of the land.

The gunner had already been on deck, but no salute was required. He had grinned. "They're not out of their sacks yet!" Even his voice had seemed louder than usual.

Midshipman Huxley murmured, "There's the flagship, Dave."

His Britannic Majesty's ship *Medusa* was a smart third-rate, a two-decker of seventy-four guns. She did not compare with the massive ships of the line, but here she seemed to dominate the anchorage. Most of the other vessels were much smaller: cutters, two brigantines, and one schooner.

Napier heard Huxley mutter, "She's like—"

He did not finish. Neither of them needed reminding, especially Napier. The memory of *Moonstone* still took him unawares, in the night watches or when some casual remark brought some part of it back to life. Like now.

He looked aft and saw the first lieutenant standing by the captain, pointing up at the topsail yards, where seamen stood ready to shorten or make more sail if the wind roused itself or dropped altogether. Did Vincent ever think about it? That more could have been done? If anything, he had avoided mentioning it.

Napier thought of the captain. He had seen the sharks, and signalled the recall immediately. But for that . . .

He cupped his hands over his eyes and stared across the water toward *Medusa*. She was moored alongside a pier or wooden jetty, the rear-admiral's flag drooping from her mizzen, and he could see a few figures working on deck and the sun reflecting on a telescope.

Lieutenant Squire said suddenly, "We shall rig winds'ls as soon as we anchor. Be like an oven 'tween-decks otherwise."

"Is that what the flagship's doing, sir?" That was Huxley, as serious as ever.

Squire grunted. "Not sure."

Napier looked away from the slow-moving schooner. "Maybe *Medusa's* preparing for sea?"

Somebody yelled from aft and Squire strode to the side and gestured to some of the anchor party. But he still managed to crack a grin.

"If the flagship went to sea, that whole bloody pier would collapse!" He clapped one of the seamen on the shoulder as he was gaping at the great anchor hanging from its cathead. "Ready for a run ashore, Knocker? Or are you too young for it?"

There were several raucous laughs, and one of the younger seamen took up Squire's mood. "Wot are the girls like 'ere, sir?"

Squire looked at the two midshipmen and winked. "Only one way to find out!" Just as quickly, he was serious again. "Stand by forrard, and warn the hands below!"

Napier saw the guardboat turning slightly, oars motionless, and someone holding up the blue flag. He thought of the charts, the countless pencilled calculations, the hundreds of miles logged and recorded, all culminating in this final position, marked by a blue flag.

He nudged Huxley again. "It's probably still snowing in Falmouth!"

Huxley gave a rare smile. "My father always said . . ." He stopped and withdrew into silence, a habit Napier had noticed that very first day when they had joined *Onward* together, he still recovering from the loss of his ship and Huxley brooding over his father's court-martial and suicide.

He said gently, "Tell me, Simon. What *did* your father used to say?" and for a moment he thought he had broken an unspoken promise.

Then Huxley answered steadily, "My father said a good navigator measured distance by the number of ship's biscuits consumed each day . . ." He faltered, but he was smiling. "Sorry about that!" And the smile remained.

Napier stared up at the yards and the topmen spread out along them, and guessed his newly promoted friend, Tucker, would be watching them, too.

Lieutenant Squire was saying, "Quiet enough. Must all be asleep aboard the flagship." He beckoned to Napier. "My respects to the first lieutenant, and tell him . . ." He stopped as another voice came from aft.

"Signal from Flag, sir! *Captain repair on board!*"

"Let go!"

Squire leaned over the side as *Onward*'s anchor dropped from its cathead and felt the spray across his face like rain; it was almost as cold on his heated skin. Mud and sand swirled to the surface as the cable took the strain.

He signalled to the quarterdeck and saw Vincent acknowledge it. It was over, but Squire knew from long experience that it was also just beginning.

"Attention on the upper deck! Face to starboard!"

Then the prolonged trill of calls in salute for the captain, and, seconds later or so it seemed, the gig pulled smartly away from the side. Squire straightened his back automatically and felt Napier move up beside him. He saw the sun glinting on the oars and then on the captain's gold epaulettes as he sat stiffly upright in the sternsheets. He seemed to be looking up at *Onward*'s figurehead, or the men on the forecastle. Maybe at Napier.

It must be difficult for both of them, captain and "middy." More than any one. To show any sign of friendship or familiarity would be seen as favouritism or bias by those eager to seize on such things.

Squire peered across at the flagship and thought he heard the blare of a trumpet. Neither captain was wasting any time.

At the gig's tiller, Luke Jago watched the steady stroke of oars and waited for it to settle into a rhythm that satisfied him. Everything smart and clean, the crew dressed in their chequered shirts and straw hats. He envied them; he was wearing his jacket with the gilt buttons, and was already sweating badly. He glanced at the captain in his best uniform; even the proud epaulettes looked heavy on his shoulders.

Jago stared past the stroke oarsman's head at the flagship's mainmast, alert for any drift that might require a shift of rudder. There was none. A good crew. He grinned to himself. *An' a good coxswain.*

He thought of Lieutenant Monteith, who had been pompously inspecting all the boats' crews as soon as the anchor had hit the seabed. "Always remember, a ship is judged by her boats. Skill and smartness speak for themselves!"

Jago had heard a seaman mutter, *"Then let 'em!"* But he had pretended not to hear. The third lieutenant seemed to thrive on his unpopularity, and Jago suspected that it was not only with the lower deck.

He felt the captain shift his position and knew he was looking astern at his ship.

A strange feeling: it always was. Adam Bolitho shaded his eyes with one hand against the fierce glare reflecting from the anchorage. He could still see the tiny figures working aloft on *Onward*'s upper yards, ensuring all the sails were neatly furled to Vincent's satisfaction. He half smiled. *And to his captain's.*

He tried not to pluck his damp shirt away from his skin. It was the same one he had been wearing when they had begun the approach to Freetown. Even his slight unsteadiness climbing down into the gig had warned him. He would have to watch his step when he went ashore. It would be the first time since Plymouth. He glanced at the stroke oarsman and saw him look away hurriedly. *And before that, Falmouth. If only . . .*

He looked ahead to the flagship, *Medusa.* Not unlike *Athena,* in which he had been Bethune's flag captain, smartly painted in her black and white livery and shining like glass in the glare. All her gunports were open, but without windsails hoisted there would be little ventilation between decks with the ship not even swinging at anchor. Maybe she was preparing for sea. He dismissed the idea. There were several lighters alongside one another, and he could just see a small stage, a "flake," hanging over the quarter, probably so that some repairs could be carried out.

He murmured to Jago, "We've done this a few times, Luke," and his voice was almost lost in the regular creak of oars. But Jago never seemed to miss anything. Unless he wanted to.

He did not take his eyes from the approach; he had seen a telescope or two being trained on his gig.

Jago answered calmly, "Be doin' it when it's *your* flag up there bein' saluted, Cap'n." He sounded completely serious.

The cry echoed across the water. "Boat ahoy?"

Jago judged the moment, then cupped his hands, his elbow on the tiller-bar. *"On-ward!"*

Adam felt the sword hilt pressing against his leg. It had been polished by Morgan, the cabin servant, and, like his dress uniform coat, had been waiting for him. He had told himself that he must never take these small acts beyond the call of duty for granted. Too many were guilty of that.

"Oars!"

Adam shifted the sword again. He had never forgotten the tale of a captain who had tripped over his own sword under similar circumstances and had fallen into the sea. He had been a midshipman at the time, and they had all laughed uproariously about it.

Now the oars were tossed, the bowmen ready to make fast as the flagship's side loomed over them. Only one deck higher than *Onward*, but it seemed like a cliff. There was the entry port, with two side-boys waiting below it. Voices, the sound of a solitary call, then total silence.

Adam stood up and half turned as Jago handed him the sealed package. He began to climb, the orders pressed firmly beneath his arm, and gripping a hand rope to steady himself. One slip now, and it would be the story of how Adam Bolitho fell into the sea at Freetown . . . But the smile eluded him. He could smell food, and recalled that he had not eaten since midnight.

He saw a line of feet, and boots as well—Royal Marines—and heard the sudden bark of commands. He was still unused to these honours for himself. Then the piercing squeal of calls, heels clicking together, and the distant shouting of commands. He stepped through the entry port and faced aft, doffing his hat as the sounds of the salute died away.

A shaft of sunlight from the opposite side of the deck blinded him, and the uniforms, scarlet or blue like his own, seemed to blur and merge. He almost lost his balance.

But a hand reached out. "Here, let me take that." And he heard what might have been a dry chuckle. "It's safe with me, Captain Adam Bolitho!"

Adam saw the hand gripping his arm now, strong and sunburned, like the man.

So many memories crowding into seconds, good and bad, which neither time nor distance could dispel. It was Captain James Tyacke, who had done and given so much, almost his life, and who had become one of Sir Richard Bolitho's firmest friends as his flag captain in *Frobisher*. He had been with him when Bolitho had fallen to a French marksman four years ago.

It was not possible.

Tyacke was handing the sealed orders to a tall sergeant of marines. "Guard 'em with your life, right?" and the man smiled gravely as he saluted.

Somewhere there was the pipe, *"Hands carry on with your work!"* and Tyacke was saying, "I hoped it was you, as soon as I was told that *Onward* was in sight. But I wasn't sure till I saw you in the glass that you were still in command." He gripped Adam's arm. "By God, it's good to see you! Come aft with me. The admiral's ashore, but he'll be back about noon."

A lieutenant was hovering by the gangway and Tyacke paused to speak with him, gesturing toward the entry port, now deserted except for the watchkeepers and a sentry.

It was the first time Adam had seen the scarred side of his face since he had stepped aboard; maybe, like most people, he had been subconsciously avoiding it, for both their sakes.

Tyacke, then a lieutenant, had been wounded at Aboukir Bay—the Battle of the Nile as it was officially called. He had been stationed on the lower gundeck when an explosion had transformed the confined world of *load—run out—fire—sponge out—reload* . . . into an inferno. Tyacke had lived. Many had not.

Now, only the overwhelming victory against the old enemy was remembered, but James Tyacke would never forget. One side of what had been a handsome face was deeply tanned, like the strong hands. The other was lifeless, like melted wax. That his eye had survived was a miracle.

The devil with half a face, the slavers used to call him.

He turned now and said, "I've sent word for your boat's crew to be taken care of. I see you've got the same fierce cox'n. Glad about that."

They walked aft together, then Tyacke halted and gazed across the water toward the anchored frigate.

"Fine ship, Adam." He softened the emphasis with a smile. "I envy you."

They walked on; Adam could feel his shoes sticking to the deck-seams, and it was still the forenoon. He said, "I saw that you were lowering the winds'ls."

Tyacke glanced at him but did not pause. "Flagship, Adam. The admiral considers 'em unsightly."

They reached the shade of the poop and Adam saw two Royal Marines, one a corporal, checking the contents of a box. He pitied them in their heavy uniforms, but to be dressed otherwise would be "unsightly" too, he guessed.

The corporal cleared his throat and said, "Beg your pardon, sir?"

Adam recognised him. "Price. Ginger Price, am I right?"

The corporal nodded and grinned, momentarily at a loss for words. Then he said, "Not quite so ginger now, sir! But I ain't never forgotten the old *Unrivalled!*"

They were both gazing after the two captains as Tyacke said quietly, "You're very like him, y' know, Adam." He did not need to elaborate, and Adam was moved by it.

He had already noticed that the flag captain's aiguillette Tyacke wore was quite tarnished compared with the other lace on his uniform coat. It might have been the same one he had been wearing on that fateful day.

The cabin door was closed behind them, although Adam had not noticed any one in attendance. He must be more tired than he imagined.

Tyacke turned, framed against the broad stern windows. "And the sword, too! I want to hear all about you!" His eyes rested briefly on the sealed orders, which had been laid on a table. He must be wondering how they might affect the entire command, or his own ship. His life.

But all he said was, "From England." Then he smiled freely. "It does me good to see you again—I can't tell you how much. And I want to apologise for dragging you aboard when your anchor'd hardly touched the bottom. I wanted to meet and talk with you before anybody else hauled you away. You've been a flag captain yourself—you won't need telling!" He unfastened his coat and slung it over the back of a chair, gesturing for Adam to do the same. "The admiral usually keeps to time, so we have a while to ourselves."

Adam hung his coat on another chair and loosened his sweat-stained shirt. Then he unfastened his sword, and hesitated as Tyacke said, "Here. Let me."

He held the sword with both hands for a long moment, then drew the blade a few inches, very slowly, before snapping it into the sheath. "Brings it all back, Adam. The man, too." The scarred face softened at some private reminiscence. "'Equality Dick.' God bless him."

The door opened and a man in a white jacket peered in at them seriously. "You called, sir?"

Tyacke smiled. "No, Simpson, but I will now," and to Adam, "Sun's over the yardarm. D'you fancy a brandy with me?"

"Thank you." But as the door closed and the cabin servant departed, Adam said, "Suppose the admiral arrives?"

"He's been ashore with some 'important officials.'" Tyacke winked. "I imagine they'll have shared a tot or two by this hour!"

Adam looked uneasily at the door. "The admiral—is he easy to work with?" and Tyacke grimaced.

"*Under*, more like." He loosened his neckcloth. "He's been in command for three months, and I know him no better than the first day." He laughed shortly. "Except that he's always *right*. You'll know the situation?"

Someone shouted, the sound muffled by deck and distance, and followed by the regular thump of feet. Marines.

Tyacke shrugged. "We have a lot of Royals in Freetown. Here aboard

Medusa, too. Just in case, as they say." He leaned forward from his chair. "Didn't someone tell me you were getting married?" He frowned. "Dear old John Allday, I think it was. When I was still a frigate captain like you, till I was shifted to *this.*" He waved one arm around the spacious cabin. "I'm luckier than many, I suppose. But . . ."

The door swung open and the servant came in quietly and set two crystal goblets down beside the sealed orders.

Tyacke nodded. "That's excellent, thank you." The servant was hesitating, and he said with a certain emphasis, "All for now, Simpson," and when they were alone again, "Here's to you and your lady." When he put down the goblet, it was empty.

Then he said, "What's her name?"

Adam gazed past him. "Lowenna. It means 'joy' in old Cornish. We were married at Falmouth, in November," and he thought Tyacke sighed.

"That's a lovely name. *I* gave up hope long ago." He was touching the scarred side of his face, a habit of which he was probably unaware. "But I didn't drag you from your own fine ship just to hear all my—"

The door opened once more, although there had been no knock. It was a lieutenant, one of the officers who had been with the side party when Adam had climbed aboard.

"Sorry to disturb you, sir, but . . ." He glanced at the two coats draped casually over the chairs. " . . . the admiral is on the jetty, sir."

Tyacke stood up without haste. "Thanks, Martin. I'll do the same for you one day!"

The lieutenant was hurrying from the cabin.

Tyacke said dryly, "Stand by to repel boarders!" and reached out to keep Adam seated. "Now we wait. You do, anyway." Then he was suddenly serious. "You don't know what this means to me, Adam." He touched the sword again. *"Together."* And the door closed behind him.

Adam refastened the sword and resumed his seat, stretching his legs, trying to relax. No matter what others might think, Tyacke was quite alone. He had asked about Lowenna, but what did he really feel? Envy or resentment?

On that last night, Adam had awakened, reaching out for her, and had seen her standing by the windows, curtains wide, moonlight like silver on her naked shoulders. They had held one another again, trying to delay the inevitable. When the dawn came he had heard her say, "Today, the sea is my enemy."

He stared up at the same white-coated servant. Had he touched his shoulder to awaken him? Was that possible? He asked, "Time to move, Simpson?"

The man seemed surprised, perhaps that the stranger had remembered his name, or even cared to use it. He said, "Heard voices, sir," and jerked a thumb up at the deckhead. "Best to be prepared."

Adam stood up and tugged his collar into shape, and paused as the servant said, "You've not had your drink, sir."

The goblet was still full, the brandy unmoving, as if the flagship were firmly aground.

Adam clapped his shoulder impetuously. "Too late now! I hope you can find a good home for it!"

The man regarded him with disbelief for a second, then grinned back. "As good as done, an' thank you, Captain!"

Footsteps outside the door: it was the lieutenant again, the one Tyacke had called by his first name. Probably his first lieutenant.

Adam patted his pockets and paused at the door to make certain he had forgotten nothing. The goblet was already empty.

The lieutenant said, "The admiral is ready to receive you now, sir."

"Wish me luck, Martin."

A Royal Marine sentry stamped his heels together, and an orderly called, "Captain Bolitho, *sir!*"

Medusa's great cabin was not unlike that of any two-decker Adam had known, or Bethune's flagship *Athena*. Although most sailors would swear that no two ships were the same. He had expected others to be present, Tyacke and perhaps a flag lieutenant, or a clerk at least, to take note of any exchange of views. But there was nobody else, and the cabin was dominated by its sole occupant.

Rear-Admiral Giles Langley was tall and square-shouldered,

thick-set beneath his immaculate uniform. His hair, reflected now in the white-painted deckhead, was very fair and trimmed short in the style favoured by the younger breed of sea officer. His eyes were in shadow, and Adam realised there was a curtain of some kind half-drawn across the stern lights and windows.

But the smile was immediate and, he thought, sincere.

"I regret the delay, Bolitho. You must be feeling the strain after your long haul." He gestured to a large table and a litter of papers, and the package, now sliced open. There were pens and ink containers close by so he had not been alone, until now.

He waved Adam to a chair but walked restlessly to the curtain and twitched it slightly. "Yours is a fine-looking ship, Bolitho. Fast too, it would seem." He did not wait for an answer. "But for the weather," he looked over his shoulder, "and the unfortunate *Moonstone* diversion, you would have arrived here even earlier, eh?"

In those few seconds Adam saw that his eyes were blue, and pale like glass.

Langley shuffled some papers. "I read your report, of course. In the little time I've had since . . ." He did not finish. Instead, he turned over a page. "Boarding party. With your own first lieutenant in charge?" The pale eyes lifted briefly. "Good man, is he?"

"He's been *Onward*'s first lieutenant since she commissioned, sir."

"Not quite what I asked, but no matter." Langley looked at him directly. "And there was only one survivor on board? The master, you thought? Did your lieutenant express any opinion?"

"That *Moonstone* had been totally unprepared, and had been fired on without warning. She was already sinking when the boarding party reached her. I signalled the recall when the weather deteriorated and was threatening my men."

Langley nodded slowly. "The lone survivor was still alive at that time." His fingers tapped the papers. "Did your first lieutenant glean any information from him?"

"Mr. Vincent was on deck when I made the recall signal. It was one of my midshipmen who was speaking with him, and who stayed with him until he died. He was all but trapped himself."

The fingers rapped the papers again. "Hardly an experienced witness, Bolitho."

Adam met the pale eyes coldly. "I trust him, sir."

Langley's smile was almost gentle. "That is commendable too, Bolitho." He was on his feet again. "You know my flag captain, I understand. A very capable officer. I don't know how I would have coped when I was given this command, without his knowledge and persistence. A pity I could not . . ." He shrugged, and the epaulettes glittered in a shaft of sunlight which had somehow penetrated the curtain.

Adam had already noticed that Langley's skin was quite pale, with little hint of colour, although Tyacke had said he had become flag officer at Freetown three months ago. Long enough to have felt the sun of Africa.

Langley said suddenly, "I'm glad to welcome you under my command, albeit temporarily. I have no doubt you'll be eager to return to England without unnecessary delay." He frowned as someone tapped at the door. "We will talk again. Possibly tomorrow. I have heard a good deal about you. And I shall discover what I can about *Moonstone*. And when I do—"

The door opened and Tyacke was standing outside, his hat beneath his arm. Langley gave the gentle smile again.

"Right on time!"

Tyacke strode into the great cabin, but perhaps because of the gloomy interior after the fierce sunlight on deck he did not appear to see Adam as he passed.

A different lieutenant was waiting to escort Adam to the entry port where the gig was waiting. *About time, too.* He could almost hear Jago saying it. A squad of Royal Marines presented arms and officers saluted, but there was no piping of the side as Adam left the ship. The admiral was in conference.

Tyacke had kept his promise: the gig's crew looked refreshed and rested, and when Jago stood in the sternsheets to greet him he could smell the rum.

Then, as the gig pulled out and away from *Medusa*'s shadow, Adam suddenly got to his feet and gazed astern, and he saluted, not the flag this time, but James Tyacke, brave and defiant. And very much alone.

6 "Don't Look Down!"

Lieutenant Mark Vincent half closed his eyes against the sun as he watched yet another work boat pull away from *Onward*'s side, and stifled a yawn. It seemed he had been on his feet since they had anchored yesterday. It felt longer. Fresh water, food and general supplies all had to be checked and signed for, and supervised in stowage by the master and the purser to their satisfaction or otherwise.

Vincent did not have to turn his head to know that the windsails were barely moving. They gave some relief between decks, but not here. He had already heard one working party complaining to the bosun about it.

"In a few weeks' time, if we're still in this godforsaken place, you might have somethin' to moan about!" Drummond had laid his hand on the breech of the nearest eighteen-pounder. "You'll be able to fry an egg on this beauty!"

And how long *were* they going to be here?

Vincent looked across the water toward the flagship. Bolitho had reported to the admiral and delivered the despatches, and Vincent had seen the flag captain through a telescope for the first time. He had felt both revulsion and pity at his hideous disfigurement. *Suppose it had happened to me?* Maybe James Tyacke had obtained no higher command because of it, despite everything he had done, and this was the end of the road . . .

He heard Lieutenant Monteith's curt tone as he finished his instructions to the midshipmen on harbour routine. Vincent was the first lieutenant and could show no favour or prejudice toward any one. They shared the same wardroom, and at sea worked watch by watch. But that was all, and his dislike of the third lieutenant remained intense. He was still ashamed that when Monteith had been wounded during the fight with *Nautilus* he had felt no sympathy, only sorrow for those who had died.

He turned quickly as he heard the captain's voice from the open skylight. How must *he* feel? Being kept here awaiting orders, and probably thinking all the time of the woman he had left behind in Falmouth? Vincent himself had had only one serious affair, which could have ended in disaster. She had been a married woman, and had proved an experienced lover, but she was the wife of a senior officer. A damned close-run thing. He had never forgotten. He almost smiled. *But I'll wager she has.*

Drummond, the bosun, crossed the hot deck and touched his hat. "'Bout ready to secure, sir. Still some new cordage to come aboard, but the lads 'ave done well."

He assessed Vincent, making up his mind. Saint or tyrant? The first lieutenant was neither. Drummond continued cautiously, "Rear-Admiral Langley, sir . . ." He did not look toward *Medusa*. "I had a mate who served under 'im before 'e came 'ere." He paused. He had only known Vincent since the old bosun had been killed. And maybe . . .

Vincent said testily, "Come along, man. Speak up."

"'E was commodore then, sir. Used to carry out inspections, no warning. Often with a newly joined ship."

Vincent was staring at the open skylight. "Well, well. I wonder if—" Then the dark face lit with a grin. "Thank you. I'll not forget this. That would be all I'd need!"

Drummond hoped he masked his surprise. It was taking him longer to understand the first lieutenant than he had expected when he had joined *Onward*. Vincent could be strict, but not aggressively so, like some Drummond had known, and he was always ready to listen when advice was required. But beyond that, he seemed to remain aloof, even in the wardroom from what Drummond had heard.

This was a small thing, but Vincent's gratitude was like a door opening. Close co-operation between first lieutenant and bosun was essential. Together, they *were* the ship. He had seen Vincent look toward the cabin skylight. Only the captain was truly alone. Drummond glanced along the upper deck and was satisfied. Smart and tidy enough again for any admiral.

He looked at Vincent's profile, edged with hard sunlight. A strong face, alert and intelligent: it was said that he had been in line for command when *Onward* had commissioned. Was he still thinking about that lost chance, still hoping? The hope might be in vain, especially these days with the fleet being cut down.

He tugged out his silver call and held it in the palm of his hand, where it looked no bigger than a toothpick.

"Just say the word, *Mister* Vincent!"

He saw Vincent walking toward the companionway, maybe to pass on to the captain the news about the admiral's little foible. Monteith's sharp voice intruded into his thoughts, impatient and sarcastic. There would be no tears if *he* fell overboard one dark night.

And there was Walker, their youngest midshipman, nodding obediently and repeating something for Monteith's benefit, while Monteith stood, hands behind his back, feet flexing up and down in their brightly polished shoes.

"I shall not ask you again, Mr. Walker!"

Drummond quickened his pace. Young Walker might make a good officer one day, given the right example to follow. Strange to realise that when he himself had been serving aboard the seventy-four gun *Mars* at Trafalgar, in the thick of the fighting in which his own captain had been killed, young Walker would have only just been born. If then. It was a sobering thought.

He gritted his teeth and felt sand or dust grate between them, but there seemed to be no wind to have carried it. He licked his lips. *Maybe cooler down in the mess.*

He heard Monteith's voice again, rising almost to a scream. "So you think that's a joke, do you? Made you smirk, did it? Then go to the maintop and stay there until I recall you!"

One of the seamen who was coiling some new rope nearby muttered, "Poor little bastard'll burn alive up there." His friend saw Drummond and spat, "Bloody officers!"

Drummond heard both of them, and was reminded of his own remark. *This godforsaken place.* Now it was mocking him, like the old warning. *Stay out of it!*

He saw the midshipman climbing slowly up the starboard ratlines, slight body framed against the sky. Monteith had already disappeared, no doubt to the cooler air of the wardroom, where he would be having a wet before making someone else's life a misery.

Drummond made his decision. He took a water flask from behind the flag locker where it was kept hidden for the watchkeepers, although everybody knew about it, and strolled unhurriedly to the mainmast shrouds.

He stared across the water toward the flagship, but nothing seemed to have changed. No boats at or near the entry port, but maybe there were some tied up against or beneath the pier. Obviously the admiral had more sense than to venture out in an open boat with the sun at its zenith.

He could feel his shirt clinging to his shoulders like a damp skin, and the sweat already running down his ribs and hips. A few faces turned curiously in his direction, but just as quickly avoided his eyes. He seized the ratlines. *In case I might find some more work for them to do.*

He stared up at the maintop, black against the burning sky. He had been at sea all his life, probably longer than any one else aboard, except for a few like Lieutenant Squire and Jago, the captain's coxswain.

He had never forgotten that one time when he had been ordered aloft by an officer. Not calm like today, but in a raging gale with a full sea running. He must have been about Walker's age. He had nearly fallen. A few seconds. A lifetime.

He could recall the comment by the tough, hard-bitten seaman who had saved his life. *When a bit of gold lace tells you to jump, look first!* He had even been able to laugh about it.

He leaned back and began to climb.

He had the sun behind him, but knew he needed to keep a sharp lookout when he reached the shade and comparative safety of the top. He held his breath and halted as something struck his shoulder from above and bounced off the ratlines. He did not need to look. It was a shoe. He wanted to call out to the boy, but the distraction could be fatal. Walker was already climbing again.

In no time, or so it seemed, Drummond had reached the futtock shrouds where it was necessary to rely on feet and hands to take the weight and to work your way out and around the fighting top, before you could begin the next stage. It was the mark of a good seaman. Drummond could feel his weight dragging at his fingers, his shoes slipping on every ratline. Not like those early days hanging out over the sea, never daring to look down.

He was pleased that he was not even breathless. It would be something to tell them in the mess at the end of the day . . .

He had reached the barricade, and gripped one of the iron mountings for a swivel gun to pull himself the last few feet. He was slow when compared with the sure-footed topmen who could make or shorten sail in minutes, and seemingly without effort. Like young Tucker, his new mate. A far cry from the poor, frightened devils who used to be dragged aboard by ruthless press gangs, never having set foot aboard ship before.

The midshipman was sitting on the edge of the lubbers' hole to avoid the hazards of the futtock shrouds. Always risky, but with Monteith watching or yelling threats from below, it was a wise precaution. Walker gazed up at him, one leg dangling through the hole as he tried to fan his streaming face with his hat.

He said quietly, "I almost slipped." He was shaking, but trying to conceal it.

Drummond knew the signs. The boy was no coward; he had proved that under the guns, and when others were falling around him. And when men had cheered him for his birthday, while hell had been exploding across these same decks.

"Stay where you are." Drummond knelt beside him. "An' take a swig of this." He grinned and felt his jaw crack. "Didn't do me no good, neither!"

He watched the boy swallow, some of the water running down his chin and neck. It would be stale after lying sealed up since . . . since when? But at this moment it would match the best wine in the fleet.

"I'll get someone to see you down to the deck. A bowline round the waist would be a good idea."

Walker seized his wrist and stared up at him imploringly. *"No!"* He faltered and tried again. "I don't want to let them think . . ."

He stopped as Drummond said, "Don't you start givin' me orders, *Mister* Walker. Not yet, anyways." He attempted to shift his own position and felt the pain jab through his muscles.

He looked across the anchorage to give them both time to recover. An entire area was filled with lifeless, abandoned vessels, masts and yards awry, untended. Awaiting sale or disposal elsewhere. Maddock, the gunner, had told him that most of them had been part of the trade. Slavers, which had been caught by some of the patrols before or after they had attempted to break out and escape.

Why any one would want to use one of them after what they had done was hard to imagine.

"They should burn the bloody lot of 'em. Their crews, too," he said now. Walker had managed to lean on his elbows, the leg still dangling toward the deck below. "You feelin' any better?"

Walker did not reply directly. "What is that boat doing there amongst them?"

Drummond wiped his eyes and squinted. Then he gripped Walker's bony shoulder. "Nothin' wrong with *your* eyesight, thank God!" He gestured through the lubbers' hole. "We're goin' down now, nice an' easy, one step at a time, see?"

Walker nodded like a puppet. "But Lieutenant Monteith ordered me to . . ."

Drummond peered down at the deck. Nothing had changed. A Royal Marine was walking slowly along the starboard gangway, keeping pace with a small craft paddling a few yards away from the frigate's side. A normal precaution: it was common enough for a would-be thief to slip aboard through one of the open ports if nobody was watching.

Everybody else would be looking at the flagship. *As I was.*

He said, "Never mind that. I want you to find the first lieutenant, an' don't take *no* from any one!"

Walker had lowered his legs, one foot shoeless, over the edge of the platform. "What shall I tell him?" He sounded calmer now, under control, but Drummond wanted to be sure.

"Just keep with me an' don't look down, right?" He glanced toward the rank of lifeless vessels. He had had only a brief glimpse of it, but it was still fixed in his mind: a longboat, double-banked, two oarsmen on each thwart, pulling steadily, even unhurriedly beyond the shabby prizes.

He replied, "Tell 'im the admiral is in sight!" He caught Walker's arm and grinned. "Don't stop for nobody!"

He watched the midshipman jump down to the deck, pause, and tear off his remaining shoe before hurrying aft. Someone shouted after him, perhaps Monteith, but he did not stop or turn back.

Drummond followed easily, and wedged the empty water flask behind the flag locker. Until the next time.

Young Walker would remember today, and be proud.

Drummond moistened his call with the tip of his tongue. To hell with Monteith!

After the uncertainty which had followed Walker's breathless arrival at the door of the captain's quarters, the speed with which the actual event unfolded was almost a relief.

A cry from the lookout: "Boat ahoy?"

And the formal response, magnified by a speaking-trumpet, *"Flag—Medusa!"* left nobody in doubt.

Adam Bolitho watched the admiral's barge turning to moor alongside, the double line of oars rising together, bowmen poised and ready to hook on. Even at this distance he could sense the strain and effort after their long pull as a diversion, chests heaving, faces shining with sweat. Jago would be observing critically, and would have a few things to say afterwards about it.

Adam had seen Vincent pass Drummond, the bosun, on the way to their stations for such an event, saw the nod and the answering grin. Like a couple of conspirators. The barge's coxswain was on his feet now, hat in hand, two lieutenants, one obviously remaining in charge, also standing and saluting. And Rear-Admiral Giles Langley's pallid face turned up toward the entry port where the side-boys were waiting, complete with white gloves, to offer assistance.

Langley ignored both and seized a hand rope, still looking up at the motionless ensign.

Langley was not lightly built, but he seemed untroubled by the climb from his barge, or the stamp of boots and attendant squeal of calls as he stepped aboard.

One of the other officers, his flag lieutenant, followed at a discreet distance, stiff-faced, accustomed to such ceremonial. Langley waited for the calls to fall silent, and the muskets to slap into position. Then he smiled and raised his hat as he faced aft. It was more of a gesture than a salute.

He thrust out his hand to Adam. "I *said* we should meet today!" and with a curt nod, "This is 'Flags.'" He did not offer a name. The lieutenant was obviously used to that, too.

Langley waved his hand expansively. "Would you steer the course, Captain Bolitho? It's not every day . . ." He allowed the phrase to dangle, perhaps a habit, perhaps for effect.

Adam strode aft, looking for flaws. The lieutenants and senior warrant officers waiting on the quarterdeck, and most of the duty watch mustered below the boat tier, the uniforms of a sweating squad of Royal Marines a vivid splash of colour amidships. A midshipman stood stiffly by each gangway, in case of any urgent message or change of procedure.

He thought of Midshipman Walker, and the quiet determination with which he had bluffed his way past the cabin sentry. And Vincent, usually so loath to reveal any emotion. He had gripped the startled boy's hand and shaken it fiercely.

"I don't care *what* you were doing up there, Walker—you came to *me!* Good man!"

Vincent was here now, much more contained, watching a bosun's mate clearing a section of the deck of spare hands who were still in working rig, or stripped to the waist in the heat.

He murmured to Adam, "I told the barge crew they could stand easy aboard us while they were waiting." Adam remembered Tyacke offering the same courtesy to *Onward*'s boat's crew. "The lieutenant declined, sir. He said he was told to stand by."

The admiral turned, lightly for a man of his girth: there was obviously nothing wrong with his hearing.

"My barge crew? They do nothing else all day. Mister . . ." He cocked his head. "Vincent? Correct?" And without pausing, "I shall want to talk to you about the *Moonstone* affair before the day is out. You were the boarding officer. When the last 'survivor' was discovered?"

The flag lieutenant leaned forward and interjected, "It was not Lieutenant Vincent who found him, sir." He was consulting an open notebook. Langley stared coldly beyond him.

"I wasn't aware that I was asking *you*."

Adam said, "I should have explained, sir," and Langley gave him the now familiar, humourless smile.

"You did, I believe." Then he said abruptly, "May we pause, Bolitho?"

Adam saw Vincent give an almost imperceptible nod and hurry aft.

Langley was looking at the windsails. "Might be a little cooler below—and we can talk." He turned just as swiftly and beckoned to Midshipman Huxley. "And who are *you?*"

Adam saw the flag lieutenant open his mouth and close it again.

"Huxley, sir."

"Oh. I thought perhaps . . ." He seemed about to walk on toward a line of seamen, but stopped and swung round again. "Huxley? I trust not related to . . ."

He left the rest unspoken, but it was enough. Huxley's face had closed, and Adam saw his fist clench before he thrust it out of sight.

He said, "I think I am very fortunate in *Onward*'s midshipmen, sir."

Langley pulled out a large handkerchief and dabbed his mouth. "Well, time will tell, as every captain must know!" He looked aft again. "I think I've shown the flag enough for the moment." He waited for Vincent to present himself. "You may carry on now, Lieutenant. A smart ship. Are *you* satisfied?"

Vincent answered without hesitation, "Ready for sea, sir."

Langley stepped into the shade with obvious relief, remarking, "As it should be."

They reached the cabin, where the screen door was already open, the Royal Marine sentry at attention, his eyes fixed discreetly on some point above the admiral's epaulette.

The flag lieutenant had his little book open again, but Langley snapped, "Not *now*, Flags! That can wait."

Inside the great cabin it seemed cool after the upper deck. The stern windows were open, and an unfinished letter on Adam's small desk was stirring slightly in the breeze.

Langley strode across the cabin and tossed his hat onto a chair, ducking his head, his fair hair almost touching the deckhead.

"This takes me back." He did not elaborate. Then he saw the bergère facing astern, in the place of honour, as Jago always called it. Langley lowered himself into it slowly and carefully, while his aide hovered nearby.

He stretched his legs. "More like it, eh?" He patted the arms of the chair and turned his pale eyes on Adam. "This could tell a few tales, I'll wager."

Adam smiled to himself. The flag lieutenant had probably recorded all the details in his little book. "It belonged to my uncle, sir."

"Guessed as much." Langley nodded and stroked the worn leather. "Sir Richard. I am honoured!" A pause. "I know that Captain Tyacke served under him, and was with him at the end." He brushed something imaginary off his sleeve. "But trying to get him to talk about their service together is like getting blood out of a stone!"

Adam saw the pantry door move an inch. Hugh Morgan was standing by.

"May I offer you some wine, sir? I'm not sure about the time, but you must have been on the move for most of the day."

Langley pouted and said genially, "Not over yet, either. Never is." He leaned further back in the chair. "Anything will be more than welcome, Bolitho!"

He gazed out of the stern windows, his pale eyes shaded by the overhang of the poop. "I often wonder what our people in London actually know of our problems out here. They worry about slavery, even though all the major powers are doing their utmost to stamp it out." He wagged a finger. "There will always be men willing or reckless enough to continue in the trade, as long as the prize outweighs the risk. Given time, I might suggest . . ." He fell silent as Morgan glided into the cabin; he could move like a shadow when required.

Langley appraised the two expensive goblets. "I could become too comfortable in your company, I fear."

Feet thudded across the deck above, and as if to a signal the flag lieutenant rose and hurried to close the skylight.

Langley said, "Just a precaution, Bolitho. Busy ears, y' know?"

Adam sipped his wine. Langley's glass was being refilled. The flag lieutenant's remained untouched.

Langley said, "I've looked into the *Moonstone*'s unexpected," he lifted a finger, "and of course tragic, loss. She had been in our service under charter or direct warrant for some years. Patrol and liaison work, and more recently transporting some natives rescued or freed from slavery and landing them close to their place of origin. Where, and if, it was considered safe. In some cases, not so easy as it sounds." He leaned forward as if to confide something. "*Moonstone* had seen better days. But for your sighting and boarding her, it might all still remain a mystery. She had been fired on, and there were no survivors save one. Yes, I read your report. Pirates, slavers, we might never know for certain. And there were sharks in the area . . ." He glanced at the screen door, which was now shut, and toward the pantry.

He said slowly, "There have been many changes here since I took command, and more since you were last here in—*Unrivalled*, wasn't it?

'Power to the Victor,' is that what they call it? Beginnings of empire. And we are a part of it." He banged his hands on the arms of the chair. "Like it or not."

He stood up, and walked to the stern bench as if to peer out at the anchorage. "Improve communications but cut the costs: a constant demand from their lordships, and from government. If only they knew or understood." He turned away from the light. "There is a new settlement to the south of us. With its own governor, and a local militia. *To save money.*"

Adam said, "Yes, I know. It is on the latest chart. New Haven."

Langley betrayed surprise for the first time. "Well, it may be a part of empire, perhaps, but this is still Africa, for God's sake!" Just as quickly he was calm again, the pale eyes steady. "I'm sending you there to meet the new governor, since he has not seen fit to offer me an invitation. *Moonstone* was under charter to him more than once. He will want to know what happened to her. And when he comes to *me* in the future . . ." The silence was significant.

He gestured to his flag lieutenant, who immediately handed him a folded sheet of official stationery. "All the necessary details are here. If the wind allows, I want you to get under way tomorrow. Make a signal to confirm it." Langley turned to his weary-looking aide once more. "Before that, I want to speak to the officer who was mentioned in the captain's report."

"Midshipman Napier, sir?"

"If that is agreeable to you, Bolitho?"

Adam scarcely heard him. Even the writing on the page seemed blurred. "I would like to be present, sir."

"Good thinking. He might forget something, or close up like an oyster. It happens at that age."

Adam folded the paper. Only the new governor's name stood out. It was Ballantyne, the name David Napier would never forget.

Nor shall I.

• • •

David Napier stepped into the midshipmen's berth and stared around blankly. It was empty and somehow spacious, his home and hiding place since he had first joined the ship, along with Simon Huxley. Always full of noisy conversation, argument, and laughter. There were just six members of the mess, but it usually sounded like three times as many.

The only sound now was the faint clink of crockery from the pantry where the messman was either putting aside the dishes from breakfast, or preparing the next offering from the galley. And it was stuffy and humid, airless after the upper deck. The windsails had been lowered and stowed, but from ladders and gangways you could see the flag and masthead pendant flapping, and hear the rattle and slap of rigging, as if *Onward* were eager to leave.

We are sailing today.

Even the ship felt different. Alive again after stagnation.

He opened his little locker and folded the unfinished letter carefully before putting it away. *Dear Elizabeth* . . . No, *my dear*. He should just forget her. She had probably put him out of her mind as soon as he had left the house.

There were some casks of wine secured in one corner of the mess. In fact, every spare space in the hull seemed to be packed with extra stores of one sort or another. How long did they expect to be away? And to what purpose?

He heard running feet, the sound of something heavy being dragged across the deck above, and a yelp from somebody who was not fast enough. It would be soon now, unless there was another mix-up over the orders.

He sat down, deep in thought, recalling his unexpected summons to Rear-Admiral Langley in the great cabin: the admiral relaxed, even casual, but always maintaining a certain distance, and not merely because of his splendid uniform and gleaming epaulettes. Sometimes interrupting Napier in the middle of a sentence to fire a question, or clarify a point with his crushed-looking flag lieutenant. But the captain had been there also, a shadow against the stern windows, saying little unless in response to some comment from Langley.

Mostly, the questions had centred upon *Moonstone*, and the boarding party, and those final moments.

"And you were alone with the last survivor? How long was that? Did he tell you his name? What manner of man was he? Where would you say he came from?"

Looking back, it had been more an interrogation than an interview.

"What did he say? Was that all he said? Was there anything else of significance? And you left *Moonstone* with the others when the order to abandon was given?"

Bolitho had spoken before Napier could answer. "He was trapped between decks. Some loose gear had blocked his escape."

"But others freed him?"

Napier heard himself say, "It was Jago, the captain's cox'n, sir!"

He had been angry, remembering Huxley's face, his despair, after the admiral had called to him and then brushed him so curtly aside.

And remembering Langley in the captain's cabin, lounging in that same old chair, to which, when Napier had been wounded and unable to walk, they had carried him. And the captain had held him, giving him strength and courage. It was like sacrilege.

Napier had remained standing throughout the interview, the old pain reawakening in his leg as if to goad him.

Langley had got to his feet and remarked dismissively, "You did your best, Mr. Napier. A pity that we are still in the dark."

It was over.

Napier had only spoken to the captain very briefly since then, after the admiral had finally returned to his flagship. He had been delivering a message from the purser. He had been about to walk away when the captain had called him by name.

"I'm proud of you, David."

Then the purser himself had appeared, and the contact was broken.

"All done in 'ere, sir?" It was the messman. "Think I 'eard th' pipe." He did not wait for a reply, but Napier had long since learned that cooks and messmen usually knew what was happening before any one else.

He glanced at his locker, hesitated, and took out the letter. His thoughts scattered as the order was piped along the deck, faint at first, but as it reached hatch or companion it was loud and clear.

"All hands, all hands! Take station for leaving harbour!"

The admiral had decided.

Proceed when ready.

7 NO MERCY

ADAM BOLITHO ENTERED HIS CABIN and walked aft to the stern windows, which were now leaning slightly to larboard. Not much, but after their slow departure from Freetown it was like a reward. He leaned on the bench seat and peered down at the water below: one of the cutters was towing astern to keep her tightly sealed after baking beside her twin on the tier. He saw the boat yawing occasionally from side to side as if attempting to overtake her parent ship.

But they were making progress. If only the wind would hold.

He opened his shirt and loosened the sleeves. It was almost cool in the great cabin, or seemed so after the small chartroom where he had been comparing notes with Julyan, the master. In there, it had been like an oven.

Julyan had sounded optimistic, even cheerful. "Wind's holding, not much, but if we keep this up we should sight the approaches day after tomorrow." Some of his confidence had faded as the rudder had quivered noisily, like something shaking the keel.

Adam rubbed his chin. Even so, three days to make one hundred miles. *Onward* was used to something better. He smiled to himself. He must be getting like Julyan, with his quaint remarks.

They had been studying the most recent chart when the master had said seriously, "If all the sea ran dry right this minute, *Onward* would be perched on the edge of a great valley, hills to larboard and a bottomless pit to starboard." It was a warning any sailor would be insane to ignore.

They had plenty of sea room, but Vincent already had the leadsmen selected to stand by for immediate soundings if the chart proved incorrect. To go from *no bottom* to only a few fathoms beneath the keel was not unknown.

The pantry door opened and Morgan looked in questioningly.

"May I?" And when he nodded, "Call me when . . ." He glanced at Adam's seagoing coat, which was lying untidily across a chair. "I can give that a shamper-up in the meantime, sir." He went out, the coat hanging over his shoulder like a faded banner.

Adam sighed. Morgan always seemed to know what was coming. He walked across to the old chair and stroked the worn leather. *How many times?*

He thought of the admiral. What was in those secret orders? Had they really required the fastest available frigate? Perhaps the only available frigate?

He recalled that final signal, *Proceed when ready,* which Midshipman Hotham had reported as soon as it had broken from *Medusa*'s yard. Langley must have gone ashore soon afterwards to one of his interminable conferences, because after *Onward*'s anchor had broken free and they were eventually clearing the harbour, another signal had been sighted. It read simply, *Until the next time.* It must have been from Tyacke.

He moved to his small desk and half-opened the drawer where the letter lay. When would it be finished? When might she eventually read it?

He heard the Royal Marine clear his throat and call, "Lieutenant Monteith, *sir!*"

Four bells chimed faintly above the other sounds. Last dog watch. Monteith would arrive flushed and breathless, apologising even though he was exactly on time. The thought irritated Adam, although he knew he was being unfair.

He looked up at the skylight, remembering how the admiral's flag lieutenant had so carefully closed it.

Monteith strode into the cabin, his hat tucked beneath one arm. "I

do apologise, sir. I was needed up forrard, but when I told them—"
He seemed surprised when Adam interrupted him briskly, waving him toward a chair.

"Never mind. You're here now. And this won't take long." He crossed the cabin, feeling Monteith's eyes on his back, and sat behind the desk. "As third lieutenant, you have the training and the welfare of our midshipmen in your care. Some are experienced up to a certain level, a few are on the first step. We all go through it, and you will recall the pitfalls and misunderstandings yourself, *Onward* being your first ship as a commissioned officer."

Monteith sat bolt upright in the chair, hands folded across his hat. "I have always tried to maintain a code of conduct and discipline, sir. If any one has claimed otherwise, I must dispute it!"

Something fell on the deck overhead and there was a gust of laughter.

Adam said quietly, "Whatever we believe or expect, today's midshipmen are tomorrow's navy. Loyalty and obedience are essential."

Monteith licked his lips and nodded, eyes fixed on Adam's face. "I know that, sir."

Adam glanced at the papers on his desk, weighed down with a piece of polished coral. There was scarcely any movement, but *Onward* was responding.

He looked directly at Monteith. "Responsibility extends in both directions, by example and by trust. Midshipman or captain."

Monteith said, "I was doing what I considered my duty, sir. Very soon now, I will be required to write a report on each of them, as laid down in Standing Orders."

"I am aware of that."

He heard hushed voices beyond the screen door, possibly Morgan, trying to think of some way to interrupt this interview. It was a waste of time in any case. Monteith would never change, unless he was threatened.

The rap on the door came as a relief for both of them.

It was Radcliffe, breathless, as if he had run all the way from the quarterdeck. His eyes flickered in Monteith's direction, and then he deliberately looked away.

"Lieutenant Squire's respects, sir." He screwed up his sunburned face as if to recall every word. "A sail has been sighted, fine on the starboard bow, steering west." He added importantly, "Too far off to distinguish, but fresh lookouts have gone aloft."

Adam saw it in his mind. A ship crossing ahead of them. Where from? Where bound? Any alteration of course would be pointless, especially now. Like the sun in these latitudes, darkness would come quickly. Like a cloak.

"Tell Mr. Squire that I'll come on deck directly."

He turned to reach for the old telescope as the midshipman scurried from the cabin.

Monteith was on his feet, standing stiffly. He looked absurdly young, like a midshipman himself. "I have always tried to do my duty, sir."

Adam brushed past him. "I rely upon it."

He had failed.

But by the time he had reached the quarterdeck, he had almost dismissed Monteith from his thoughts. He looked up at the sails, feeling the warm air on his shoulders. The wind, what there was of it, was still holding, but the canvas was barely moving.

Squire was waiting with a telescope beneath his own arm. "I've sent Midshipman Hotham aloft, sir. Any one who can read and send signals as well as he does might see what others miss."

Adam moved toward the small group around the wheel, and one of the helmsmen called instantly, "South by east, sir!"

Vincent was here now, and Adam saw him pausing to flick some crumbs from his shirt.

He stared abeam at the endless barrier of land, like the edge of their world. Bleached and almost colourless under the glaring sun. It was closer now, less than five miles away. When the daylight was gone, it would be dangerous to tack any nearer.

The other vessel would be out of sight by now, heading into the great ocean.

As if reading his thoughts, Vincent said, "Probably seeking more sea room."

Adam hardly heard him. He said, "I'm going up." He knew Squire in particular was staring at him as he slung the telescope across his shoulder.

"I wouldn't have called you, sir, but—"

Adam looked up at the maintop, thinking of Walker, ordered aloft by Monteith as a punishment and beginning this unforeseen chain of events. He saw Jago standing with Drummond, the bosun, arms folded, and sensed his disapproval.

He gripped the ratlines and started to climb. The sun burned his back, and the cordage felt as if it had been lying across a stove. He glanced abeam again, pausing to wipe the sweat from his eyes with the back of his wrist. They had the sea to themselves, as far as he could see in any direction.

He had reached the maintop and saw Midshipman Hotham lower his own telescope at his captain's untidy arrival. There were two other lookouts with him, one of them Tucker, the new bosun's mate.

Hotham said, "The other vessel is almost out of sight, sir." He tapped his telescope. "Two-masted, probably a brig. Local, maybe?" He reached out as if to emphasise the point and stopped himself, but was unable to hide his excitement. "But over there, sir!" He pointed toward the uneven coastline. "*Flashes,* sir. Thought the sun was playing tricks on me. But they were flashes!"

Tucker said, "I saw 'em too, sir."

Hotham rushed on, ignoring the interruption. "On an' off. Like sunlight reflected from a mirror or a piece of glass. But then it stopped, or was lost in the inshore mist. But I did see it!"

Adam rested his knee against the barricade and felt the whole mainmast shivering against him. And the keel beneath that. His ship.

He focused the glass and saw the nearest land spring into detail, the curve of the next spur of headland. And after that? He thought of the sailing master beside him in the airless chartroom, as they had transferred their calculations to the new chart. He had marked this same thrust of headland. Not much, but still dangerous for any vessel so close inshore.

The most recent chart had shown a tiny landmark, which had not been on the previous version. A mission of some kind, either religious or simply supplying aid or sustenance to any trader or sailor who might venture ashore in this "godforsaken place." It could certainly be used as a guide.

Tucker said slowly, "Maybe it *was* hidden in the mist, sir."

Adam closed the telescope. "Not mist this time. It's smoke." He looked at Hotham again. "Flashes? You're certain of it?"

The midshipman hesitated, but only for a moment. "I've seen the army making signals like that. I'm certain, sir."

Adam started to climb down. A clergyman's son. What would his father say if he could see him now? *But no matter what he thinks he saw, it is my decision.*

Vincent was waiting, his face full of questions.

Adam said, "We will hold our present course until sunset. Then I intend to come about and close inshore." He looked at him directly. "And anchor."

"Landing party, sir?"

"At first light, weather permitting." As if he were thinking aloud. "Two boats, the cutter towing astern, and the gig. Easier. Any sign of trouble—"

Vincent said, "We'll be ready, sir!"

Adam gripped his arm. "Not this time, Mark. I need you here with me. Remember? The ship comes first."

He looked toward Squire, who had not moved since he had watched his captain scrambling aloft. "Join me in the cabin, both of you. And I'll explain what I have in mind."

Only then did he release Vincent's arm.

As he walked toward the companion he could hear the low murmur of their voices. What was there to discuss? Right or wrong, it was decided.

. . .

"Landing party mustered and standing by, sir." Vincent's voice was clipped and formal, loud in the uncanny silence.

Adam waited for his eyesight to adjust to the darkness on deck. Even Vincent's face was barely visible.

He had stolen a few precious minutes to revisit the chartroom. There was only a small shaded light above the chart table, just enough and no more. The order to darken ship had been piped at sunset, when *Onward* had altered course and headed toward the original sighting, and the master-at-arms and ship's corporal had maintained a regular patrol above and between decks to make certain it was carried out.

They had anchored, and the silence was unnerving. Even the sound of the cable running free had seemed dangerously loud, and the leadsman's regular chant as they approached the inshore waters seemed to invite discovery.

It was the middle watch, almost over now. Adam stared through the darkness toward the land, imagining he could smell it, but he knew it was about two miles distant, if his calculations and Julyan's were correct. The sailing master had seemed satisfied. *By guess and by God,* as he had put it.

The cutter and gig were moored alongside. It would be a long pull for the oarsmen, with extra men and weapons adding to the weight. Squire would be in command. Not an easy man to know, but he was brave, reliable, and popular. His experience as a master's mate, ashore and afloat in a surveying vessel taking part in Sir Alfred Bishop's expedition, made him the obvious choice. His service throughout the expedition had gained him a commendation from the great man himself, and a promotion to commissioned rank which still seemed to surprise him.

He would be leading in the cutter, which mounted a swivel in the bows as additional protection, with the gig staying as close astern as possible. If Squire ran aground on a sandbar before reaching a suitable beach, the gig could tow or kedge him free. Monteith would be in charge of that. There was no alternative.

It might all prove to be a mistake and a waste of time, and Rear-Admiral Langley would not be pleased about that.

Two midshipmen were also among the landing party, Huxley and David Napier, requested by Squire because he had worked alongside both of them while anchoring and getting under way. Adam had mixed feelings about Napier. Experienced, yes, but it was too soon after the *Moonstone* affair. But any exclusion would be seen as favouritism, and Napier would be the first to protest.

Many of *Onward*'s company had been standing by for most of the night. Some may have snatched a catnap curled up against a gun or in some corner of the hull, waiting for the call. No hammocks had left their nettings, in case of some emergency when all hands might be needed. A sudden shift of wind, or the leadsman's cry, warning of unexpected shallows. Like the edge of Julyan's "great valley," Adam thought.

They were ready. It was *now*.

Vincent had reported that there had been no shortage of volunteers, but Squire had only chosen a few extra men, including a squad of Royal Marines. Adam could still hear the disappointment, and see it on Lieutenant Sinclair's face, when he had been told that he was staying aboard and Sergeant Fairfax would be in charge of the "lobsters."

He glanced toward the land, very faintly visible now, darker than the sky.

And the air was still cool. But in another hour, less . . . He felt something like a shiver, and repressed it. He said quietly, "So let's be about it, shall we?"

He had gone over it in his mind again and again. Weapons, powder and shot, a day's ration of food and water. Bandages. He heard a few hushed voices, a slap on the back. Even a quick laugh.

The gig cast off first, oars moving slowly to carry her clear of the side. Jago was at the tiller. Not a volunteer: he had insisted. Napier was with him, Monteith's decision. Next the cutter, muffled oars taking the strain, the coxswain the usual man—Fitzgerald, a true Patlander as Jago called him—waving to someone still invisible in the darkness. His loose white shirt was ghost-like against the black water. It would be Jago's guide as he was following astern.

Vincent said, "I've doubled the lookouts, and the anchor watch is standing by. Now all we can do . . .”

Adam looked up at the sky, which seemed lighter, although that was impossible, and considered Vincent's voice. Efficient but envious. When he looked again, the two boats had disappeared, and he felt Vincent move toward the side.

Like me, he wants to be with them.

David Napier crouched in the gig's sternsheets and watched the regular thrust and heave of the stroke oarsman, slower than usual, but very steady. With extra hands aboard there was scarcely room to move. He eased his injured leg as much as he could; at least that was not playing up.

Monteith was sitting beside him, shifting occasionally to peer around the oarsmen as if in search of the cutter. It was rarely visible, except for a phosphorescent splash of oars, and the pale blur of Fitzgerald's shirt.

Once he snapped, “Look out! We're losing her!” and Jago had broken his silence.

“I've got her!” The barest pause. “Sir.”

Napier could feel spray splashing across his legs as the oars dipped steeply into the swell. Like tropical rain. How much worse it must be in the cutter, with a much heavier load to carry. He had seen the swivel gun mounted in the bows, but had heard Sergeant Fairfax say, “There's another one to take its place if need be.” He had even chuckled. “No time to load an' prime if we have to fire!”

No wonder the cutter had displayed so little freeboard. Squire must be thinking of that right now in this deeper swell.

Napier shifted again and felt the curved hanger's hilt rub against his thigh. The gunner had issued it to him when the landing party had been arming, blades freshly sharpened on a grindstone. Like *Nautilus*. Like *Moonstone*.

The gunner had watched him unbuckle his dirk. “Take this, boy. You might need something stronger than that do-little sword today!”

He looked toward the shore, and tried to see it in his mind. The sky was lighter, but only slightly, like the edge of a frayed curtain. There should be a small spur of headland to starboard, if the cutter was on course. And a beach, which might still surprise them. He would talk it all over later with Huxley, who was up there with Squire. It was hard to determine what they had in common, except for the unbreakable bond of friendship, which neither of them had ever questioned.

Jago said curtly, "Alterin' course to starboard."

Monteith almost stood up, but seemed to change his mind. "Are you certain?"

Jago either did not hear him or ignored him.

Napier offered, "I can still see the cox'n's shirt, sir."

He sensed that Jago had leaned across the tiller-bar and guessed he was grinning. Or swearing under his breath. They had hardly spoken since the hands had been mustered for "this adventure," as Lieutenant Squire had called it.

"Any trouble, you keep with me!" That was all, but from Luke Jago it was everything.

"*Oars!*"

The blades rose dripping on either side, while the gig swayed and slowed almost to a halt.

Jago said, "Cutter's run aground." He stood, one hand on the tiller. "Got clear again. Give way, *together!*"

The stroke oarsman gripped his loom and leaned back, and in those few seconds Napier was able to see the gleam of a medallion as it swung freely across his shirt. The features of the men around him were faintly visible for the first time since they had cast off.

A bosun's mate named Sinden muttered, "Not much bloody longer!"

Monteith rapped out, "Silence in the boat!" and did not see Sinden's gesture behind his back.

Napier seemed to have lost track of time. It was measured by each thrash of oars, and the surge against the hull, the occasional heavy breathing when Jago called for a brief pause if they were overhauling the cutter.

Napier stared past the oarsmen and saw the land, not high ground but a ragged barrier of trees.

"*Oars!*" Jago had turned his head, either to look or listen.

Monteith said sharply, "I gave no order!"

Jago did not move. "Mr. Squire just made a signal. We're arrived, sir!"

With the oars stilled, Napier thought he could hear the murmur of sea against beach, then the silence was completely shattered as some of the cutter's crew and passengers splashed over the side in readiness to haul their boat to safety.

It was not simply a landfall. The place seemed to be reaching out as if to encircle them . . . He told himself that would change when true daylight showed itself.

Monteith got to his feet and peered toward the land. Fitzgerald's shirt, the signal, had vanished. He said, "Stand by to clear the boat!"

He clambered over a thwart, but Jago reached out and restrained Napier. "Not yet."

Monteith did not wait, and jumped or fell into chest-deep water.

Jago said calmly, "Give the officer a hand, lads!" Then, "Clear the boat. Sinden, take charge up yonder."

It seemed to take an age before both boats were safely hauled ashore, but the oar-blades were still dripping when Squire was satisfied. He stood with his back to the sea and waited for a sodden Monteith and the two midshipmen to join him.

To Sergeant Fairfax he said, "As planned, have your lads take cover. Weapons uncocked, remember?" and Fairfax responded with a touch of outraged dignity.

"They *are* Royals, sir!" But he hurried away, and his white belt was soon hidden.

Squire said, "When it gets lighter we'll move inshore. There's a small cove beyond those trees." He grinned. "Or should be!" He touched Monteith's wet sleeve. "Never mind. Sun'll be up soon!"

They all tensed as a flock of birds broke from the undergrowth and rose, flapping and crying, toward the sea.

Squire said, "We don't need an audience!"

Someone laughed quietly.

Jago had joined them, his broad-bladed cutlass casually over his shoulder. He gestured in the same direction. "Th' mission must be over there as well." He did not look at Monteith.

Huxley was gazing after the disturbed birds as they circled and then vanished against the sea. He whispered to Napier, "I have to stay with the boats, Dave. I'm sorry you're stuck with *him*."

No name was necessary.

Squire was elaborating on his plan. "We can make our way along the shore now. It shouldn't take long. We'll know better once we fix our position more exactly." If he was grinning it remained invisible in the dimness before dawn. "And the ship will be able to see *us*."

He turned abruptly, lightly, for a man of his powerful build. "What is it?"

A seaman said, "I kin smell smoke, sir. Burning."

Squire sniffed audibly. "I can, too." He looked at Monteith. "We'll separate here, Hector." He waved to the bosun's mate. "Probably nothing, but we'll find out!"

Monteith loosened his belt. "If you ask me . . ."

No one did.

Napier turned to follow. He had never heard any one address the third lieutenant by his first name before. *Hector.* Coming from any one else . . . He froze.

It was a scream, terrified or in pain. A woman. And then utter silence.

He felt someone brush past him and knew it was Jago. "Best keep on the move, sir. It'll be sun-up in no time, an' we'll be sittin' ducks!"

Monteith was staring down at the beach as if to look for Squire's party, but they had already disappeared toward the higher ground. Napier looked at the nearest ridge of trees. No longer a black, formless mass but taking shape against the sky. He had been holding his breath since the scream, and drew it in sharply at what might have been a sudden gleam. But it was the first hint of sunlight.

He felt his shoe catch on some fallen frond, and heard it crackle underfoot. He said, "I agree with Jago, sir."

Monteith swung round. "Don't you *dare* to give me instructions!

When I need advice from you—"

There was a solitary tree directly ahead of them, the uppermost branches a green pattern against the sky, the lower still in deep shadow. But the shadow was moving.

"*Down!*" Jago seemed to lunge into the shadow even as he sent Monteith sprawling; Napier felt his strength and fury as he thrust him aside, and saw the blaze of metal as the great blade flashed between them. Then Jago recovered his own balance and hacked again at the writhing figure on the ground.

Then, very deliberately, he reached down to hoist the lieutenant to his feet.

"Easy does it, sir." As Monteith stood gazing at the body, he added quietly, "That's stopped '*im* farting in church!"

Monteith said nothing, and looked ready to vomit as Jago stooped and wiped his blade on the dead man's clothing.

"Too close for my likin'." Jago touched Napier's arm. "You're doin' well, Mr. Napier."

Napier wiped his mouth on his cuff. In the strengthening light he could see their attacker's curved blade in the sand, the severed hand still gripping it.

"Thanks." Too little, but it was all he could manage.

The shot that followed was not close, but on this tiny beach it could have been a thunderclap. Shouts and the sound of running feet, bodies stumbling and crashing through and into the undergrowth, and a second shot.

A solitary, authoritative voice rang out. It could have been on the quarterdeck of some flagship, or the barracks square at Plymouth. "Royal Marines, *fix bayonets!*" The familiar rasp of steel. "*Advance!*"

Sergeant Fairfax's squad of volunteers sounded like a regiment.

Squire strode toward them and nodded briefly to Monteith, who was biting his lip.

"Took 'em by surprise. Won't give 'em the chance to draw a second breath!" He clapped Monteith on the shoulder. "Bloody well done!" But he was looking at Jago.

Then he said quietly, "Lost one, I'm afraid. Seaman McNeil. A good lad. One of the best."

Napier could remember his face. He had been aboard *Onward* when she had first commissioned.

Squire seemed to square his shoulders. "We'll take him back with us." He looked around at their faces. "Be ready. And no quarter, right?"

Napier gripped the unfamiliar hanger and followed Squire onto firmer ground. Monteith had stopped to examine his pistol, which had dropped to the sand when Jago had pushed him aside, saving his life. At any second Napier expected another challenge, or more shots. The sound of their feet trampling over the rough ground sounded deafening, and once again the bright birds broke cover noisily and scattered throughout the trees. He looked back, but the two boats were out of sight. He thought of Huxley and the two men with the swivel gun, alone now except for the dead McNeil.

He saw Squire raise his hanger and gesture toward a gap in the trees, where the gleam of blue water was sharp-edged in the dawn.

"Be still!" Sergeant Fairfax had appeared from nowhere, his uniform blazing against the undergrowth. He dropped to one knee, musket raised and unmoving.

Napier looked around nervously. There was nothing. Even the sea was out of sight.

Then he heard it. Like ragged breathing: someone gasping. Louder now; he could scarcely hear the click of Fairfax's musket. The unsteady breathing stopped instantly.

Squire said, "Halt or we fire!" He did not raise his voice, but it seemed to hang in the humid air like an echo.

"No! No!" The voice was closer, unsteady. "Don't shoot. I'm only . . ." The rest was lost as something fell heavily amid the scrub.

Silence again, then somebody behind Napier murmured, "Speaks English, thank God."

Sergeant Fairfax snapped, "Stay where you are!" and stood slowly, but his musket and fixed bayonet did not waver. "*Easy,* I said!"

Napier heard Squire mutter something as he got to his feet, pistol drawn and ready, and saw Jago step into a flickering patch of sunlight, his cutlass at his side.

He spoke slowly, calmly. "Come 'ere, matey." His hand moved slightly toward his belt. "Nice an' easy now."

Napier saw Squire move fully into the filtered sunlight and come face to face with the shadowy figure. Grey-haired, gaunt in patched clothing, eyes wide as two more marines appeared behind him.

One called, "Nobody else up there, Sar'nt!" But they kept their eyes fixed on the stranger.

Jago held out his hand. "The musket, eh?"

Napier saw the man's confusion, but he did not resist as Jago took the musket and said, "Empty. Never been fired, by the look of it!"

Squire cleared his throat. "Where are you from?" He must have seen the bulging eyes fixed on the uniforms as more of Fairfax's men emerged from cover. "We are your friends."

Monteith said, "How can we trust him? If I had my way—"

The ragged figure did not seem to hear him. "I have work at mission. They are always good there . . . They help others." He covered his face with one hand; he was trembling. "There was shooting. And a fire."

Squire moved closer, and halted as the other man cowered away from him. Napier did not move, dared not. The man seemed to be English, a sailor perhaps. Or had been, until something had brought him to the mission.

The voice faltered on. Remembering, maybe reliving. "All gone now. A ship." He repeated, "All gone now!"

"It looks like we're too late." Squire sounded angry. With himself. "The captain will be wondering what the hell's happening!"

The stranger was staring at Napier fixedly, as if he were seeing a vision. "You are young. I remember when I . . ." He reached out as if to grasp his hand or arm.

Jago murmured, "Easy does it, matey," and his fingers flexed on his cutlass. "Where do you come from?"

"I told you! Th' mission!" A spark of impatience or sudden determination, but he did not look away from Napier. "I will take *you*. Show *you*."

Squire opened his mouth as if to countermand it, then he said very softly, "It's not an order, David. We'll be with you."

Napier did not trust himself to answer. Men had already died. And for what? He looked steadily at the ragged man and tried to shut his mind to everything else. He said simply, "Show me."

They turned toward the wash of dawn sweeping the eastern sky, and he imagined he could feel its growing heat on his face. For a moment longer he thought the man had not heard him, but then they were walking together, side by side, and he heard him utter one word.

"Home."

In a few seconds they were completely alone, or so it felt. Every so often he glimpsed blue water between the trees, but if he looked back over his shoulder, the beach and the distant ship were invisible.

At any moment . . . He had to control his thoughts. Fear was always the enemy. Time and distance meant nothing. When had he last been able to sleep without the picture of the stricken schooner in his mind? The feel of a dying man's grip on his wrists . . .

He said conversationally, "My home is in Cornwall. Do you know it?"

No answer, but the bony hand dragged at his arm. "This way."

Out of nowhere, a pair of giant rocks appeared, long fallen from the hillside, and it was as if he had been cut off from every hope of aid. Separated. Even the sounds of their feet across loose branches, the whine of insects, their own breathing seemed louder in the stillness. His mind was screaming. They were alone. *Any minute now* . . .

He tripped and felt the bony, steadying hand, heard the whispering voice. "Look yonder." And, carefully, "Da-vid."

Napier stood very still, unable to accept that they had arrived so suddenly. Like a great curtain being dragged aside, light and colour replacing the shadows and pitfalls of the jungle. A small cove shaped like a horseshoe beneath a hill the twin of the one behind them. And beyond, the ocean.

And here was the mission, or what remained of it. Small buildings no more than crude shacks, and a main structure which had once been painted white, as a simple landmark for passing vessels. It was charred beyond recognition, and the smell was sickening.

He realised he was alone. He swung round and tried to tug the hanger from his belt. A trap, a betrayal? But he knew it was neither.

He could not take his eyes from the smoking buildings, and a painted sign he could not read from here, which was surmounted by a wooden crucifix flaking in the sun.

The ragged man had returned. "Others are following. I tell them to wait."

Napier imagined Squire's reaction. He would soon close in. He asked, "All gone from here?"

"They came to rob and steal. Need stores for voyage. To carry slaves." The gaunt shoulders lifted. "The ship sailed, but some of them stayed here. It has . . . happened before."

Napier thought of the shots, and the scream. "Is any one alive?"

The man did not reply immediately, but was staring, like Napier, at the charred building.

"Mister Dundas is a strong man. *Fine* man." He shuddered. "Man of God." He straightened and seemed to compose himself. Then he touched Napier's forearm, as if to lead him. "We will go down. Your comrades will wait no longer." He gave a ghostly smile. "Da-vid."

They left the shelter of the trees and walked down through trampled grass toward the mission. Napier stayed close beside him. Suppose the man was completely mad, or driven beyond reason by what he had seen or imagined?

There was a body lying against a length of fence, a black man, shot in the face, one fist still gripping an axe. Napier heard the flies buzzing as they passed.

"I was afraid. I ran away when they attacked the mission. I came to find you. I saw you land."

Napier looked at the heavy door of a single structure separate from the burned remains of other buildings. A chapel of sorts. A notice was displayed nearby, with the same name, William Dundas, and a few lines of scripture in English.

The door was badly damaged and scarred by several shots. There was complete silence.

Napier said, "You brought me. I only hope—" and the grip tightened on his arm.

"I deserted them. I must do it!" The man's eyes were running in the drifting smoke. Or they were tears? Then he walked up to the door and shouted, "Ahoy! It's Wolsey! I am with friends! The navy!"

Napier watched him twisting his head in all directions, screwing a corner of his coat into a tight ball, his composure gone. To his relief he saw bayonets glinting beyond the broken fence, and patches of scarlet moving. And here came Jago, grim-faced, lifting one hand as he strode toward the building.

Napier heard the first tentative scrape of metal, and the heavy-timbered door was opened wide. The interior was completely dark, pierced here and there by thin beams of light through what must be shutters or other defenses. Napier stood with his back to the sun, every instinct warning him that he was a perfect target, but unable to move.

A few figures staggered or pushed others aside to reach the door, natives, perhaps workers at the mission, and several children, running out into the sunlight and huddling together, hiding their faces as they were confronted by seamen and marines.

But many of the others inside did not move. Nor would they.

Napier felt Squire's heavy hand on his shoulder as he brushed past. "Well done, David. Your guide kept his word!" He waved toward his men. "Otherwise . . ."

It was a grim sight. Some had crawled here for help, or to die. Others seemed too dazed to understand what was happening. In a corner of the chapel a white woman knelt on the floor, a grey-haired man propped against her.

Napier dropped to his knees beside them and tried to take the weight from her, but she pushed him away, struggling and hitting him with her fists, screaming, "Don't touch me! I can't . . ." She broke off in a fit of coughing.

Napier put his arm around her shoulders, conscious only of her rage and fear. She was wearing a loose white garment that might have been a man's shirt, and her arms and legs were bare. He knew that she wore little else.

He felt the weight lifted clear and heard someone mutter, "'E's dead, poor bastard!"

The woman began to struggle again, her nails reaching for his face. "My father! *Not dead!*"

Men were making their way deeper into the building, more light guiding them as shutters and doors were forced open. The woman was quite still now in Napier's arms, and was staring into his face. There was a bruise on her cheek, and a wound across her neck. There had been a lot of blood, too. Hers.

She said suddenly, *"Where were you?"* Her voice was taut, like a knife-edge. The bare arms and legs were very tanned, and she was English.

He said quietly, "We came as soon as we knew," and tightened his grip again as something dropped and broke and a man swore, angry or unnerved.

She had dark hair, loose and tangled, but when he moved to push it back from her face he felt her flinch as if expecting a blow. Pain, or worse. But the eyes remained unnaturally steady, fixed on his face.

"Wolsey found you. He came back."

"He's here with me." He stroked the hair from her face and she did not resist this time.

"I should have known. Been ready. But they never gave us a chance. My father tried." She seemed to shiver. "He always *believed.*"

A shadow loomed over them: it was Squire, his eyes everywhere, wary but very calm. "We'll soon have you out of here, my dear."

He crouched unhurriedly and took one of her limp hands. "Our doctor will soon have you as right as rain." She began to protest, but he continued, "You must be Mr. Dundas's daughter." He was turning over her wrist, revealing the deep rope burns; she appeared to have been cruelly tied and dragged. "We'll take care of you." He released her hand, quite gently. "So what do we call you?"

She moved her head stiffly, and her eyes left Napier's to focus on Squire's face. "Claire Dundas."

Squire looked over his shoulder, frowning at the interruption as Monteith appeared and stood framed in the doorway.

"All mustered." He looked at the grey-haired man, lying dead on a frayed carpet. "Sergeant Fairfax reports that the intruders have gone."

Squire hid his impatience. "And what do *you* say?" He did not wait for an answer, but rose and peeled off his uniform coat. "Here, my dear. A bit too hot for later, but you put it on now, eh?"

She stood swaying on her feet, and when she obediently held out her arms Napier saw another wound on her naked shoulder. She had been bitten.

She tugged the coat around her until the lapels overlapped her slim body. Without taking his eyes from her, Squire said, "I'm sending Jago with the gig and McNeil. Tell the captain, 'bosun's chair.' He'll know what to do."

The girl called Claire said dully, "McNeil. A Scottish name."

Squire looked back at the dead man on the floor. "Yes. Like Dundas."

Napier reached for her arm. "Come outside with me."

He saw her turn toward her father's body and Squire said gently, "I'll take care of him for you." She attempted to pull away and almost fell. Napier took her hand again, but he was looking at Squire. So familiar and easy-going. A true sailor, he thought.

He was far more than that.

Sergeant Fairfax was waiting with two of his marines, a length of shutter carried between them.

Fairfax touched his hat. "Ready for the lady when you give the word, sir!"

Fairfax was a senior sergeant, and had never given up the hope of promotion. He watched them lifting the young woman onto a layer of blankets. He had seen plenty of people in shock during times of war, on land and at sea. Most of them recovered. There was little alternative in the navy, much less in the Corps.

The marines were lifting their makeshift litter, and carrying it with care, the woman partly shrouded by the lieutenant's coat. She was staring up at the sky, heedless of the burning sun. There was blood on one bare ankle, but she was safe. Fairfax kicked bitterly at a loose stone. Safe? How could she feel safe after what she must have endured?

He shouted, "Come on then, we don't have all day to find them boats!"

He saw one of the seamen glare at him, and was glad. He heard a shout and saw Midshipman David Napier waving from a gap in the trees. Nothing more was needed: the ship was in sight. Their part in this venture was over.

Squire was standing beside the woman now, speaking with her even as she dragged her hand from his. Sergeant Fairfax knew from hard experience that it was only just beginning.

8 Not a Race

Lieutenant Mark Vincent turned away from the group of men around the wheel as he heard the captain's voice. Or perhaps someone had prodded him warningly. He must have been half asleep on his feet.

He touched his hat. "South by east, sir. Full and by."

Adam walked to the compass box but did not consult it. Instead, he stared up at the spread of canvas, almost fully braced to contain the wind and hold *Onward* on course. The wind had backed slightly so that the deck was tilting to leeward, but only enough to allow them to gain more sea room. He looked at the masthead pendant: it was streaming, although the air across his neck was clammy.

He looked at the foredeck, seeing it as it had been a few hours before: boats being hoisted, exhausted sailors being lifted bodily over the side, too weary or subdued to respond to their welcome. Hard to believe they had watched those same two boats vanish into the darkness before dawn this very day.

He recalled the gig returning from the beach, and Jago's grim description of the sequence of events. And later, when the bosun's chair had been hoisted aboard, the girl in Squire's coat losing her self-control as hands had reached out to carry her below. Murray, the surgeon, had been with her from the first.

Someone had asked Jago if he wanted anything, and he had retorted, "Just get me away from that hell-hole!" He spoke for all of them.

Adam gazed forward along the full length of his ship. Beyond the quarterdeck rail, every space seemed to be full of silent people.

Vincent said quietly, "As ordered, sir. Lower deck cleared."

Adam nodded. "Better now than later."

He moved to the centre of the rail and felt for the small prayer book inside his coat. It would be pitch black within a couple of hours. The sea was darker, almost bronze toward the horizon, and the land was already losing shape and definition.

He could see the bosun with some of his men on the larboard gangway, bare-headed and looking aft toward their captain. And the two flag-draped corpses. Adam thought of the dead man's daughter, lying down below at this moment. Would she ever be allowed to forget, let alone forgive?

He knew Squire was standing close by, and Monteith, the latter strangely withdrawn since he had climbed aboard. David Napier seemed composed enough.

Another shadow merged with Adam's own. He knew it was Jago.

They had shaken hands when he had returned with the gig, and the news. Jago had gauged the moment, as usual. "You'll be needin' a shave, eh, Cap'n?" But the strain was very evident.

Squire had described Jago in stronger terms. "He was like the Rock of Gibraltar! Right from when we cast off!"

Jago murmured, "Got the book, Cap'n?"

Adam glanced at him and smiled. "Thank you." He pulled it out of his pocket. All those other times. Faces, memories, pain.

He heard Vincent call, *"Uncover!"*

Most of them had already removed their hats. Others were still half-dressed from working ship, getting *Onward* under way again.

He thought again of the girl named Claire. She was about the same age as Lowenna. It never left him. How it must have been, for the one he loved.

In spite of the silence the ship became a part of it, the sound of the wind, canvas, loose tackle, but Adam's voice carried and every word was clear.

The days of men are but as grass:
for he flourisheth as a flower of the field.

United again, all six of *Onward*'s midshipmen were mustered on the larboard side of the quarterdeck with Hotham, the senior, in charge. He was finding it difficult not to look around as he listened to the captain's voice speaking the familiar words. It was unusual to see the entire ship's company gathered together all at once, except when they were at action stations or on occasions like this, which fortunately were rare.

Faces he knew well, others hardly at all. Voices and accents from every part of Britain. When he wrote to his father he would attempt to describe his emotions, before and after he had sighted the flashing reflection which, in turn, had caused the captain to alter course and send a landing party to investigate. People had died as a result, including one of their own, and Hotham felt a deep sense of guilt because of it. If he had kept quiet, would they still be alive? Would it have made any difference?

And there was an intense pride, rivalling the uneasy guilt. From the moment the boats had cast off and pulled away into darkness, an eternity before sunrise or so it had seemed, he, Charles Hotham, clergyman's son, had been appointed acting lieutenant, until the two lieutenants who had gone with the boats returned.

He had not been called upon to perform any duty which was foreign to him, and those around him had barely noticed his temporary promotion. But he had *felt* it, the weight of honour and responsibility. And he still did.

Hotham looked around at his fellow midshipmen, some of whom looked even younger without their hats. Radcliffe, their newest member, had already shown his disrespect by offering a sweeping bow and addressing him as "sir."

But one day, maybe soon, he might be summoned to face the Board—the Inquisition, as they called it—and gain the glittering prize of promotion, a commission. The events of this day might just tip the balance in his favour.

David Napier was standing nearby, Huxley beside him. Napier could see the captain's dark hair catching the last of the bronze sunlight as he looked keenly across the crowded deck and the full length of the ship. He was holding the prayer book and speaking the words, but Napier had not seen him consult it.

Napier did not look toward the land. It was shadowed by the twilight, and he wanted to shut it out of his mind and never see it again. But he knew he never would. Small, stark pictures burned like flames in the darkness of his thoughts: Jago pushing Monteith off balance and hacking down the attacker in the shadows. *But it was my life he was saving.*

And the strange, ragged man named Wolsey, who had risked everything to come to them for help, and had chosen a midshipman to be his companion even to the mission. Mission of death . . .

And yet, just when the boats were about to leave the beach and return to *Onward*, shining on the clean sea in the sunlight like a perfect symbol, Wolsey had turned and disappeared. Back to the mission, his only home.

Lieutenant Squire was standing on the gangway; perhaps he had asked to perform this duty. For a second or so, their eyes met. Like that final moment of decision.

> *We commend unto Thy hands of mercy, most merciful*
> *Father, the souls of these our brothers departed, and we*
> *commit their bodies to the deep.*

The combined shrill of calls broke the stillness and Squire dropped his hand, the signal for which the burial party had been waiting. Napier heard an improvised grating being raised and tilted, and then a second, and when he looked again, the flags were empty and rippling in the light wind. It was over.

A solitary call followed: he knew it was Drummond the bosun.
Carry on.

Some of the men on deck were going below to their messes; others seemed reluctant to leave and stood in silence by the same gangway. Squire glanced down at his own uniform. He was wearing his best coat, at odds with his breeches, which were still badly stained from the ordeal ashore. Maybe there was a tailor at Freetown where he could replace the coat used to cover the missionary's daughter.

He looked toward an open hatch. She might have heard the brief ceremony, despite her pain and hideous memories, and understood that they were honouring the dead in the navy's way. *Our way.*

He thought of the old coat again and knew he would never discard it.

Nor would he forget her.

There were only two lanterns burning in the great cabin, but compared with the complete darkness of the previous night it seemed like broad daylight. Adam Bolitho could see himself mirrored in the stern windows among the familiar items of furniture, old friends in this sanctuary.

He was very tired, drained, but his mind refused to relax. He thought of the entire ship in darkness when they had come about to head for that little-known beach where they had landed the boats. Stealth had seemed impossible. Even the small compass light, shaded though it was, had seemed as blinding as a beacon.

Astern now, the sea was black; only the reflections in the salt-stained glass seemed real.

He braced his legs as the deck tilted slightly. Perhaps the wind had freshened, although he doubted it. There was an empty plate and a wine glass on the table. He could scarcely remember anything about either, except for Morgan's persistence and concern.

Tomorrow, unless the wind and weather turned against them, they should sight their new landfall around noon. Julyan was optimistic, but even he had seemed subdued after the sea burials. Maybe he was like his captain. No matter how many you witnessed, each one seemed like the first.

He made an effort to concentrate. It would mean anchoring, and the depths in this area were uncertain. As the approaches to Freetown must have been years ago.

Tomorrow he would finish writing his report, when his mind was clear again. He thought of the seaman who had gone over the side, McNeil. He had always seemed in good spirits. One of Squire's men. His entry would be the briefest. *D.D.* Discharged—dead.

He felt the air stir slightly as the door opened, and knew it was Jago. Apart from cabin servants he was the only one never announced by the Royal Marine sentry.

Jago closed the screen door behind him, and looked at him questioningly.

"I was told you wanted to see me, Cap'n?" He jerked a thumb in the direction of the sleeping cabin. "Thought you'd be countin' sheep by now!"

Adam gestured to a chair. "We'll all be busy enough tomorrow. There's something I want to discuss. To *ask*. Before I write my report for the admiral."

Jago sat down on the edge of the chair, eyes expressionless. He said, "I see you didn't call me for a shave, Cap'n," and rubbed his own jaw. "Needs a trained fist!"

Adam had cut himself. Even the hand guiding the razor had been weary. But he knew that Jago was ahead of him.

"I heard what you did ashore, Luke. It was what I've come to expect of you."

Jago leaned forward in the chair, and Adam could see the strain as well as the strength. The man who should hate and offer no loyalty to any officer. An official pardon could never wipe away the scars, mental or physical, of an unjust flogging.

Jago said, "I think I knows what you mean to ask, Cap'n. A road we've been down afore, as I recalls." Then he smiled, for the first time since returning aboard. "Remember what I said when we went over to th' flagship. I wants to see *your* flag up there at the mast'ead, when I'm *an admiral's coxswain.* Then, if you offers me promotion . . ." It was a broad grin now. "Time to ask me again!"

Adam shook his head. "You deserve it."

Jago turned as if he had heard something, and said quietly, "An' so do you, Cap'n."

There was a tap at the door.

"Surgeon, sir!"

Morgan was halfway there, muttering, "Don't they realise! We've not had a moment!" and sighed as Adam said, "I was expecting him." Then, "Give my cox'n a wet, will you?"

Murray stalked into the cabin, very hawkish and alive. "I apologise for keeping you waiting, sir. I was not sure. And I still am not." He was wearing one of his stained surgery smocks.

Adam said, "How is she?"

"Recovering. It's still too early to judge. But she's young and she's strong. Given time . . ." Murray held up his hands and stared at them. "These are supposed to heal, but every time I touch her she must relive the ordeal. Beaten into submission, abused and violated. The damage to her mind may never mend." He looked up, his eyes calm again. "I told her that you wished to visit her. I'm sorry it's taken so long."

"I'll be guided by you. The last thing I want is to jeopardise her recovery."

The cabin skylight was still open and they heard someone call out and laugh.

Murray said curtly, "The best sound I've heard since we up-anchored!"

Jago said, "I'll wait here, Cap'n," and picked up Adam's coat from a chair and held it out for him. "So she'll *know*."

Murray opened the door. "She's in my cabin." Impatient or apprehensive; it was hard to know. Adam had already heard about the cabin: Vincent had told him. It would be quieter, safer.

One of Murray's loblolly boys was sitting outside, and he got to his feet as they appeared in the narrow passageway. Murray's cabin adjoined the sick berth, but was not a part of it.

Murray murmured something and the man shook his head.

"We cannot stay too long." Murray paused. "She may have changed her mind." He regarded Adam steadily. "Trust me." He opened the door.

There was one small light but, like the sick quarters, everything was painted white. It was enough.

She was lying on a cot covered by a sheet which she was holding closely beneath her chin. One arm was bare, the linen bandage around her wrist livid against her tanned skin, hiding the rope burns where she had been tied and dragged. She turned her head toward the door, eyes open and unblinking.

Murray said, "I've brought the captain to see you, Claire. Remember how we talked about it. Only a short visit. Then perhaps you'll go to sleep."

She turned her head away slightly, her profile in shadow.

Murray repeated, "Captain Bolitho. He commands here."

Her lips moved as if they were forming the name. But her eyes were shut.

Adam saw the dark hair was clinging to the pillow. Still damp; it had been washed. And on the one visible hand the nails were clean. When he had seen her carried aboard they had been black with dried blood, probably from the face of one of her attackers.

She said, "Bo-lye-tho." Her eyes were open again. "I wanted to see you." There was another pause. "To thank you. He said you would come."

Adam glanced at Murray and saw his almost imperceptible nod. She was talking about her father.

She tried to twist her head to gaze at him again, but pain seemed to prevent it. The sheet had slipped from her shoulder, where he saw another bandage.

"Bless you for what you did. I know you gave him to the sea. He'll be safe there."

Murray's eyes told Adam that it was time to leave.

She reached out suddenly as if to seek his hand, and he clasped it instinctively. Murray did not protest.

She said, "*Thank you*, Captain Bolitho. I shall never forget." A tear ran unheeded over her cheek. "Or forgive!"

Adam stood up, gently releasing her fingers, and saw her grope for his hand again. "Try to rest, Claire. We shall anchor tomorrow, and then . . ." Her fingers gripped his with unexpected strength.

"*No!*" The damp hair spilled across his sleeve. "No, not there! Later!"

Murray took the hand and felt the pulse discreetly.

"She must rest now," and when he had pulled the door to behind them, "I'm glad you came. And so is she."

They stood in the passageway and Murray lowered his voice. "She wants to remain aboard with us until we return to Freetown. She has friends there. That was as much information as she gave me."

Adam said, "Send somebody to call me if I can help," and looked at Murray directly. "At *any* time."

The surgeon touched his forehead, sketching a salute, but it was more than that. "Aye, aye, sir!"

His cabin door was still partly open and Murray thought he heard her call out, a little more strongly now. He turned, but the passageway was empty. Bolitho had gone on deck, and not aft to his own quarters.

He was the captain again.

Squire closed the telescope and slung it over his shoulder. With the sun almost directly overhead and the heat oppressive, it was hard to concentrate, and he was bone-weary. After the bustle and excitement of their final approach and anchoring off New Haven, the ship seemed strangely still and quiet. It was the afternoon watch, but except for those required on duty most of *Onward*'s people were asleep, and deserved it. There was a lingering aroma of rum in the air, an extra tot from the captain. His way of saying thank you, Squire thought. Probably why Bolitho had gone immediately ashore: to pay his respects to the governor while his gig's crew were still smart and sober. *Onward* had anchored a cable's length from the elbow of land Julyan had described, which shielded the anchorage beyond.

It had been an unusual experience. With the sun so intense and the inshore water so clear, it was possible to see the frigate's shadow full-length as she passed over some of the sandbars.

Squire moved into the welcome shadow of the mizzen mast and glanced at the wheel. It gave some hint of the current, jerking slightly as if controlled by invisible helmsmen.

The anchorage was like a mill-pond, and seemed a safe mooring, but he knew two rivers converged here and emptied into the sea. When the rains came it must be a real challenge for any master.

He had seen a few boats paddling out to investigate the frigate, one or two coming close enough for those aboard to wave or hold up baskets of goods for sale or barter—pottery, vegetables and carvings for the most part. But they kept their distance, discouraged by seamen or marines stationed at intervals along either side.

Bolitho had made it quite clear. No one was to be allowed aboard. This was an official visit, and Squire had seen the sealed package handed down to the gig before it had shoved off.

Greetings from the admiral at Freetown. Although Squire had heard there was no love lost between Rear-Admiral Langley and the governor here. No doubt Langley would be more concerned by *Onward*'s failure to appear within the time expected, and if not, his flag lieutenant would soon remind him, if he valued his own future.

He felt his shoe stick to the deck seam. The ship had been washed from beakhead to counter when they had altered course to enter the anchorage. Now even the scuppers were as dry as tinder. He heard footsteps and turned to see the surgeon crossing the deck toward him, avoiding the softened seams.

"I'm afraid the captain's still ashore, Doc. Not returning till the last dog, as far as we know. Is something wrong?"

Murray was hatless and holding one hand across his eyes to shield them from the sun, but the strain seemed to have fallen from his long face like a cloud.

"This time it's you I came to find." He glanced incuriously toward the shore, as if he had not seen it before. "Experience or instinct: I often ask myself, where do we draw the line?" He turned his back on the land, dismissing it. "She wants to see you, although at this stage it might destroy any progress she has made. Such as it is."

Squire said uncertainly, "I didn't realise she knew my name."

"She did not. But her description was enough!" Murray paused. "Will you see her? It might do more harm than good."

Squire muttered, "I don't know. After what she went through—" and said nothing for a moment, recalling her anguish and the brief moment of peace and communion when he had given her his coat to hide her shame from those trying to help her. "It might bring it all back when she sees me."

Murray shrugged. "I don't know what the purser will say, but I raided his slop-chest for some clothing. Not what she has been used to, but it's fresh and clean. It might make a difference."

Squire waved to Lieutenant Sinclair who was speaking to some of his marines. "Bob, call me if I'm needed"—and indicated the surgeon— "You know where I'll be."

Sinclair raised a hand and Squire thought he had forgiven him for choosing his sergeant for the landing party instead.

It was cooler below deck, but not much, despite the hastily rigged windsails. Squire hardly noticed. Claire Dundas might be feeling stronger, safer, but one sight of him and it could all be torn apart.

They reached the cabin door and Murray exchanged a few words with one of his assistants, who was rolling and repacking bandages like those they had carried in the cutter. Then to Squire he said, "Not too long. And don't touch her," before tapping at the door. "Claire? Me again!"

Squire still hesitated. For a moment he thought Murray had left another one of his assistants here while he was on deck. She was dressed in white, the shirt probably a midshipman's, fastened to her throat, and breeches which had clearly been taken from the slop-chest. She was sitting upright in Murray's armchair, facing the door.

Murray said, "Don't keep the lieutenant too long, Claire. He'll be wanted on deck shortly," and gestured to another chair. "Call me if you require anything. I have to pull out someone's tooth—but it will not take long." It sounded like a warning to Squire.

She said, "It was good of you to come," and turned to watch Murray depart: he left the door open. A lock of dark hair fell aside slightly and Squire saw the bruise on her forehead.

"I wanted to see you. I've been wondering about you, ever since . . ." He said nothing more, recalling Murray's warning. "You look wonderful." He moved to the other chair and saw she was staring at the door again. This was a mistake. He had wanted to tell her he had thought of nothing else since she had been carried aboard.

She said softly, "I wanted to see *you*. To explain." Her eyes were restless, flickering around the cabin. "To . . . thank you." She looked at him suddenly. "After the way I treated you. And the risks you took for us . . . for me."

Squire stood up and saw her tense as he took a small package from his pocket.

"I wanted to bring you this." He opened it carefully, not looking at her; perhaps he had already made things worse. "It was in my old coat." He laid the bracelet on the table beside her. "I thought you might be looking for it."

She reached out, her lips moving, but he heard no words.

Her hand faltered. "I thought they'd taken it." Then she shook her head, heedless of the hair falling over her face. "No. I remember putting it in your coat when you tried to help me." She fumbled with the bracelet. "*He* gave it to me."

She was sobbing harshly, but there were no tears.

Squire wanted to help her, but he heard the surgeon's warning. She was fumbling at her cuffs, one after the other, and he saw the thick bandages around her wrists.

He said carefully, "I can put it in the strongbox, until . . ."

She stared at him with that unnerving directness.

"*You* keep it for me. It will be safe with you." She thrust the hair from her face. "Until I leave the ship—Lieutenant Squire." She laid the unfastened bracelet on the table, and he could see her shoulders beginning to quiver. "What . . . do your friends call you?"

"Friends?" He wanted to smile, make a joke of it, but nothing would come. "Jamie."

She touched the bracelet, and almost dropped it.

Instinctively, Squire did not move. But the restraint cost him more than Murray would ever guess. He felt her fingers on his as she laid the bracelet across his calloused palm.

The door was slightly ajar, and Murray's voice said from beyond it, "I think you're needed on deck."

He came in, glancing somewhere between them. "And it's time *you* had a rest, young lady." He was holding a pair of felt slippers. "But first try these on for size. Tilley, the sailmaker, made a few alterations. I made a sketch for him."

She leaned down and slid one onto her bare foot. "How wonderful. Please thank him for me, will you?"

She picked up the second slipper; they were the kind worn by powder-monkeys whenever they were ordered to the magazine. Maddock, the gunner, was never without a pair himself. To forget could invite disaster, where one spark from the sole of an ordinary shoe might explode into an inferno.

She touched her cheek with the back of her hand. "So kind. I don't know what to say."

Murray turned and deliberately slipped his arm through Squire's, but did not look at him. "We've not forgotten what it feels like to be young. Have we?"

A warning, between friends. Murray wanted to stop him from making a fool of himself, before it was too late.

Squire said, "If I'm wanted on deck . . ." but could not help looking back. "I'll put the bracelet in the strongbox. Just in case."

She stared at him, and nodded slowly. "I understand." She did not smile. "Thank you, Lieutenant."

Like a door being slammed shut.

Adam Bolitho shifted slightly on the hot thwart to gaze at the full expanse of the anchorage as the gig pulled past the headland. Plenty of eyes must have observed *Onward*'s slow and cautious approach; he had seen sunlight blinking from telescopes ashore and afloat most of the way.

A longboat had come out to meet them, perhaps surprised that *Onward* did not anchor closer to the shore, with its scattering of buildings and long, ungainly pier. The boat had signalled for them to follow, a uniformed figure standing to wave aside any dugout that hovered too closely.

The main fortification was timber-built, with a stockade and a battery of small cannon. In stark contrast, the flag that flew above them, making a brilliant splash of colour, was the same as the one hoisted at *Onward*'s own jackstaff when her anchor had been secured. Maybe Freetown had begun like this, and other footholds in wilderness that Rear-Admiral Langley would dismiss as the encroachment of empire.

Jago said, "'E's turnin', Cap'n."

The other boat was losing way, its oars in confusion. The man in uniform was on his feet again, bowing and baring his teeth in a grin. At one end of the pier were more uniforms, and bare-backed figures who were apparently repairing the lower structure close to the water.

Adam said, "You must stay in the boat this time, I'm afraid." He glanced along the slow-moving looms, at the faces he knew so well. "I'll send word if I'm delayed."

He felt the body beside him stir suddenly; he had almost forgotten that Monteith was aboard. Tense, his sword gripped between his knees, still going over the events at the mission. Doubts, fears, it was not possible to tell. Yet.

Jago called, *"Oars!"* He may have glanced at Monteith, but he did not wait. Monteith was, after all, in charge of the gig for this formal visit. When he had been piped over the side, one of the duty watch had slipped and allowed a coil of rope to fall across the gangway. At any other time Monteith would have yelled at him, and for far less.

Whatever it was, it must have happened ashore. Squire had said nothing, and Jago would keep it to himself as usual. Unless . . .

The oars were inboard, the bowmen hooked onto the pier. Another uniformed figure was peering down at them, head and shoulders silhouetted against the sky.

Adam stood up and reached for the thick envelope, the reason for this visit.

He looked at Jago. "Remember what we talked about, eh?" and Jago's tanned face broke into a grin.

"Ol' John Allday would never forgive me, Cap'n!"

Some of the bare-backed men on the lower pier had stopped work to look down at the gig and the newcomers. There was a shout, and the sharp crack of a whip. The onlookers vanished.

Adam glanced at Monteith, who had not moved. "Ready?" He did not wait for an answer. Monteith was probably recalling their talk. *Leadership by example.* He stared up at the pier, angry with himself. *So do it!*

He climbed up into the sunlight and felt the wood still wet under his hands. It must have been scrubbed in readiness for their arrival. Monteith was close behind him, perhaps relieved to be away from the gig, which must be the key to whatever memories were remaining in his mind. Adam straightened as he was confronted by a stocky man in an unfamiliar green uniform. The New Haven militia.

A smart salute, and a voice as English as one of his own seamen's barked, "On behalf of the Governor, sir, I am to bid you welcome!" He waited for Monteith to join them. "If you will step this way, sir?"

Adam looked back at the gig and saw Jago nod. That was all.

They walked along the pier. Some of the timber was scarred and well-used; other sections looked freshly laid. Across from the anchorage, there were low sheds along the distant waterfront: slipways for building and launching coastal craft. In a few years' time, this might become another Freetown.

He quickened his pace. Their guide was keeping well ahead of them, perhaps deliberately.

There were others working beneath the pier. A guard, too, with a whip dangling across his shoulder.

The guide said, "Felons, sir," and almost smirked. "No different from England!"

They had reached the main building. Like the pier, it must have seen faces from every part of the world.

"Your boat's crew, sir? They'll not be coming ashore, will they?"

"I don't intend to keep them waiting." It came out more sharply than he had intended, and Adam saw the man flinch. Perhaps Monteith was not the only one.

"If you'll come this way, sir." The guide broke off, obviously disconcerted as someone stepped from the shadow of the broad entrance and came striding toward them. "My apologies, Sir Duncan—I brought them along the pier!"

Adam was not sure what he had been expecting, but Sir Duncan Ballantyne was not it.

Tall and lean, he strode toward them, both hands outstretched. "I should have sent one of our boats, and not forced you to drag all the way along that relic!"

He grasped Adam's hand and shook it vigorously, apparently untroubled by the sun in his eyes. "Captain Bolitho!" He nodded toward the water. "And His Majesty's Ship *Onward*—a frigate, no less. We are indeed honoured!"

Ballantyne slipped his arm familiarly through Adam's. "Something to kill our thirst would be in order."

He paused to say something to one of his men and Adam took the opportunity to study him more closely. The eyes were, and the hair had once been, as dark as his own. He was said to be sixty years old, but he had the bearing and agility of one much younger. He was casually but, Adam guessed, expensively dressed in riding breeches, with tall boots that shone like glass, and a silk cravat tucked into a matching shirt.

But the face told another story, deeply tanned, dominated by a strong nose and a beard, neatly trimmed to contain the grey. A face it would be impossible to forget. It reminded him of some of the old paintings he had studied as a boy, portraits of those who had defeated the Armada.

Ballantyne glanced casually at Monteith. "You are welcome too, of course. You can amuse yourself while we talk." And to Adam, "Something tells me that your visit will be a short one." He took his arm again. "Maybe next time, eh?"

Inside the building he turned to face them. "I heard about the mission, and I have sent some men to investigate the matter. I knew William Dundas, of course. Not well, but as much as he would allow. His kind are always at risk, as I'm sure you know."

He pushed open another door. Here it was cooler, and a long

bamboo-mounted fan was moving slowly back and forth on the ceiling.

Ballantyne sat down and waved Adam to another chair. He said, "News travels fast in these parts," and stamped one booted foot. "By horse and by coaster." He waited while a black servant knelt to tug off his boots.

Adam held out the envelope. "I was told to give this to you personally, Sir Duncan," and Ballantyne wagged a finger at him.

"Not here, together. Plain 'Duncan' will do well enough!" He laughed. "I'm not even used to the title myself yet." He was turning over the envelope. "I can guess the contents. For an admiral and the like, Freetown has become a stepping-stone . . ." The silken shoulders lifted in a shrug. "To promotion or oblivion!" He leaned forward as another African entered, carrying a silver tray and a pair of glasses. The servant must have caught his foot on the carpet, and the glasses clinked dangerously. "Easy, Trusty! Take your time!"

Adam realised that he was quite young, perhaps the same age as David Napier. He was nodding and smiling now, the glasses safely deposited on a heart-shaped wooden table. An older man brought the wine. Adam rubbed his forehead. He was still tired; he had not even noticed Monteith being shown to another, adjoining room.

Ballantyne sipped the wine slowly. "Fair enough. Under the circumstances."

When they were alone again, Adam said, "How did he come by a name like 'Trusty'?" and for a moment he thought Ballantyne would choke on his wine.

He laughed and dabbed his mouth. "He's a good fellow. Obedient, loyal, and usually careful." He recovered. "I gave him the name. Trusty was my little pony, given me by my old father when I was a lad. I never forgot him. I probably couldn't pronounce *his* real name, even if I knew it."

Adam had noticed how Trusty had watched Ballantyne's mouth, and Monteith's too as he had left the room. "Can he neither hear nor speak?"

Ballantyne was studying his glass. "He was involved in some kind of family feud in a village not far from here. From which I rescued him."

He seemed to recall the question. "I believe him to be deaf. And they tore out his tongue." He turned, frowning as someone else appeared in the doorway, then he rose and strode across to him. "What is it now?"

The newcomer was in uniform and, Adam thought, senior to the man who had met them on the pier. He could not hear what was being said, but Ballantyne was obviously displeased.

"Of course I have not forgotten! I have been busy, too!" and then, "No, the captain will *not* be involved." He waited for the door to close. "I sometimes have to ask myself . . ."

Then he smiled. "I must leave you and change," he looked down at his immaculate breeches, "into something more formal. I am required to attend an execution. No time to show you the welcome I would have wished!"

Adam saw the boy, Trusty, hurrying to find Monteith, responding to some signal from his master. Perhaps Ballantyne really had forgotten his grisly appointment, but it seemed unlikely. He was regarding the empty glasses on the table, and the admiral's sealed envelope, still unopened beside them.

"I can't tell you how much I regret this interruption." He tapped the envelope. "I shall, of course, reply to *this* when I have given it some thought." He paused. "Rivalry is no bad thing. It can often be the spur, when one is needed." He reached out and took Adam's hands in a grip like iron. "Meeting you, albeit briefly, has meant so very much to me. I hope it will not be long before we greet one another again. This is not a race: we're on the same journey!" He laughed. "Given the chance!"

They walked out into the sunlight and Adam was surprised to see that the gig had moved to a smaller jetty almost hidden by the line of guns.

Ballantyne said, "I sent word to your crew. One walk along our pier is enough for anybody. Next time, Adam, remember."

Adam walked slowly toward the jetty, strangely unwilling to leave, without understanding why. So many questions remained unanswered, and he knew they were both to blame.

Monteith hurried from somewhere to join him. He sounded out of breath. "Only just told you were leaving, sir!"

Adam shaded his eyes to gaze up at the flag again, and beyond to the clouds gathering on the horizon. A chance not to be missed, for several reasons.

"We will up-anchor directly and be clear of the land before dark."

He could still hear Ballantyne's words. *This is not a race.* He had known of William Dundas's death at the mission, but had not mentioned his daughter, Claire.

Neither did I.

He stared across the burning water and saw *Onward* for the first time. He must find time to prepare himself. Langley would want all the details. And the results, if any. And his impressions of Sir Duncan Ballantyne, too, more formally dressed as he watched an execution.

Jago was on his feet, hat in hand, the gig's crew sitting with their arms folded. He swore under his breath as Monteith hesitated and almost stumbled while he moved aside for the captain. Didn't he know after all this time that a captain was always the last to enter, and the first to leave his boat? Maybe he'd been having a few too many wets ashore. *Not likely. A real drink might kill him.*

But he forgot Monteith as he watched Bolitho pause and look back at the thatched building with the flag flying above it. They had been together longer than many. He thought back over their talk about promotion, a conversation they had had more than once, and about the life they shared.

Luke Jago was sharing it now. He could see it on the captain's face, like all those other times.

"*Out oars!*"

Adam turned toward him until their eyes met.

Another bloody Friday, Jago thought.

9 JUSTICE OR REVENGE

HUGH MORGAN, the cabin servant, lurked behind his pantry door and watched his captain's shadow move past, pacing toward the stern windows again. After all their months together he thought he knew most of Bolitho's moods: with *Onward* cleared for action and shuddering to the crash and thunder of a broadside, or reeling through a storm in Biscay or the Western Approaches. Or simply waiting, like this, on edge without knowing why.

They had entered harbour quite early, in the forenoon watch, with all the usual bustle and what seemed conflicting orders, to the stamp of feet and sound of gear being hauled across the deck above and other shouted demands. Now it was afternoon, and would soon be the first dog watch. Morgan's ears recorded these things without careful attention; they were part of his daily life.

He had been on deck when they had entered harbour. The experience was always different. Even the harbour itself and the anchorage seemed larger than when they had left it for the outpost optimistically called New Haven. He had already heard several of the sailors suggesting other, less pleasant names for it.

The guardboat had guided them to their new anchorage, closer to the moored flagship, *Medusa*. Morgan had heard Luke Jago remark that it would be harder for the admiral to launch another surprise attack without being spotted by the duty watch. He had said a few other things too, less polite. Jago might be a brave and loyal friend to his captain, but he would never be asked to wait and serve at the table.

The officer in the guardboat had apparently brought word from the flagship requesting Bolitho's presence aboard during the afternoon watch. The admiral was otherwise engaged with "important visitors."

He clucked with disapproval. What did the admiral think he was saying? The landing party, the slaughter at the mission, the sea burials, and the captain was still waiting. Dress uniform coat folded over a chair, sword and belt lying across the bergère where the admiral had sprawled during his visit. *I'll wager his servant could tell a few tales if he ever got the chance . . .*

The shadow stopped moving, and Morgan opened the pantry door.

"Can I tempt you with something, sir? A glass, maybe?"

Adam shook his head, although he appeared more relaxed. "I expect the admiral is reading my report. Unless the officer of the guard dropped it overboard!"

Morgan sniffed and brushed some invisible dust off the small desk. More likely the admiral was still enjoying a lavish meal with his guests. Morgan had made a habit of studying the various officers he had served over the years and considered himself to be quite an expert at it. When he had been on the quarterdeck briefly this morning it had been a case in point. A new frigate was anchored in *Onward*'s previous place, a fifth-rate of thirty-eight guns. So new, in fact, that she was not yet fully registered in the Navy List, described only as *Portsmouth, building*. Her name, *Zealous*, was shining in the early sunlight. He had heard Bolitho say, "A fine command for somebody. A lucky man, whoever he is!"

Julyan, the sailing master, was more outspoken, as usual. "Has a friendly hand on his shoulder, if you ask me!"

Morgan had seen the first lieutenant's face at that moment, clearly recalling how close he might have come to being given command of *Onward*.

Adam walked to the centre of the cabin and glanced up at the partly opened skylight. He could smell fresh paint: one of the cutters was being freshened up after running aground during the landing, Drummond, the bosun, silencing a few audible grumbles with, "Keep you out of trouble for a bit longer, eh?"

So unlike New Haven. Here, the local boats pulled and paddled as close to the warships as they dared, displaying their wares and offering their services. In a couple of craft, each with the sternsheets protected by screens, there had been women, reclining and smiling.

Drummond had said, "You'll get more than a smile if you take a run ashore with any of that lot!"

Adam had reached the stern windows again, and stared across the water toward the other frigate. To casual onlookers she might appear a twin of *Onward*. He could remember . . .

Morgan called, "The surgeon, sir!"

The sentry was holding the screen door wide open, and Adam could see members of a working party lingering and watching as Murray took the young woman's hand to guide her over the coaming.

Murray said, "I was just told, sir," and stood aside for her to enter the cabin. "Otherwise I would have waited."

Adam held out his hands. "A boat has arrived for you. I sent word earlier." He felt her hands close around his. They were warm now, but she was shivering. "It *is* what you wanted, isn't it?"

She nodded slowly, the hair on her forehead parting to reveal the bruise. "It is for the best. My friends there will expect it. After that, I will have to make plans."

He walked with her to the stern. "I am waiting to present myself to the admiral, otherwise I'd escort you in person."

She gazed unblinkingly at the waterfront and the buildings shimmering in the heat. "I can see the parent mission from here. My father was once . . ." She did not finish it. "So, good-bye, Captain Bolitho. I will not forget you, or your men."

Morgan stood by the screen door, blocking it, and muttering angrily to someone outside. Then he turned and said apologetically, "The lady's boat is alongside, sir." He peered around. "Is there anything I can do?"

She was about to say something, then her expression changed. "My bracelet! Your lieutenant found it and put it in the strongbox." She unfastened her cuff and touched the bandage. "All my worldly goods."

They walked away from the cabin, toward the shaft of sunlight streaming down the companion ladder.

Adam offered his arm but she said, "I can manage, Captain!" Then she twisted round toward him. "One day . . ."

The silence was intense, as if the ship was holding her breath.

She smiled. "I *am* ready."

Drummond was here now, his silver call swinging from his neck. "Sorry, sir. Took me all aback!"

Adam was still not accustomed to him as bosun, but it was rare to see Drummond disconcerted by anything or any one.

They climbed into the light, where some of the senior hands had formed an impromptu guard of honour to the gangway, and a bosun's chair had been rigged by the entry port. Somebody ran from the opposite side and slithered to a halt. It was Midshipman Hotham, a signal slate wedged beneath one arm. He could barely take his eyes from the girl in sailor's garb.

"Signal from Flag, sir! *Captain to repair on board.*" He swallowed. "Shall I acknowledge, sir?"

Nobody moved, and Adam heard the newly arrived boat being warped closer alongside.

He took her arm and turned her toward the watching faces. He said quietly, "Let him wait."

Someone had climbed up from the boat, and was holding out some sort of afternoon shawl and a wide-brimmed straw hat with ribbons. Claire spoke to him by name. As she tied the ribbons beneath her chin, she waved the shawl aside. "I feel more suited to this, thank you." She was still smiling, but very close to breaking down.

Vicary, the purser, pushed some seamen aside and held out a small package. "From the strongbox, ma'am." He smiled also, which was rare for him. "I was asked to make certain you received it."

She said nothing, gazing past him toward the boat tier. Squire was standing there with his working party, all of whom were waiting simply to see her depart.

Adam knew it was as near as Squire would come, and that Murray was hovering watchfully, and yet it was as if they were alone together. She unwrapped the bracelet and held it as though for Squire to see, then she kissed it and put it inside her midshipman's shirt.

Two seamen helped her climb into the bosun's chair; others seized the tackle and waited for the order to hoist.

A voice yelled hoarsely, "Give 'er a cheer, Onwards! We don't want 'er to go!"

The response was immediate and deafening. Even the cook and his helpers emerged from cover and were waving and shouting with the rest. Adam felt her gripping his arm, as if unable to break the final contact; her dark eyes were filling her face.

Across the water, men aboard the new frigate had manned the side to join in the farewell, although they could not have understood it.

She said, "I pray that if we meet again . . ." She could not continue, but pulled Adam's hand to her mouth and kissed it. Then she waved at the upturned faces and tensed, holding tightly as Drummond shouted, "*Easy*, lads! Hoist away!"

Her shadow crossed the hammock nettings and dipped slowly over the side. Only then did Murray speak.

"A brave young woman. She wasn't expecting a farewell like that. I shall join her now." But he lingered, watching the men beginning to disperse, some still peering down at the boat with its insignia, a blue osprey, painted on either bow. Some of them had already seen it at the smouldering mission, amidst its grisly remains.

"I shall miss her, and that's the truth." Murray strode toward the entry port without looking back.

Vincent had climbed onto the gangway, and beyond him Adam could see the Royal Marine guard and side party already in position.

"When you are ready, sir."

Morgan had brought the sword, and helped him to adjust it, his face troubled. Routine was taking over again, and most of the decks were clear. Adam glanced aft where Squire was now standing alone, looking toward the shore. Once, he raised his arm as if to wave, but let it fall back to his side. Her boat was well clear by now, and Adam saw Murray sitting beside her in the sternsheets. She did not turn her head.

He walked toward the entry port where Drummond and his mates were waiting, calls moistened and poised.

"Attention on the upper deck!"

Adam returned the salutes and raised his hat to the flag as he went down the side, where Jago had moored the gig without wasting a moment, always with one eye on the flagship.

"Busy day, Cap'n?"

"And not over yet." But Adam's eyes were still on the other boat, even as it disappeared beyond a clutter of moored barges.

Jago waited until he was seated before adding warily, "She'll be lookin' for justice, I reckon." His words were almost lost in the ripple of movement beneath the gig, but moments like these were never shared. And the captain knew it.

He realised that Adam had turned to face him, and his voice was cold and calm. "If she were my girl, only revenge would suffice."

"Welcome back, Captain Bolitho!" The flag lieutenant touched his hat as Adam walked away from *Medusa's* entry port, and the stamp and shrill of salutes. The first lieutenant was in charge, and had explained that Captain Tyacke was escorting the admiral's visitors ashore. He seemed surprised and pleased that Adam had remembered his name when they had only met once, and very briefly.

The flag lieutenant turned aft and said, "We have all been extremely busy—" One bell chimed from the forecastle. "The admiral will receive you now."

They had reached the shadow of the poop when he added suddenly, "I watched you enter harbour and anchor today. It was later than expected, of course."

Adam retorted, "*We* were quite busy, too!" It must have taken more out of him than he knew. "Forgive me. No reason to bite your head off."

The lieutenant said with dignity, "I was going to say, sir, that I read your report. It made me very proud."

Two Royal Marines snapped to attention, one shouting, "Captain Bolitho, *sir!*"

The flag lieutenant murmured, "I shall be close by if I'm needed, sir," and effaced himself.

A servant Adam did not recognise opened the screen door to the great cabin and he saw Rear-Admiral Giles Langley sprawled in a deep leather chair beneath the skylight, his heavy coat with the gold epaulettes tossed across a cabinet, and his discarded shoes even further away, as if he had kicked them off.

Langley did not stand up. Instead, he waved languidly toward another chair and said, "Come and take the weight off your feet, Bolitho!" He patted the front of his own straining waistcoat, grinning. "Not that you need to, by the look of it!"

He snapped his fingers. "A glass for the captain!" and laughed, but broke off in a fit of coughing. "An' another for me. I deserve it!"

Adam looked around the cabin. It was much as he remembered it, but the stern windows were not now hidden by curtains, and the sun reflecting from the anchorage seemed dazzling.

Langley's fair hair had been neatly trimmed and was even shorter than on the previous visit, and his eyes were gleaming like blue glass in the glare. The servant had been carrying out a wastebasket, the contents of which might have been bottles. Langley and his guests had not been too busy with affairs to enjoy themselves.

Langley patted the arms of his chair. "What d'you think of this beauty? Got the idea after visiting *Onward*." His mood changed just as quickly. "I read your report, of course. Just as well I sent you down there. Otherwise it might have taken months before the facts became known." He frowned so deeply that his eyes almost vanished. "And the missionary's daughter? Ashore now, recovering?" He did not wait for an answer, a habit of his, apparently. "Probably never will." He dabbed his eyes. "There to help others, but when *they* need it this is too often their reward!"

"She is at the Osprey Mission, sir."

"Hmph. Best solution. A civil matter, as far as we're concerned. Our work is still at the sharp end."

He heaved himself abruptly from his new chair and took several deep breaths. "And you spoke with *Sir* Duncan Ballantyne?" He moved to the broad stern windows and leaned against a frame. "Gave nothing away, I take it?"

"He's sent some of his militia to the mission, until . . ."

"Yes, yes, but what's *he* like? Friend or foe? Or just another opportunist lining his pockets under the King's protection?"

The servant padded softly back into the cabin and placed two crystal goblets on a table.

Langley turned sharply. "Over *here,* man!" and Adam could see the sweat shining on his forehead. The servant was filling the glasses. Brandy: he had smelled it as soon as the door had opened for him. "You can leave it!"

Langley's mood seemed to change again, and he waved his goblet expansively toward the harbour. "What d' you think of that new frigate, eh? A damn fine sight, especially these days. His first command, too."

Some of the brandy was running down his wrist, staining his sleeve. Tyacke was probably used to this sort of behaviour. He could cope with just about everything.

Adam said, "Who is her captain, sir?"

Langley shrugged vaguely. "Somebody called de Vere. George de Vere. Know him?"

"There was an Admiral de Vere, but . . ."

Langley snorted with laughter. "His uncle, no less! Fair sailing for some, eh?" He swung round angrily and snapped, "What is it now, dammit? You don't buy a dog and bark yourself, do you?"

It was the flag lieutenant. "I am very sorry, sir. I didn't mean to interrupt."

"Well, you have! What's so important this time?" He attempted to thrust his foot into one of the shoes and almost lost his balance.

The flag lieutenant said, "*Onward*'s surgeon is come aboard, sir." He did not take his eyes off the admiral, but he was speaking to Adam. "He wishes to see the captain."

Langley grunted. "Sawbones. I hate 'em!" Then he waved dismissively. "Well, send him in."

Murray stepped into the cabin and bowed, ever so slightly. "My apologies, sir." He was looking at Adam. "I thought it might be urgent, sir."

"I gathered that!" Langley had picked up a telescope and was training it toward something on the frigate's quarter.

Murray said in a low voice, "We had almost reached the Osprey stairs when," he paused as the telescope stopped moving, "I thought she was having a relapse. I had to restrain her." He glanced at Langley's powerful shoulders, framed against the restless water. "She had seen a ship she seemed to recognise. Said it had been near the mission. It's here now."

Langley lowered the telescope. "She's quite sure of that? Women often make mistakes about . . ." He snapped the telescope shut and strode across the cabin. "Dundas's daughter? Where is she now?"

Murray said, "With me, sir."

Langley sat down. "Well! That will have all the tongues wagging!"

"I was careful, sir."

But Langley was already on his feet again. "And she's the only available witness!" He returned to the quarter windows. "Today, of all bloody days—" He turned, his face in shadow. "She will have to identify the vessel herself."

Murray said curtly, "I am not at all certain we can ask that of her."

Langley snapped, "Don't *ask*. Tell her!" and looked up at the skylight, suddenly calm again. "You are my senior captain, Bolitho, until James Tyacke returns. And you are directly involved, in any case." His mouth moved in what might have been a smile, but Adam could not see the expression in his eyes. "I leave it in your hands. But this is not a battle, remember?"

"I shall send word, sir."

The flag lieutenant followed them from the cabin, still glancing nervously over his shoulder.

Adam said, "I shall want my gig," and to Murray, "I am sorry you had to endure that."

Murray walked lightly, keeping pace, his hawkish profile withdrawn. "I am still not convinced . . ."

"I doubt she would have been mistaken. So let's find out, shall we?"

Medusa's first lieutenant was waiting for them on deck. "Your gig is here, sir." And to Murray, "The schooner you were asking about is the *Delfim*. Came in yesterday, taking on cargo." He looked toward the flag lieutenant, who was still hovering nearby as if listening for a summons from aft.

Adam saw Jago standing in the gig, two of his crew holding the hull steady.

The first lieutenant added, "*Delfim* is under Portuguese colours, sir." He shaded his eyes to look across the water at *Onward*. "Do you need some extra hands?"

Adam shook his head. "Time might be getting short." He was thinking aloud. "A few spare cutlasses would be welcome."

"Good as done, sir." He gestured to a bosun's mate. "What about the young lady?"

Adam said, "I'm afraid she's a part of it," and looked over at the gig once more. Claire was sitting in the sternsheets, the wide-brimmed hat obscuring her face; she could have been an ordinary passenger. Even the oarsmen were sitting on their thwarts, apparently unconcerned.

"Watch your step, sir. The officer of the guard will be doing his rounds in the last dog."

Adam walked to the side. "I hope it won't come to that."

Nobody moved as he climbed down the side; there was no ceremonial this time. Murray followed him into the boat and sat beside Claire Dundas.

"I am not in favour of her coming to confront these people."

The wide-brimmed hat turned slightly. "I *want* to be with you," she said. "Don't you see?"

Adam leaned over but did not touch her. She was very calm; even her breathing was controlled.

He said, "Trust me," and thought he saw Jago nod. "Trust *us.*"

They were moving, and faces were watching them from the flagship's open gunports, men stopping work on the forecastle to saunter alongside, keeping pace until the gig gathered speed. It had to be now. Few secrets in a busy harbour could be kept for long.

The girl reached out and laid her open hand flat on Murray's arm. "If?"

He covered it with his own, and said only, *"When."*

They were pulling abeam of some moored lighters, and there was the *Delfim*, lying alongside another landing-stage. She was a topsail schooner which, properly handled, could give a larger vessel, even a frigate, a run for her money.

The small figurehead the girl must have seen and remembered was a leaping dolphin, like a miniature replica of *Onward*'s own. A bare-backed figure was stooping beneath the foremast, polishing something that occasionally caught the sunlight; he did not look at the gig. Some tackle was already coiled nearby. The loading, or unloading, was finished.

Adam stared along the boat, watching the regular stroke of oars, the familiar faces looking aft but somehow avoiding his eyes.

Jago said, "They've got a brow lowered, Cap'n. Larboard side, forrard."

Adam glanced at the tapering bowsprit, and the gleam of water between hull and scarred timbers. He snapped, *"Now!"*

Jago was ready, swinging the tiller-bar hard over before easing it against his hip, his eyes fixed on the narrowing gap ahead.

"Boat yer oars!" He swore under his breath. "Stand by to fend off forrard!"

But for some it was already too late. An oar blade splintered before it could be withdrawn, and one of the bowmen was struck by his loom as it jammed in its rowlock, and was sent sprawling.

Adam clambered over the side and steadied himself against the end of the brow. A grapnel slithered past him but held fast as the seamen hurried to join him, each one snatching a cutlass as he jumped ashore. One man stayed in the gig with Murray and the girl.

There were shouts and the sounds of running feet, and Adam saw men coming from aft.

Something slithered over the side, a boathook or boarding pike. It was gone.

Adam reached the top of the brow and heard someone yell in English, "It's the navy, fer Christ's sake!"

Others had appeared on deck, staring at the sailors and the bared cutlasses, and one said, "What is the meaning of this?"

Adam rested his hand on his undrawn sword. "Are you the master?"

The man shook his head, staring at Adam's uniform, noting his rank. "Bosun." He waved vaguely at his men. "An' most of them are Portuguese." He folded his arms. "This vessel is registered as such." Then he twisted round as he noticed the three people still in the gig. "What's all this, a joke or somethin'?"

Jago called, "In position, Cap'n!"

The bosun said hoarsely, "You're goin' to be real sorry for this, *Captain*—"

"I command here!"

The newcomer had appeared through a hatch, half dressed, with a towel hanging carelessly around his neck. He was pulling it slowly up and down. "I am Pecco!" His eyes flicked around at the armed seamen. "Arthur Pecco. And who might you be, may I ask? A full captain, no less!"

He did not wait for a reply. "I know this intrusion is your right. And I understand, in these difficult times. We have finished loading." He shrugged. "Coconut oil. You can look for yourselves, if you must. But I am about to step ashore. We sail tomorrow." He made a crude gesture at one of the crew. "Don't stand there dreaming, Miguel! Work!"

Adam said, "I wish to see your charts. And the log."

Adam heard Murray clear his throat, and when he had Adam's attention he gave an imperceptible shake of the head. The girl had boarded also and was standing a pace behind him, gazing fixedly at the schooner's master.

"So if you will excuse me, Captain, I have work to do."

He grinned and dabbed his cheek with the towel. There was a trace of blood on it.

Like facing an enemy, Adam thought, out of nowhere. Gunports open, ready to fire. And in his mind he saw Luke Jago, razor poised for the much-needed shave. He said, "Did your man have a beard, Claire?"

"What the bloody hell are you saying? I'll see you broken for this!"

Jago was there. "Keep yer mouth shut, Mister Pecco."

The girl's voice was very quiet, but not subdued. "Yes, it's him. I should have known immediately."

"What is she saying?" It was almost a scream.

Adam put out his hand protectively, but she was very calm, and her eyes remained on Pecco.

She said softly, "I remember the beard. How could I forget?" Her fingers were unfastening the buttons of her shirt, and before Adam or Murray could stop her she had dragged it down over her shoulders and turned them toward him. "I felt it when you did *this* to me!"

She tore the dressing away, so that the scars seemed raw and untreated where she had been bitten. She was saying, almost to herself, "He was the first." She did not look down as Murray gently fastened her shirt. "Then he watched the others . . ."

Adam said sharply, "Search him!" He beckoned to one of his men. "Take a message to the officer of the guard."

Jago said, "Here now, by the sound of it, Cap'n." There was a jacket in his hand, but he was holding up a medallion on a thin chain. "Yours, missy?"

She snatched it and pressed it to her lips. "My father's."

The *Delfim*'s master tried to push one of the seamen aside. "You'll never prove a charge of slavery against me!"

Jago seized his arm and twisted it behind him. "No need, *matey!* You'll swing for murder!"

Murray had managed to pacify the girl and had seated her on a hatch cover. He pulled a flask from his pocket, and said, "Against doctor's orders, but it will help."

There were more shouts as booted feet thudded across the brow and onto the deck. Marines.

Murray said, "I'll take you to the mission, Claire. It's safe now."

She was staring at the scarlet uniforms as they hurried past, and whispered, "Where's the one you call Jamie?" Then she collapsed.

Adam saw Murray supporting her head on his folded coat, while he murmured and stroked the hair gently from her face.

"Up to us now, sir."

And Adam heard the voice in his mind respond.

It is up to me.

Captain James Tyacke waited for his cabin door to close, then seized Adam's hand and shook it warmly.

"I hate to drag you aboard at this hour. I've only just returned myself!" He strode to the stern windows and stared across the water. It was still broad daylight, but darkness came suddenly, and they both knew that all the lanterns would be burning within the hour.

In another part of the flagship's hull someone was singing, in time to the scrape of a violin.

Tyacke said to the window, "Our lord and master has gone ashore again. I don't know where the man finds the strength," and faced Adam once more. "I heard about this proposed passage in *Delfim*. I think you've done more than enough already." He half smiled. "I wish I was going with you."

Adam said quietly, "I've chosen some good hands, and I'm leaving my first lieutenant to carry the load."

"Vincent. A good fellow."

Adam recalled Vincent's expression when he had been told. He was far from pleased.

"You'll take extra care, I hope." Tyacke might have been thinking aloud. "That poor woman you rescued—is she reliable?"

Adam thought of her confrontation with Pecco, if that was his real name, the naked courage in her face. "I trust her."

Tyacke looked at him keenly, eyes very blue in the ruined face. "I'll make damn sure no unauthorised vessel leaves harbour before, or when, you do." He tugged out his watch and opened its cover. "Meanwhile, I'll be right here." Then, "You've been a flag captain yourself, so I don't have to remind you. If you do the right thing, your superiors will get the credit. If you fail, you'll take the blame."

He closed the watch gently and held it for a moment. "A gift from Sir Richard, bless him."

They walked to the door together. It was time.

Adam said, "And these important guests of the admiral's? Hard going, was it?"

Tyacke was feeling his pocket as if to ensure that the watch was secure. "Guests? Useless popinjays, as far as he's concerned. Only one of them matters, just between ourselves." He paused. "I'll leave you here," then seemed to recall what he had been about to say. "The Honourable Sir Charles Godden, no less. I see you've heard of *him*."

Adam said nothing.

"Well, he's now become head of the First Lord's advisory staff. Member of Parliament as well. So our lord and master may have other things on his mind."

It was like hearing Duncan Ballantyne's own words. *Promotion or oblivion.*

Adam clipped the sword to his belt and said, "Sir Richard is still with *both* of us!"

He was suddenly impatient to begin.

10 BLADE TO BLADE

LIEUTENANT JAMES SQUIRE stifled a curse as he stubbed his foot against an iron ringbolt. By the time they all became used to the commandeered schooner the whole affair would be over. He tugged down his hat to shade his eyes from the reflected glare and examined her critically. She was about eighty feet in length and twenty at her beam.

He stifled a yawn, and it was not even the forenoon watch. They had cast off at an hour most landsmen would still consider the dead of night. Even the sounds had seemed louder: squealing blocks and muffled oaths as they edged away from other, sleeping vessels and hoisted the big gaff-headed mainsail. It had taken time, as all but a handful of *Delfim*'s original crew were ashore, under lock and key. Culprits or hostages, their fate would be decided later.

He tried not to look at the schooner's master, standing beside Bolitho and an armed seaman.

Another footstep interrupted his thoughts. This time it was Murray, the surgeon. They had all been too busy to speak much, but Squire had asked him about Claire Dundas. Murray had evaded the question, saying only *in good hands* or *a very brave young woman*. In other words, nothing.

It was one of the seamen who had described the moment when Pecco had been identified as the man who had gone to the mission and raped her like a wild beast. Bolitho had not mentioned it. He was embarking on a chance operation which might prove either dangerous or complete folly.

Squire unslung the telescope from his shoulder and trained it toward the coast, in the far distance an uneven panorama of green and brown, with the hint of misty grey further inland that might have been a mountain ridge. And to starboard, the endless ocean.

He saw some of *Onward*'s seamen resetting staysail and jib. Christie, a senior gunner's mate, shouted, "Move yer bloody selves! Gawd 'elp us if we runs into some real sailors!"

It was oddly reassuring to hear them laugh.

He looked at the compass beneath the sails' shadow. One of Pecco's men was at the spokes, and Bolitho and Tozer, master's mate, were comparing notes. He thought again about the mission, the girl struggling in his arms, her shock and incredulity when he had wrapped his coat around her. She must have been expecting another assault.

Jago appeared in an open hatchway, grinning and hitting a metal basin with a ladle. "Up spirits, lads!" An even wider grin. "Stand fast, the 'Oly Ghost!"

The age-old signal for a rum issue, but it could still bring some smiles.

Squire saw some of them lift their tots like salutes as Bolitho walked past them. But what was he thinking? Did he fear failure or personal loss, or death? And what of his lovely young wife?

"I need you in the chart space, James." His tanned face relaxed into a smile. "Or should I say . . . Jamie?"

Later, Squire was still remembering it with a mixture of embarrassment and pride. No wonder men would follow their captain to the gates of hell. *So would I.*

Luke Jago leaned against the bulwark, chatting idly to the gunner's mate crouched beside one of the *Delfim*'s stocky twelve-pounders. She mounted eight of them, all carronades, four on either side. In these waters every vessel needed some kind of protection if the worst happened, and it was certainly possible. Jago was past being surprised by anything.

Christie glanced up at him quizzically. "Load 'em with canister, the cap'n says. Close action, d' you reckon?"

Jago swore and slapped an insect crawling across his bare arm. "Catch bloody fever more like, Ted!"

Christie looked toward one of the main hatch covers. "I went below with Mr. Squire. She's bigger than she looks. Mixed cargo, passengers mebbee—or slaves." He lowered his voice. "What d' *you* think, Luke?"

Jago watched the schooner's master, Pecco, being taken forward under arms. "I'd trust a rat from the bilges more 'n that scumbag." He touched the hilt of his heavy cutlass. "One sign o' treachery, an' 'e gets it first! Then the sharks can 'ave 'im!"

Christie grinned. "Glad you're on *our* side!" Then he murmured, "Heads up!"

It was Lieutenant Sinclair, who, with twenty of *Onward*'s Royal Marines, had been ferried aboard at nightfall. He looked like a stranger in a grubby shirt, without his scarlet coat and smart crossbelt. But somehow he was still a Royal Marine. He seemed preoccupied in making sure that his men were as comfortable as they could be below deck, and they obviously respected him. Jago shook his head. *As an officer.*

Sinclair glanced at the nearest twelve-pounder and said casually, "If we get that close, I'll be relying on our bayonets!" He sounded almost unconcerned.

Not much of a choice, matey, Jago thought sourly.

Sinclair was saying, "We'll be tipping some of the cargo over the side soon. Give us a bit more freeboard. We'll need it when we move closer inshore." He strode away. Smartly.

"Not a bad fellow," Christie said, and paused.

They chorused together: *"For a lobster!"*

A voice, or perhaps a touch on his outthrust arm, and Adam Bolitho was instantly awake. He did not recall the moment he had fallen asleep.

So many times, so many different ships . . . faces . . . demands.

It seemed completely dark, then he realised that the only lantern was close-shuttered, and what light remained was partly hidden by the figure bending over him. It was Murray, his hawkish face in shadow.

He said only, "Squire said to call you, sir."

Adam cleared his throat. It was painfully dry. "Thank you, Doc. All quiet?"

It was something to say, to give himself time while the shipboard sounds and movements brought him back to reality and purpose. The chair in which he had fallen asleep was as hard as iron. But sleep was necessary for him, and for those who might have to depend on his ability when the time came. Today.

Murray said, "No trouble, sir. But trust would be something else again."

Adam's eyes flicked around the box-like cabin, the chart space where Pecco, the schooner's master, lived his solitary life. Adam had examined the available charts, and the crude map Pecco had drawn for him. Like a flaw in the coastline, with a protective scattering of tiny islets that might spell disaster for any larger vessel or complete stranger. He had discussed his final plans with Squire and Tozer, the master's mate.

Pecco insisted he knew nothing about any slavers, only that he had heard it was a regular and safe rendezvous for several of them. He had offered the information as if bargaining for his own security, but would be doomed anyway if the slavers or those who controlled them ever learned of it.

Adam said, "I have no choice. But trust has to play its part, I'm afraid."

Murray straightened up and reached for his familiar satchel. "I'll be ready, Captain." He moved away, out of the lantern light, and halted. "Seventy-odd years ago my grandfathers trusted in loyalty and obedience, at Culloden."

The door creaked open and Jago peered in at them.

"Standin' by." He glanced at the uniform coat which was hanging from the deckhead. "Not this time, eh, Cap'n?"

Adam faced him. They might have been alone together, the marines squatting outside the cabin invisible. "Don't you ever change, Luke!" He picked up his sword, and added curtly, "Be ready with the flag."

He felt his way to the ladder and opened the hatch. The sky was still black, so that the tall spread of canvas stood out like wings against a sprinkling of pale stars. There was no moon. The compass light was tiny, but by its faint light Adam saw the faces turn toward him as he appeared on deck.

All the previous day, from the moment they had cleared the approaches to Freetown, they had sighted no other vessel, large or small. Somewhere far astern was a brigantine named *Peterel*, but Captain Tyacke had made sure no other ship would leave harbour in an attempt to overtake this schooner, to divert it or warn others of their intention.

Within the hour the dawn would show another empty sea, and a stretch of coast unknown except to the few who had braved it, some of them to their cost.

Squire called hoarsely, "Sou' west by south, sir! Steady she goes!"

But it sounded like a question.

Adam plucked the shirt away from his skin; it felt clammy, almost cold. "Bring our prisoner on deck."

He walked a few paces to the side and stared toward a mass of land darker than the darkness: one of the islets he had checked and checked again with the master's mate breathing down his neck. They had no option. A straightforward and safe approach would be seen immediately by any vessel anchored there. Even *Delfim*'s master seemed uncertain.

He looked along the deck, faintly visible now in the first paleness of the coming day. A few dark shapes were standing or sitting in readiness to shorten sail, to alter course, and, if so ordered, to fight.

"All carronades loaded, sir. Canister." That was Christie, gunner's mate, one of the shadows.

He heard Squire clear his throat as he stood beside the compass box. Keeping his distance, or unwilling to distract him? He looked toward the land again, and thought he could see it lying like an unbroken barrier beyond the fin-shaped jib.

"I am *here*, Captain."

"Are you ready?"

Pecco moved closer to the compass and tapped it with his knuckles. Adam thought he saw one of the nearby seamen reach out as if to prevent him.

Pecco said, "I gave my word, Captain. Will you give yours?"

"Any aid you give will be made clear in my report."

Pecco breathed out slowly. "Then I must take the helm, Captain. I have the *feel* of her."

Adam could sense both Squire and Tozer watching him. Their lives, too, were at stake. He saw Pecco look up at the canvas, still taut despite the nearness of land, and heard him say quietly, "I had no part in the killings at the mission." He might have shrugged. "And the woman . . . Maybe I had a few drinks too many. At least she is alive."

He eased the wheel to starboard and leaned forward to watch the compass. "South south-west." He lifted his eyes briefly from the compass and seemed to grimace. "Not an easy passage!"

The canvas reacted very slightly until the schooner was back on course. The sound was not loud enough to muffle a metallic click as the armed seaman cocked his musket.

"Deep ten!" The call came from forward as one of *Onward*'s best leadsmen took his first sounding. He barely raised his voice, but in the tense silence it was as if he had shouted.

Pecco muttered, "You take no chances, Captain."

Adam gazed up at the masthead beyond the tattered Portuguese flag, and saw the first hint of blue. It was unnerving, with the sky almost hidden by the land as it crept out of the dimness like a groping arm. Or a trap.

"If the wind holds, Captain, we might need to shorten sail. We must alter course very soon now. We will sight a wreck to larboard." Pecco even sounded as if he were smiling. "If some fool has not removed it!"

"By the mark, seven!"

Adam remembered other times, in other ships, when he had seen the vessel's own shadow passing over the seabed. Not merely a warning but a threat. He could sense the others moving closer, even Murray, watching and recalling his own retort about loyalty and Culloden.

"By the mark, five!"

The leadsman was wasting no time. Skilled enough to make an underhand swing with his lead-and-line, he was feeling his way. Thirty feet beneath the keel. And the next cry . . .

"And *now*, Captain . . ." The wheel was turning steadily to larboard, as if they were steering headlong toward solid ground.

Adam tried to see the chart in his mind, and remember the sketches made by the man who was at the wheel beside him. He had nothing more to lose but his life. He swung round as the wheel began to turn faster. Pecco was using all his strength. There was a glint of light from the compass box, then, like a curtain being dragged aside, the sun was upon them.

Pecco shouted, *"Now!"* and Tozer joined him, adding his weight and experience as the spokes were dragged in the opposite direction. There in the sun, between mainland and islet, was the shining curve of the channel. The tall sails hardly appeared to shift; a square-rigger would have been hard aground by now.

Adam heard Jago urging more hands to trim the staysail and jib, and as they ran to obey some fell headlong over yet another unfamiliar obstacle.

Pecco steadied the wheel and looked up at the flag. "Never easy!" Then his eyes met Adam's. "I know what you thought . . . It was in my heart." He watched Tozer take over the wheel, and added simply, "Remember that, when the time comes."

Adam trained his telescope on the widening stretch of water directly ahead. He did not recall having picked it up, and was disconcerted by the surprising heat of the metal and the dryness of his throat.

Pecco was clinging to a backstay, his face devoid of expression. Neither guilt nor triumph.

And there, fine on the larboard bow, was the wreck: it must have caught fire before running aground in the shallows. It lay like a blackened carcass, the timbers like charred ribs. Nobody spoke or moved as they glided past, and when the leadsman called from the forecastle it seemed an intrusion.

"An' deep ten!"

They were through, undetected, and ahead was the sheltered inlet. It needed skill and strong nerves, but there always had to be a "first time."

Adam raised the telescope again and saw the nearest beach leap into focus in the lens, some ragged undergrowth almost to the water's edge in places, elsewhere pebbles, washed white by sun and salt. His grip tightened. Two canoes pulled well clear of the water. Furrows in the sand where they had been dragged ashore. *Recently.*

"Seen them afore, Cap'n." It was Jago, powerful arms crossed, but fingers still close to the cutlass.

The canoes were typical of those used to ferry wretched captives from stream or beach to the ship destined to carry them into slavery. Adam could never understand how so many survived. Slavers were known to sail from this coastline to destinations as far away as Cuba and Brazil. It was inhuman beyond belief.

Pecco said suddenly, "Another two miles. Maybe less." He spread his hands. "There may be nothing to discover."

Jago murmured, "Then pray, you bastard!"

Squire strode aft. "I have two good lookouts aloft, and both boats ready for lowering. There's not much else—"

Adam's expression silenced him. "If I should fall . . ." he said.

Squire said only, "Then I'll be lying there beside you."

They both looked in the direction of the forecastle as the leadsman completed another sounding.

"By the mark—" It was as far as he got.

The explosion was more like an echo than gunfire, and for a few seconds Adam was reminded of the early fog-warnings, the maroons he used to hear as a child in Cornwall. Local fishermen always claimed they did more harm than good.

Squire exclaimed, "So much for trust!" and was reaching for his pistol even as Adam stepped between him and Pecco, who was cupping his hands around his eyes and shaking his head in protest.

"No, no! Not us, Captain! Lookouts in the hills!" He gestured wildly. "If a trap was intended they would have been waiting in the channel!" Now his eyes were fixed on the barrel of Squire's pistol. "I tell the truth!"

Adam said slowly, "Another ship. My guess is she's Captain Tyacke's brigantine." A few more seconds while he groped for the name. "The *Peterel*."

Squire uncocked his pistol and thrust it into his belt. He said, not looking at Pecco, "Your lucky day!"

Pecco said, "I have done all I can!" He pushed past two seamen and vomited in the scuppers.

Adam swallowed and looked away, forcing himself to concentrate on the strip of headland, which was tilting toward a widening expanse of water beyond the jib. "Warn all hands below."

Jago said, "Done, Cap'n." Aside to the gunner's mate, he added softly, "Now or never, eh, Ted?"

After the slow and torturous passage past—and sometimes among— the offshore islets, their arrival was startling in its suddenness. From *Delfim*'s deck the anchorage was a lagoon as large as an enclosed lake, but from the yards and upper shrouds the keen-eyed lookouts could see the final outcroppings of land, and beyond, like a blue-grey barrier, the great ocean.

Once lying here, a ship would be invisible to any passing patrol or casual trader. In the strengthening sunlight the water seemed calm and unmoving, but the sails were taut and straining, and the tattered Portuguese flag was streaming.

Adam moved a few paces away from the wheel and trained his telescope across and ahead of their course. Individual faces stood out, gazing at the islets or beyond at the green mass of the mainland. One frowning in concentration or apprehension, another with lips pursed in a silent whistle. Men he had grown to know and understand. Who trusted him, because they had no choice.

And the doubts, which always remained in close company, the ambush when you least expected it. Like his own *if I should fall*. Who else would these men look to?

He thought again of his uncle, Sir Richard Bolitho, his last words on that fateful day. *We always knew.* His coxswain, John Allday, had heard him, and James Tyacke had written it in the flagship's log immediately after the action. *We always knew.*

He wiped his smarting eye with the back of his hand and focused again, and for a moment imagined his mind was too strained to concentrate. A ship was almost broadside-on, filling and overlapping the field of view, stark against a backdrop of trees and a narrow strip of beach.

He held his breath and steadied the glass. He was not mistaken. Some of the trees merged with the ship: loose branches which were lashed to her yards and shrouds. A simple camouflage, but enough to confuse even the most experienced lookout aboard a passing man-of-war, or the brigantine *Peterel*, which Tyacke had sent to offer support if required.

He held out the telescope to Squire.

"We were right."

He heard him adjusting the glass but held the image in his mind: the crude but effective disguise, some fronds and loose fragments in the water alongside drifting slowly clear, or already snared by her anchor cable.

She was preparing to get under way. To escape.

She was a big schooner, three-masted, unusual in these waters, and she looked almost cumbersome in this confined anchorage. But once out on the ocean and under full sail, she would soon show her paces.

Adam peered at the compass and saw Tozer give him an assertive nod. Very calm. Julyan would be proud of him.

Squire said, "She's moored from aft, too. Not enough room to swing!"

Adam took the telescope, still warm from Squire's grip. *No more time.* The big schooner's stem and foremast loomed into view. There were men hurrying about her deck, and the anchor cable was already bar-taut, and possibly moving. Someone running across the forecastle slithered to a halt, peering toward *Delfim*, which would be fully visible by now. A flash of light, and another: telescopes being trained, but little else.

Tozer muttered, "They know this ship, right enough."

Adam turned as a seaman shouted, "What th' hell! Stop him!"

Pecco ignored the muskets as he ran to the side and yelled, "No! Stop, Luis!" and something in Portuguese.

One of *Delfim*'s crew had broken free and was waving his arms and shouting, until a sailor leaped from behind the capstan, belaying pin swinging like a club, and brought him down.

Pecco stood looking at the man sprawling by his feet. "You were *wrong!*"

Adam trained his telescope on the other schooner once more. There were men already aloft on the yards and others manning the braces, as if nothing untoward had happened. But the main deck was not cleared for sea. Even as he watched he saw naked bodies, Africans, scrambling up from holds and hatchways, some driven by whips and blows, others clinging to one another with terror.

Squire exclaimed, "Slaves! The bastard! What better cover?" Then, "Their anchor's hove short, sir!" He glanced bitterly at the compass. "Those scum know we can't open fire with all those poor devils as targets!"

Adam looked at the sails, and the vessel anchored across the gleam of open water beyond the last islet. And once able to make full sail . . .

He said, "Clear lower deck!" and saw Jago watching him. Waiting, as if he knew. "Run up the Colours!"

He moved closer to the wheel even as a call shrilled from below *Delfim*'s deck, as if she were indeed a King's ship.

"She's up-anchored, sir!"

Adam had already seen the big schooner's topsails come alive, a long masthead pendant reaching out like a lance.

There was a bang, and the deck quivered under his feet.

"Do we fight 'em, sir?"

Adam glanced at Pecco. "Stand by! We're going to board them, right now!"

More shots, and he saw that the slaver's topmen had been joined by others with muskets. He felt a few of the balls hitting the deck, jagged splinters lifting like quills as seamen and marines ducked for cover.

He knew the gunner's mate was crouching by the forward carronade, never taking his eyes from him, even as someone cried out and fell nearby, and remained there motionless.

Adam shouted, "Full elevation, Christie! Knock out all the quoins!" and saw him nod, teeth bared in concentration. Without the wedge-shaped quoins beneath their breeches, the stocky twelve-pounders should rake the rigging and yards, leaving the hostages untouched.

The first carronade responded instantly, bringing down most of the remaining branches and foliage, and blasting away some of the shrouds. Three bodies fell to the deck below, or into the water alongside.

Pecco, face desperate, was hauling down the Portuguese flag, flinching as the second carronade fired and ripped into the big schooner's topsails. Between shots they could hear the shouts and screams of the slaves who had been herded between forecastle and mainmast, then they were silent. Shock or disbelief, and perhaps the sight of the White Ensign and whatever it might mean to them.

Adam felt a shot hammer into the planking near him, but he did not move. Nothing else mattered now.

"Wheel hard a-starboard! Stand to, lads!"

It seemed to take an age, but he knew it was only seconds before the bows began to respond, until *Delfim*'s bowsprit and jib-boom were swinging toward and across the slaver's taut canvas.

More shots, but haphazard, or perhaps they were firing on the slaves.

Squire yelled, "Ready, lads! Grapnels forrard!"

Adam gestured to Tozer, who had been joined by two more seamen at the wheel. "Helm a-lee!" He reached out and seized a stay, bracing himself for the collision.

But it was more of an embrace: a splintering crash as the jib-boom and bowsprit drove through the other ship's shrouds like a giant lance, and the final, shuddering impact as the bows of both locked together. Vague figures had become the enemy. Yelling and screaming, some falling into the sea between the hulls, escaping one fate for another as some of the released slaves began to shout, even cheer.

Adam heard Lieutenant Sinclair's voice even above the noise, breathless after running with his men to the point of impact.

"Royal Marines, stand to! *Ready to fire!*"

Adam drew his sword and shouted, "Boarders away!" as he jumped onto a broken grating and across a huge tangle of canvas. He felt someone reach out and prevent him falling. He did not turn to look but knew it was Jago, knew his cutlass, and the smell of the last "wet" on his breath.

He stared up and behind him at a line of Royal Marines, heads and shoulders and trained muskets. Some had even found time to don their scarlet tunics, although most were hatless. Seamen were swarming up to join him, cutlasses and boarding pikes dispelling any doubt or argument.

There was another deafening shot and an instant response of shouts and cries from slaves and captors alike.

He heard Squire's powerful voice, and Tozer's; he must have just left the wheel.

Squire climbed over a shattered spar and stood by him, breathing heavily. "That was the ship's master. Killed himself, the bastard!"

He was trying to sheathe his sword, but there was blood on the blade and it refused to budge.

A few scattered shots followed, and then, as if to some invisible signal, weapons were clattering across the deck and some of the slaver's crew were running toward them as if to seek protection from the advancing line of scarlet and blue. With Squire beside him and Jago at his back, Adam made his way toward the poop.

At the foot of the mizzen mast Jago shouted, "A moment, Cap'n!" His voice seemed very loud, as if all movement had stopped.

Adam handed his sword to a grinning seaman and thrust his arms into the sleeves of his coat, which Jago must have had slung over his shoulder despite the chaos surrounding them.

A few more weapons fell, and someone nearby was murmuring, maybe praying, in Portuguese. A man who might have been the schooner's second-in-command was offering the hilt of his sword and gesticulating toward his captain's corpse, sprawled near the big double wheel, a pistol still gripped in his hand. He had no face.

Adam looked away as someone grasped his arm. He saw Jago's sudden, defensive movement, then he lowered his cutlass and said, "Lucky it was *you*, my son!"

It was a young African boy, naked but for a ragged shirt, staring up at Adam or his uniform with wide eyes. There were bloody welts on his arms where he had been chained or beaten. Adam felt the heavy silence around him as he reached down to clasp the boy's shoulder. Like Trusty, the one without a tongue.

In the unreal stillness they all heard the distant cry from one of Squire's hand-picked lookouts, who must have watched the boarding and its aftermath from aloft, unable to help or take part.

Squire lifted his stained blade and signalled toward the overlapping masts. "He's sighted the *Peterel*, sir."

They were no longer alone.

Adam heard a groan, and saw the surgeon bandaging a marine's bloody head. He had not known that Murray had followed him aboard. The marine, a corporal, saw his captain watching and tried to grin. Then he died.

Adam heard the two hulls creaking together, and the clatter of untended tackle. It was over. *So many times.* He steeled himself.

"What's the bill?"

Squire regarded him steadily. "Five, sir." He saw Murray hold up his free hand. "Six." He gave their names, knowing his captain would be seeing each face.

Adam stared up at the shot-holes in the topsails overhead, the dark stains left by canister. He said, "They did well. Tell Lieutenant Sinclair," and stopped as Squire shook his head.

"He's dead, sir. They just told me."

Adam walked to the side, and looked down at the swirling arrowhead of water with its litter of branches, and one corpse caught among them.

Squire glanced over at the crowd of captives, separated by a thin line of marines. Then he asked quietly, "When *Peterel* is within signalling distance—"

He felt Adam's hand close on his arm. There was blood on it. "Make to *Peterel . . .*" Adam hesitated. Strain or emotion? This was not the time. *"Welcome. Mission successful. We will proceed when ready. Together."*

Squire had found a slate somewhere and was deliberately repeating the signal. But Adam was gazing at a body covered by canvas, a pair of polished boots protruding, gleaming in the sunlight. The cost of freedom.

He reached out to stop Squire but he had gone, and the blood remained.

11 SUNSET

HARRY DRUMMOND CLIMBED through *Onward*'s main hatchway and paused to clear his mind. Most of the routine work had been completed during the forenoon watch, and with a heavy meal under his belt a doze in the mess would have been welcome. But as bosun he needed to be seen and heard, as he had learned the hard way.

He wiped his mouth with the back of his hand and stifled a yawn. Too much grog. But it was Tilley, the sailmaker's, birthday—as good an excuse as any.

He glanced up at the shrouds and stays, the neatly furled sails gleaming in the sun, unmoving, like the flags and masthead pendant. As for the ship herself, she could have been aground.

He looked aft, but the quarterdeck appeared to be empty. Not for long. Vincent, temporarily in command, never seemed to rest from his extra duties. Maybe he did not know how. Was he still brooding about how nearly he had been given command? Dead men's shoes . . .

Close by at her own anchorage was the new frigate *Zealous*, her captain's first command. Young, too, from what Drummond had heard. That would be lying heavily on Vincent's mind.

He shook himself, tasting the grog again.

He saw a seaman standing by an upturned boat, which had been propped over some old canvas to protect the deck. It was the gig, and Drummond had been thinking about Luke Jago and wondering how he was faring aboard the little schooner as one of the captain's prize crew. A hard man to know, unless he let the barriers fall. But Drummond had not forgotten that when he had been appointed, replacing the bosun who had been killed, Jago had been the first to befriend him. They never discussed it, but there it was.

He saw the same seaman now cleaning a brush, and found himself smiling. The old Jack's yardstick: *if it moves, salute it! If it doesn't, paint it!*

He heard voices: one of the gun captains giving instructions to some of the new hands, making sweeping gestures and ducking beside an eighteen-pounder. He was probably describing the clash with *Nautilus*. Hardly a battle. *If he had been at Trafalgar . . .* Drummond shaded his eyes and looked over at the flagship. His own ship, *Mars,* had been in the thick of the action, her decks smeared with blood, the enemy sometimes broadside to broadside. Even their captain had fallen, beheaded by a French ball.

He was suddenly angry, and could not contain it. He shouted, "Winning, are we?" But he was immediately ashamed of himself.

He turned as a shadow fell across the deck. It was Maddock, the gunner, and he was smiling. "We were all like that when we were young. So long ago I can hardly remember!"

Drummond saw the familiar felt slippers tucked in Maddock's belt. He was on his way to the magazine. Nobody would bother him there. Strangers and visitors to their small mess hardly ever realised Maddock was so hard of hearing. He had even made a short and witty speech today to mark the sailmaker's birthday, and got through it without interruption.

He said now, "I just met the first lieutenant, Harry. I think he wants to see you when you're free."

Drummond laughed, his moment of temper forgotten. "That means *now!*"

Maddock yawned too; it must be contagious. "He's in the cabin, getting a bit of peace. While he still can."

Drummond knew there were only two possible reasons. With Squire, Sinclair of the Royal Marines, and Murray, the surgeon, all away in *Delfim*, the wardroom would be a place to avoid. Julyan, the master, was ashore dealing with some new navigational aids, and Vicary, the purser, was dull to say the least. That left Lieutenant Monteith. That was reason enough.

A marine strode toward them and clicked his heels together. "Beg pardon, sir, but the first lieutenant . . ."

Maddock held up his hand and grinned. "You were right, Harry. He meant *now!*"

Lieutenant Mark Vincent loosened his coat and walked through the great cabin to the stern windows. Even with windsails rigged and most hatches and doors opened, it seemed airless, and the anchorage was still, the reflected glare painfully bright.

There was an occasional sound or sensation around or beneath him, and in his mind's eye he could place and define it. He knew every part of *Onward,* possibly better than any one. Except her builder.

Something fell on deck and he heard the Royal Marine sentry outside the screen door move away to investigate, then somebody laughed and was hissed into silence again. He glanced at the neat pile of papers brought for his signature by Prior, the captain's clerk. Quiet and confident, and, for all Vincent knew, watching him and making comparisons. He sat down abruptly and tried to relax, but he was not tired, which surprised him.

For an entire week the ship had been under his command, and as a result he had shared every watch with Monteith and Julyan, keenly supported by Midshipman Hotham, who had once more been appointed temporary acting lieutenant.

Vincent saw a jug of water on the little desk. The surface was barely moving. Suppose . . . He shut his mind to it.

Every day had been full: dealing with the ship's routine and the harbour requirements and formalities, discipline and defaulters, but only a few of the latter. They knew him too well by now. He had even met the new frigate's captain when he had gone aboard *Zealous* with some local information, more out of curiosity than anything else. Pleasant enough,

and friendly up to a point, but the courtesy of the visit had not been returned. He was young, younger than Vincent, and the significance had
been obvious to them both.

He was on his feet again, pacing. The pantry door was shut, but he
knew Morgan was not far away. A good man, none better . . . He put
that, too, from his mind. He had selected Hugh Morgan himself for the
position of captain's servant, even before *Onward* had been fully commissioned. *Even then, I was behaving like a captain.*

He pushed at the other, narrow door until it was half open. Bolitho's
sleeping cabin was almost box-like. But at least it was his own. He
looked at the portrait that always hung there, seen only by Morgan and
a few interlopers. *Like me.* Andromeda, awaiting her own sacrifice to the
sea monster. He reached out and lightly touched the canvas, as guilty as
a schoolboy. What must she have felt as she had posed for it? What did
she think now, with Adam Bolitho away at sea, not knowing . . .

He was closing the door, flushed and unsettled, as Morgan padded
past with an armful of clean shirts.

"He'll be back soon, sir." He did not move. "Will you be dining with
any guests here tonight, sir?"

There was a tap on the screen door. Morgan tutted. "Never any
peace!"

"Officer of the guard, *sir!*"

Morgan was laying the shirts carefully on the seat of the bergère.
Then he looked up, staring at the door. "He's back!" He hurried to open
it, but halted as the air seemed to quiver to a dull boom.

Vincent's eyes remained on the officer in the doorway, a lieutenant
like himself. It was the signal from the headland.

He turned without speaking and looked for the last time at the
cabin. Like a dream, it was over.

Midshipman David Napier walked across the quarterdeck, gazing at
the anchorage. There were still a few lights showing ashore and on vessels at anchor, but that would soon change. All hands had been called
at dawn and the air was still fresh and cool, the decks wet underfoot,

washed down by seamen half asleep as hammocks were being stacked
in the nettings, still warm from their bodies. The midshipmen's berth
had been like a furnace in the night, despite the open ports and hatches.

Napier saw someone stooping over coiled rope and grinned. It was
his friend Tucker, the bosun's mate.

"This makes a change!"

They both looked toward the as yet invisible headland. Napier said,
"Bit of a breeze now. That will help them."

Every one was thinking the same. How soon? What was the cost?
When you fought together as one company, it was different. Fighting
guns or the sea itself.

Tucker murmured, "Stand by."

It was Lieutenant Monteith, peering around at the men working
below the braced yards and furled sails, which were already sharpening
against a clear sky. He saw Tucker and snapped, "I'll need *you* to chase
up the jolly-boat's crew, in case . . ." He did not finish, but beckoned
imperiously to Napier. "And I want a few words with *you*." He gestured.
"Even the flagship's not wide awake yet!"

Tucker said, "Can I send the men under punishment to breakfast,
sir?"

"Ask the master-at-arms. I can't deal with everything!"

Napier followed the lieutenant down to the wardroom. It was deserted, the table laid for one person. A messman was collecting the
empty dishes.

He stopped as Monteith said, "Another cup, Berry. The last one was
stone-cold."

The man nodded and hurried away.

Monteith sat down and wiped his face with a handkerchief. "You
have to watch some people all the time!"

Napier glanced around. Lieutenant Vincent must still be in the great
cabin, but did he ever sleep? Even during the night he had heard him
about, sometimes just prowling along a gangway or the main deck. He
had always liked the first lieutenant. Strict when necessary, but he was
fair, and always ready to listen. Unlike some . . .

Monteith was saying, "As you probably know, I am writing your monthly report. I'm afraid it's something we all have to go through." He shifted in the chair and gazed at him. "You must have learned a good deal by now." He ticked each point off on a finger. "Your previous experience when *Audacity* was lost in battle, then aboard this ship." He gave what might have been a smile. "And with me and our landing party. I shall put that in my report, of course."

Napier felt his leg beginning to throb. Not like those early days. *He will always have a limp.* But Monteith, although aware of his discomfort, did not ask him to sit down.

Monteith leaned back expansively. "You have a good relationship with the captain, I believe." He waved any response aside. "It can be a hurdle, of course, but in your case it must offer reassurance, surely." He turned abruptly toward the door. "What is it *now?*" then waved at the table. "Hot this time, I trust?"

Berry, the messman, said nothing. He had heard it all before.

Monteith sipped the coffee and collected himself. "I expect you told Captain Bolitho of our experiences at the mission, eh? A close thing. I expect he was worried about you. But as you were with me—" He broke off. "What the hell is it *now?*"

Berry might have shrugged. "Somebody left a message for you, sir." He pulled an envelope from his apron.

"And you didn't see who it was?"

"Must've been while I was fetching your breakfast, sir."

Monteith snatched the envelope from him. "I shall speak to the first lieutenant about this!"

A fine shaft of sunlight had driven the last shadows from the wardroom, and Napier could see the envelope trembling in Monteith's fingers, with his name and rank printed in bold letters across it.

"Shall I carry on, sir?"

Monteith glared at him. "I haven't finished yet!" He tore open the envelope. "If this is some sort of joke—"

He shook it angrily over the table, and for a few seconds nothing happened. There was no letter or note enclosed.

As if from another world they heard the shrill of calls, and the cry, *"Clear lower deck! All hands muster by divisions!"*

The waiting was over.

Napier held his breath, and watched something drift slowly from the torn envelope until it landed on the table.

It was a white feather.

Midshipman Charles Hotham was about to raise his telescope again, but changed his mind as he heard Lieutenant Monteith come to stand beside him on the quarterdeck. A moment earlier, with all hands hurrying to their various stations, he might not have noticed, but he could hear the sharp, uneven breathing as if Monteith had been running, or was agitated about something. He knew Monteith had been in the wardroom, which was no distance away, where Hotham assumed he had been complaining to David Napier about something. Monteith made a point of it. If and when the time came for Hotham to leave *Onward* for his own promotion, he would miss Monteith least of all.

And would that day soon come? He tried not to hope too much. Being made acting lieutenant, even if temporarily, must count for something. He smiled. Especially as he had to suffer for it from the other young members of his mess.

He heard the murmur of voices from the assembled figures on the main deck. Excitement, anxiety, or both.

Monteith said, "Silence on deck," but without his usual irritation. Hotham glanced at him curiously, and saw that he was looking at the shore, or perhaps in the direction of the flagship, and that a crumpled handkerchief was dangling loosely from a pocket, although Monteith prided himself on his appearance and was always quick to point out any failure to "measure up," as he put it, among the midshipmen.

He saw the Royal Marines paraded in a small section by the starboard gangway, Sergeant Fairfax, stiff-backed, in command. They would be at full strength again when the prize crew returned. *Unless.* Hotham tried to close his mind to the possibility. Like the ill-fated mission, when his own sighting of that crude distress signal had begun a chain of events none of them could have anticipated. And some had died because of it, and because of him.

He adjusted his telescope hurriedly, although there was no need. He saw Vincent now, standing by the quarterdeck rail, hands clasped behind his back. Julyan, the sailing master, stood nearby, but alone.

Hotham breathed out slowly and raised his telescope. A big East Indiaman had anchored two days ago to land a mixed cargo, but was said to be leaving today. He felt himself tense as he saw the sleek bows of the brigantine listed as *Peterel* begin to pass her. Still not much wind, but enough to fill her sails, which were very clean and bright in the morning sunlight.

By moving the glass he could just see the topmasts of the schooner about which they had been told earlier, anchored where she would not impede incoming vessels or those wishing to leave, like John Company's big ship. And to put her under closer guard.

Hotham looked toward the flagship, unwilling to take his eyes from the new arrivals even for a few moments. *Medusa* had hoisted an "affirmative" to a brief signal from the brigantine, which was hidden by the set of her canvas.

He tried to ease his grip on the telescope. There was the renegade schooner, no more than a cable astern of the small man-of-war. He watched the hull and rigging leap into life, holding his breath as the deck moved slightly beneath his feet. Waiting for the image to settle. Faces: people he knew. He could hear their voices in his mind. Hastily sewn patches on some of the sails, scars on the hull, splinters untended and out of reach. And above it all, a large White Ensign.

He lowered the telescope. It had misted over, to his annoyance: the sun, or his eagerness to see every detail. Then he saw Adam Bolitho standing beside the wheel, another officer, who could only be Squire, close by.

Hotham jammed the telescope under his arm and wiped his eyes with the back of a sunburned hand. It was not mist on the lens.

He heard someone call, "Give 'em a cheer, lads!" It was probably Tobias Julyan, shouting from the heart.

Then another voice, sharper: Vincent, the first lieutenant. "*Belay that!* Stand fast and uncover!"

Hotham reached for his own hat, but he had just removed it to wave with every one else when he saw that the clean White Ensign aboard the schooner had been lowered to half-mast. Then he could see more clearly, every sense sharpened. There was another ensign spread on the schooner's deck, not large enough to hide the bodies of men who would never see another dawn.

The heavy silence was shattered as Sergeant Fairfax broke ranks and marched to the side, where he halted and threw up a smart salute. There were no words, but he was speaking for all of them.

Luke Jago felt himself tense as the first heaving-line lifted from *Delfim*'s low forecastle, but fell short, splashing into the water. *Too soon, too eager.* The same jetty they had left only a week or so ago seemed crammed with people, black and white, while others had climbed on the roofs of nearby buildings, some waving, others watching in total silence.

A second seaman was standing by with a line coiled and ready, then Jago saw a uniformed figure reach out and take it from him. It was Squire. His eyes met Jago's, and there was a brief smile. Squire had not forgotten. Nor would he.

The line snaked over and was seized by many willing hands, taking the strain of the main cable, still only a reflection.

They had anchored overnight, but they had been kept busy, with boats arriving from shore and more marines sent to take custody of the *Delfim*'s crew and tend to the immediate needs of the freed slaves. Their own prize crew had been reunited with their mates. He did not look at the dead men partly covered by the ensign.

Jago could not remember when he had last been able to rest, let alone sleep. He had always prided himself that he could do either standing on his feet. But after this . . .

This morning's move to enter harbour had kept all of them hopping. Past a big Indiaman, her company preparing for sea but still waving as the smart little *Peterel* had cleared the way, then coming abeam of the flagship, her decks lined, officers saluting, sailors and Royal Marines at attention, and from somewhere, the local garrison probably, a trumpet sounding, paying its respects.

Other, more painful moments remained uppermost in his mind. When the fighting had ended he had seen the gunner's mate looking across the deck, his eyes finding his friend, the master's mate. His face had said it all. And a tough seaman, one of *Onward*'s topmen, kneeling beside a mate who was now a corpse lying under the ensign.

It was done. Until the next time.

"Try and keep still, will you?"

Jago saw the surgeon crouching by a man who had been injured by a wood splinter, who was now trying to rise and join the others standing by for going alongside. The sawbones had been kept busier than most of them, he thought, and had not escaped wounding himself. One wrist was bandaged, and Murray looked unusually dishevelled and impatient as he was attempting to examine his patient.

Jago watched the strip of water narrowing as more muscle was lent to the mooring ropes, and the furled canvas cast shadows across the up-turned faces. He recalled the moment when he had steered his gig toward their first encounter with *Delfim*, and the impact of the girl showing her scars to the Portuguese master and identifying him as her assailant. Had she seen them enter harbour this time, he wondered?

He turned abruptly, not troubling to shade his eyes from the glare, and saw *Onward*. Her decks were full, but those waiting were silent. Thankful to see them back again, trying not to show it. A sailor's pretense.

He heard a telescope snap shut and someone mutter, "I can see Mister bloody Monteith as large as life! Bin makin' Jack's life a misery while he was playin' top dog!"

Another voice: "Don't know 'is arse from 'is elbow!"

Not loud, but enough for Jago to hear it.

Maybe Monteith had always been like that. Jago had known other "young gentlemen" who had shown their true colours after taking the first, vital step from white tabs to wardroom. He thought of Midshipman

Hotham, acting lieutenant during this brief and bitter operation. Clergyman's son or not, how would he perform when the time came?

He heard Tozer, the master's mate, call out something and saw him standing with Bolitho and gesturing toward the jetty. There was more activity, men clearing a space for any one who had been hurt. And for the dead.

He recalled Bolitho's face when he had told them he was taking the dead men back to Freetown for burial. Foreign soil, no matter what the charts might call it. But Jago knew the real reason. They had given their best and paid for it, and they would not be left to share the same ground as scum like slavers.

There was other movement now, seamen and marines forcing a passage through the line-handling party and onlookers, presumably for somebody important. He felt the instinctive resentment soften slightly as he recognized the upright figure of James Tyacke, the flag captain. A good one, to all accounts. *For an officer.*

Jago realised that Bolitho was looking directly at him. Like those other times, good and bad, moments of pride and fear, fury and compassion. And he felt his hand lift in their private salute.

He watched the flag captain pulling himself aboard, and waving aside all attempts at formality. Much as old John Allday had described him. As if he sensed Jago's scrutiny, Tyacke paused and looked across at him, the terrible disfigurement pitilessly revealed by the reflected glare. There might have been only the two of them.

"Kept your eye on him for me, did you, Jago? Knew I could rely on you!" Then Tyacke strode across the remaining few yards and grasped Bolitho's hands in both his own.

Christie, the gunner's mate, nudged Jago in the ribs. "I'll stand right next to *you*, Lukey, when I'm lookin' for promotion!"

Jago felt the deck shudder as *Delfim* nudged alongside and her moorings were secured, and as if to some signal, hesitant at first, a burst of cheering spread across the whole anchorage. He was thankful for the noise: Tyacke's obvious sincerity had left him at a loss for words.

He heard the squeak of halliards, and knew the ensign had been rehoisted to its peak. They were back. It was the way of sailors. And he heard Squire calling for him.

Until the next time.

Adam Bolitho stood alone by the *Delfim*'s taffrail and gazed along the deserted deck. He could still feel the warmth and intensity of Tyacke's greeting, and it had moved him deeply.

He knew that Squire was waiting for him to leave with the last of the prize crew, but the schooner already felt empty. Dead. She would remain under guard to await auction or the breaker's yard, with those others he had seen across the anchorage. Even the jetty was empty. He had waited until the dead seamen and marines had been carried ashore; somebody had even folded the spare ensign and left it beneath the mizzen, a reminder, if one was needed.

Tyacke probably knew him better than many, and had kept his questions to a minimum, letting him do the talking, phase by phase. They had seen Pecco, *Delfim*'s master, taken ashore under guard, to be detained separately from the other prisoners. Adam had described their difficult approach to the rendezvous with the slaver, and how Pecco could have betrayed them at any moment.

Tyacke had said only, "I'm not sure how his loyalty will be valued by higher authority, Adam."

"I gave him my word."

Adam came out of his thoughts as he heard Squire's heavy tread across the splintered decking.

"The boats are here to take us across to . . ." he seemed to hesitate, "*Onward*." It was rare for Squire to show emotion.

"I was glad to have you with me, James. I've said as much in my report."

Squire walked beside him past the abandoned wheel, and said quietly, "Surely you're not expected to visit the flagship, when you've only just—" He broke off as Adam grasped his sleeve.

"Not until tomorrow forenoon, James! The admiral is being most considerate!"

Squire stopped near the capstan and looked up at the ensign, which seemed particularly vivid against the clear sky. "Shall I haul down the Colours, sir?"

For a moment he thought his question had gone unheard, or that Bolitho was still preoccupied with something else. But when he turned and faced him, Adam's dark eyes were unwavering in the hot sunlight.

"At sunset, when the flags of all our ships are lowered." He stared across the water, Squire thought toward his own command. "Then it will be up to us."

As they made toward the waiting boats, Squire was still sharing the moment. It was not a threat. It was a promise.

Adam waited for the screen door to close behind him and the sentry to resume his place outside before walking aft to the stern windows. An hour or more had passed since he had climbed aboard, and his mind was still dazed by the reception. Calls shrilling, faces eager or apprehensive, impetuous handshakes, all order and discipline momentarily forgotten. But now he was feeling the aftermath, and for the first time he was alone.

Even the cabin seemed different, unfamiliar, but that was all part of it. It was in fact exactly as he had left it, and had seen it in his mind in those rare moments of peace. The strangeness was within himself.

He stood for a moment beneath the skylight and felt the warm air on his face. There was an unmoving shadow across it—another sentry overhead to ensure that the captain was not disturbed.

He leaned on the bench and stared through the glass. The jetty and the schooner were hidden from here. He should be glad. He stretched his arms until his hands jarred against a deckhead beam. When had he last slept? He stared at the coat flung carelessly across a chair; he could not remember having dragged it off. Had Morgan been here, he would have folded it with care. He felt his mouth crack into a smile. Morgan *was* here, doubtless sealed in his pantry and listening for every sound.

Adam looked at the old bergère, in shadow now. If he sat down now, it would finish him. He moved restlessly to the desk and pulled out its smaller, less comfortable chair, feeling his chin scrape against his neck-cloth. But the effort of enduring a shave, even under Jago's skilled hand, was too much for him. And God knew Luke Jago needed rest more than most. He was probably on his back right now, the strain and sudden death safely stowed away under the hatches of his mind, and likely with a few wets to help. And Squire too, with the prize crew. But with Sinclair gone, it would be different in the wardroom.

He gripped the edge of the desk, staring with burning eyes at the opened letter. Her letter: Tyacke had handed it to him when they had met, instead of leaving it for the mail boat to deliver later. Or maybe he had come simply to reassure himself that *Onward*'s captain was not one of those lying covered by the ensign.

And tomorrow they would be buried. Someone would remember them.

Adam spread the letter on the desk but could not focus on the words. He had already read it in minutes snatched between one duty and another, all the demands which had awaited him on board; he had even found time to call young David and tell him Elizabeth had asked to be remembered to him. Just a brief contact, captain with midshipman.

He felt the hot air stir against his skin, and heard the quiet Welsh voice. "Shall I fetch another brandy, sir?" Adam saw Morgan's eyes flicker to the discarded coat, probably noting his unshaven face as well.

"Another?" he said.

Morgan smiled gently. "With all respect, sir, I think you should try to sleep a while."

"*Not yet!* I must wait until sunset!" Then, "You didn't ask for that, Hugh. Forgive me." He smiled. "So I *will* have some more brandy, and thank you."

The door closed, and he tried to focus on the writing, hearing her voice in the words. *My own darling Adam. I am lying with you now—just reach out for me . . .*

Later, when Hugh Morgan returned to the great cabin under protest, to report that Sunset had been piped, he found his captain asleep across the desk, the brandy untouched. He thought of the lovely girl in the painting in the adjoining cabin. "Flaunting herself," as his old mother in Wales would have called it.

And aloud, he said quietly, "Not for a while yet, Captain. We need you right now!"

12 Voice from the Past

Adam Bolitho walked out on to the dusty road and heard the graveyard gates clang shut behind him. He had already noticed that they had
not been painted for a long time, and were showing rust.

He looked toward the harbour and the tight cluster of masts, a few
moving, taking advantage of a slight but steady breeze, others anchored
or alongside, their work done for the day. Beyond the sheds and slipways he could see the flagship's masts and spars rising above the rest,
with all her canvas furled and still, no "unsightly" windsails to offend
the admiral.

He knew it was wrong, but he was glad to be alone, if only for a short
while. The burial service had been brief, almost impersonal, but how
could it be otherwise? It had been conducted by a senior chaplain with
a hollow, monotonous voice, but in fairness he had known none of the
men being buried this day. How could he?

Faces in battle, or laughing together at some well-worn sailor's joke.
Or seen across the table, for promotion or punishment. *His men.* Who
had followed him and obeyed without question. And had paid the price.

Their personal possessions would be collected and auctioned; the
wardroom, too, would donate something. As usual, time and distance
were the enemy. How long would it be before their relatives and loved
ones were told?

What if it had been me?

How would Lowenna have been told? A courier or some local

authority, maybe an incoming ship, or by the official letter. *The Secretary of the Admiralty regrets to inform you . . .*

He stopped and looked down at his feet; they were covered with mud, and some of it had spattered his stockings. The ground had been soaked with water before the burial, to the point of being almost awash. The gravediggers would have been helpless otherwise: the sun-baked earth was like rock.

The sight of his shoes transported him to somewhere else a world away: Cornwall and the coast he knew so well. Walking along one of those narrow country lanes after a downpour. Where you could still smell, among the fragrance of the fields, the sea, and taste its salt on your mouth when you spoke, or laughed with the woman you loved.

He was conscious of the clip-clop of hooves and the scrape of wheels, and realised he had been hearing them for some time beyond his thoughts. He moved to the side of the road, but the vehicle was slowing. Stopping.

"Well met, Captain Bolitho! For a moment I thought I had taken the wrong turning."

It was a small carriage drawn by two horses, probably because of the steeper inclines of the road. And despite the familiarity of the greeting, the face staring from the open window was that of a stranger, lean and narrow with deepset eyes, the hair completely grey, the voice confident and cultured.

"I understand you're heading for the harbour?" The door creaked open. "I'm going that way. Please join me."

Adam shook his head. "I cannot. My shoes are . . ."

The man pushed the door back as far as it would go and held up one of his feet. "Mine too. But I'm glad I was there."

And Adam remembered seeing him in the graveyard, almost hidden among the officials and visitors, but somehow remaining remote, apart from them all.

He thrust out a hand as hard and lean as himself. "I'm Godden, by the way." He smiled, and seemed younger. "I was hoping to meet you, but time ran out. Today changed that." He slid across the bench seat so that Adam could climb in beside him. The coachman who had jumped down to hold the horses was waiting silently. "Carry on, Toby!"

The carriage turned back on to the road, and Adam's mind groped with the sudden shift of events. The man sitting beside him was not merely "Godden." He was the Honourable Sir Charles Godden, the admiral's "important guest," who had had every one on the move since his arrival in Freetown.

Godden said, "I have been hearing quite a lot about you, Captain Bolitho. This recent venture must seem a reward for all the work supported by Rear-Admiral Langley and his staff. Do you see any end to the slave trade in view? It is illegal in most countries, but the business goes on, although the admiral seems to think it is already in decline . . . almost finished except in name."

Adam hesitated. This meeting was no accident, and it was more than a mere courtesy.

He said carefully, "There are always men willing to take the risk, if the money is ready and sufficient. Slaves are being taken from these shores as far away as Brazil and Cuba, despite the efforts of the patrols and the threat of punishment if caught."

He stared through the window next to him. Even so diplomatic a comment sounded disloyal, against the code of duty and loyalty as a sea officer.

Godden said, "Politics and the navy have much in common," and tapped some dried mud from his shoe. "Robert Walpole is regarded as Britain's first true prime minister." He paused. "Except by the Irish, of course!" He became serious again. "Walpole was a man I would have dearly liked to know. We could all still learn from his example. His family motto, for instance. The part I remember is, *Fari quae sentias.*" He twisted round and gripped Adam's arm. *"Speak as you feel!"*

He rapped the inside of the roof. "Here, Toby!"

The carriage juddered to a halt, dust settling around it in a yellow cloud. Godden turned easily in his seat, his eyes in shadow. "I know a good deal about you, and I have learned more since I arrived here." He seemed to sense a challenge, and added, "Not from staff officers."

He tapped his chest. "Or politicians like me. But from ordinary, decent men like the ones you lead. Who trust you."

Adam opened the door and said sharply, "And who die because of me!"

He stepped down into the road so that *Medusa* seemed to be towering over him. Solid, real.

They shook hands, but only their eyes spoke. Then Adam turned toward the steps to the jetty. His arrival would already have been reported.

I should have walked.

But the words were still ringing in his mind: *Speak as you feel.*

Lieutenant James Squire halted in a patch of shade by an unfinished wall and looked across the graveyard, deserted after the orderly departure of the uniforms and the local people who had occupied most of the spare ground, watching curiously. Now it was over, the graves neatly marked and numbered to await the stone or wooden crosses. He stretched and felt his tendons crack. By which time *Onward* should be at sea again. *Never look back.* He had seen a lot of good men die over his years at sea, and a few he still remembered.

He heard two of the gravediggers talking to one another, one of them smoking a well-used pipe. To them it was just a job of work, and rightly so.

He felt in his pocket to ensure he had the signed papers Bolitho had told him to collect while he was reporting to the admiral. He felt his sunburned face crease into a frown. The admiral should have been the first here to show his respect. Gratitude. He thought of Luke Jago, and what he might have said. *That will be the bloody day!*

He glanced down at his shoes; the mud had dried on them like iron. He recalled that the senior chaplain had been careful to stand on a rug throughout the service. He thought by contrast of the sea burials, the captain speaking the familiar words.

He turned, caught off-guard by a woman's voice.

"Over here, if you're certain . . ."

Two of them, one who was still pointing toward the graves, dressed in a white cape like a nun or a medical attendant, round-faced, smiling tolerantly. The other was Claire Dundas. Her arms were full of blossoms, a splash of colour against her plain gown. Her companion was carrying a kind of frame of neatly tied canes.

Claire looked across directly at him, her face partly hidden by flowers. "I thought we were too late."

Squire heard the other woman say, "Don't forget, Claire dear, the doctor wants to see you on the hour."

The girl ignored her. "I saw you sail into harbour." She did not look at him. "I had a telescope."

Squire strode across the uneven ground and reached without thinking for her hand. The blossoms remained between them like a barrier.

She said quietly, "I prayed for you," and gazed away, almost guiltily. "For . . . all of you."

"I haven't forgotten. I was hoping to see you somehow . . ." Squire broke off awkwardly and touched the ribbon around the flowers. "These are fine. Are they lilies?"

She smiled for the first time, perhaps with relief that he had changed the subject. "No, only vines. Bleeding Heart, they're called here." She shook them gently, and only then looked at him. "They will not last long, but I just thought—" She did not go on.

He knew he was staring at her but could not help himself, as if the woman in white and the gravediggers were invisible, remembering how she had struggled and fought to free herself as he had tried to carry her to safety, her nakedness scarcely covered by his uniform coat. He could see the scar on her wrist, fading, but still visible enough to remind her. And although she had arranged her hair differently, he could still see the dark bruise on her forehead.

He said, "I must see you. Not here." He took her wrist and felt her tense. "Not like this, Claire."

The other voice intruded. "We really must leave now. They will be expecting you."

He released her wrist and stooped to pick up some of the vines which had dropped between them. "I've been so worried about you." He looked up into her face, in shadow against the clear sky.

She said, "You saved my life." She broke off, and took a few paces as if to join her companion. "I will never forget . . . Jamie."

Squire watched them leave. She did not look back, and the vines lay where they had fallen.

A voice muttered, "'Ere, sir, I'll put 'em on show," and there was an intake of breath as Squire thrust some coins into his fist. It must have been more than he realised.

It was over. It had never begun.

Rowlatt, the master-at-arms, watched impatiently as the harbour launch thrust away from *Onward*'s side and headed toward the shore, faster this time, having unloaded the seamen and marines from the funeral muster. Then he strode aft toward the quarterdeck where the first lieutenant was inspecting an unexpected delivery of purser's stores. So much for a day of mourning . . .

Rowlatt waited for the lieutenant to look up from the cargo list, and touched his hat. Vincent was probably glad of the interruption. Pinch-gut Vicary, as the purser was known, was not the liveliest company on any day.

"All aboard?"

"Mr. Squire is returning with the guardboat, sir."

Vincent made a non-committal noise. Squire must have remained to the end, while the captain presented himself as ordered to the admiral. He yawned, irritated that he was too tired to control it. But he knew there was a deeper reason. It was envy.

He saw Midshipman Walker loitering, gazing intently at a small boat pulling unnecessarily close along the larboard side. A Royal Marine was keeping pace with it on the gangway, but when he waved for the helmsman to stand clear he was given a huge grin and a display of cheap ornaments.

Vincent glanced at the nearest pile of stores. That must be stowed away without delay. "Mr. Walker, find some spare hands."

He saw him hurry away. Walker must have had his hair cut: it made him look younger than ever. Thirteen, or was he fourteen now? The boy who had been forever seasick, even in a flat calm. The other midshipmen had tired of making jokes about it, and of cleaning him up. Now it was unknown.

Rowlatt asked, "Th' cap'n, sir—is he due back on board soon?"

Vincent nodded. Rowlatt always had a reason. He was never lacking when it came to discipline and routine. A first lieutenant's right arm, and usually hated because of it.

"I want a close watch kept." He gestured in the direction of the flagship. "He'll want some rest after all this." Rowlatt said nothing, and he thought, *and so shall I!*

Vincent thought longingly of the wardroom. But if he went below now . . . He swung round, startled, as the cry came from forward.

"Boat ahoy?"

Rowlatt snapped, "Must be a mistake, sir!"

But the reply was clear enough. *"Aye, aye!"*

A visitor. An officer.

Vincent swore under his breath. "Who the hell?"

Midshipman Walker hurried over, holding a telescope outstretched, and Vincent took it, calm once more. He should have known. He trained the glass with care, the fixed grin of the would-be trader leaping out at him until he found the other boat, bows on, filling the lens. One of *Medusa's* own gigs, the flagship's distinctive markings unmistakable in the sunlight. And one passenger, wearing the scarlet uniform of the Royal Marines. More to the point, there was a pile of kit in the sternsheets, some of it personal.

Images of the wardroom flooded Vincent's mind again, and the habits and characters of the men who lived there. Robert Sinclair had been buried today: no time wasted. This must be his replacement arriving. He saw the newcomer being met at the entry port by Monteith, who had appeared a few seconds earlier, and who was now directing him aft. Sergeant Fairfax was nearby, but keeping his distance. His life, too, would now be changed.

The first few moments were always the worst.

The marine, a lieutenant, strode aft, his eyes not leaving Vincent until he had halted smartly and saluted. An open, youthful face, the hair beneath his hat fair and neatly trimmed. The scarlet uniform was well-cut but looser than some, as if he had lost weight since he had last visited a tailor. The sword, too, was well-worn, even tarnished. He was older than he looked, Vincent thought.

He returned the salute. *About my age.*

"Lieutenant Devereux, sir, come aboard to join. Regret the delay. All boats in use." He held out the familiar stamped and sealed envelope. Good or bad, a new beginning.

Vincent offered his free hand. "I'm the senior here. Welcome aboard."

The smile, like the handshake, was firm but unconsciously so, not done to make an impression.

"The captain is not aboard at present. But you probably know that."

Devereux nodded, and winced slightly, touching his face. "I know, sir. I caught sight of him just before I came over."

Vincent waited, giving himself time. The gesture had drawn his attention to a deep scar on the left side of Devereux's face, not large but deadly, an inch or less above the jawbone.

Devereux said lightly, "Sun's a little hotter than usual," but the smile was gone.

Vincent said, "Did you get that out here?" and Devereux lowered his hand.

"No—back home. In Chatham, as it happens."

Vincent gazed along the main deck, where a few men were still clearing up from the day's work. "I hope she was worth it?"

Devereux looked at him in silence, then said abruptly, "*I* thought so." His jaw lifted, so that the scar seemed to speak for him. "It was self-defense, of course."

Vincent touched his arm. "I'll have your kit taken below." He glanced at the official envelope. "Paul, isn't it?" He gestured toward the companion ladder. "I'll show you our quarters. The formalities must wait until the captain returns."

Even now he could feel the stab of resentment.

. . .

The flag lieutenant paused outside *Medusa*'s great cabin as Adam wiped the last of the dried mud from his shoes on to a rope mat.

"Don't trouble yourself about that, sir. You're here, that's the main thing!" He nodded to a Royal Marine sentry, and added in an undertone, "*He* will see you now."

Once through the screen door, the cabin was much as Adam remembered it, well furnished, spotless, and somehow unlived-in. At the far end, in the centre of the broad stern windows, Rear-Admiral Giles Langley stood with his back to the gleaming panorama of water and moored vessels, his fair hair almost touching the deckhead.

As Adam walked aft Langley seemed to come to life, and strode to meet him.

"Good to see you again, Bolitho. Only sorry I had to drag you aboard without giving you time to breathe." He gripped Adam's outstretched hand and stared intensely at him, his pale eyes unblinking. "You look damn well despite it all. Proud of you." Then, "Pity I couldn't have joined you at the sad but necessary ceremony." He waved vaguely around the cabin. "I'm sure you understood."

He waited as a servant darted forward and moved his chair away from a shaft of sunlight. So that was what was different. The curtains which had covered the stern windows, obscuring the impressive view of Freetown, were gone. Perhaps the admiral had become more accustomed to the searing light and the climate.

They sat facing one another, a small table between them, while the servant spoke to someone else in hiding beyond the same door. There was a clink of glasses, and Adam found time to wonder what was keeping him alert. And for what?

Langley said bluntly, "I hear you fell in with Sir Charles Godden."

"Apparently he was at the funeral service, sir, although he did not announce himself."

Langley smiled coldly. "He was, in a carriage. But I doubt it was by coincidence. Not in his nature." He turned his head and rapped out, "I shall send word if I need you, Flags."

Adam had not realised that Langley's aide was still in the cabin. No wonder he looked so hunted. And where was Tyacke?

Langley asked, just as brusquely, "What did you make of Godden?" and did not wait for an answer. "Had everybody jumping here from the minute he stepped ashore. He and his little group of cronies—they've done well for themselves. I can't even guess what the bill will come to! And he was here looking for ways to *save money!*" He laughed, almost jovially, but his eyes were very keen. "Well? Did he impress you? A few minutes beside someone in a carriage you had never met before. Or are likely to meet again."

"I think he was sincere—even eager to learn how we feel about our role here."

Langley snapped his finger and thumb. "What we're costing his precious government, more likely! Better friend than foe, in *my* opinion."

He leaned over and tapped the little table. "Don't take all day, man!"

Adam could smell the brandy from where he was sitting.

Langley took out a handkerchief and dabbed his face. "But he's nobody's fool. I can see why he's got where he is. Knows about our anti-slavery patrols and the results, good or bad. Knows of our co-operation with the ship-owners and traders here." He winked. "Or lack of same!" He shifted in his chair as the servant approached with a tray and a full decanter, and two fresh glasses. There were wet rings on the tray left by previous ones.

Langley said, "Not sorry to see him go. Now we might get some results." He lifted his glass. "He knew a little too much about *you*, anyway!"

Adam felt the brandy sear his tongue. "Not from me, sir."

"No, no. Had it all written down, for God's sake!" Langley laughed again, and nearly dropped his glass. It was empty. "He asked a lot of questions about . . ." He snapped his fingers again. "Ballantyne, and his affairs at New Haven. Another *carpet knight*, eh?" He grinned and touched his lips. "And you did not hear that!"

The servant was refilling the glasses, his features expressionless. He was probably used to this behaviour but Adam had never seen Langley like this. It was more than relief.

Langley was saying, "What now, Flags? I thought I made it clear . . ." He wiped his face with the handkerchief. "Not time already?"

The flag lieutenant closed his little book. "Colonel Whitehead from the garrison is due to arrive shortly, sir. You said—"

"Slipped my mind, dammit." He looked at Adam and shrugged. "Had to see you first, Bolitho. We've both been through it of late." The pale eyes flickered around the cabin. "They all like to visit the flagship. Makes 'em feel important!"

Another servant had appeared carrying Langley's cocked hat and sword, but he was pushed rudely aside as the admiral strode toward the quarter gallery. Langley paused and rubbed his hands together. "Must clean up and pump the bilges before they arrive. Not much longer, eh, Flags?" The door slammed behind him. Adam thought he looked as if he were going to vomit.

The lieutenant waited for the servant to lay hat and sword on the bench beneath the stern windows and leave before saying quietly, "*Medusa* is being paid off." The well-thumbed notebook had fallen to the deck, but he did not seem to notice. "Finished!"

Adam was on his feet, his mind quite clear. Like all those other ships he had seen in harbours at home. Some with famous names, legends, and remembered not only by those who had served and fought in them. At the Saintes and Camperdown, at the Nile and Copenhagen, and at Trafalgar. Now awaiting that final voyage.

He walked slowly aft. From here he could see the berth where the *Delfim* had been moored, when Rear-Admiral Giles Langley had dissociated himself from the plan to seek out the slaver's lair, for which he had since taken the credit.

And what about Tyacke?

He turned and faced the flag lieutenant, who was glancing around the cabin as if he had never seen it before. Langley had left even this to him.

There were voices beyond the screen door, laughter: the visitors. *Makes 'em feel important.* Not any more.

He shook the flag lieutenant's hand. "Let me know if . . ."

"Thank you, sir. I'll signal for your boat."

Adam thought of Jago, and said, "He'll be here. Waiting."

The door had opened a few inches, and he could see the red coats of the visitors, the scarlet of the sentry.

Jago would know already, and by tomorrow everybody would.

He left the cabin, noticing that the notebook still lay where it had fallen.

The flag lieutenant said, "I will tender your apology."

But the cabin was empty.

13 PRIDE AND ENVY

LUKE JAGO WIPED HIS GLEAMING RAZOR and held it to the light before laying it on a tray.

"Feel better, Cap'n? Ready for a new day?" He watched with approval as Adam stretched his arms and nodded.

It was early, with the morning watch still in force.

Adam felt the deck move slightly and saw Jago's razor slide across the tray. *Onward* was coming alive again. The pantry door was closed, but he knew that Morgan was not far away. Like the rest of them: waiting.

Jago said, "Meetin' at eight bells, Cap'n? I'll be standin' by, just in case." He did not go on. He did not need to.

Adam glanced aft toward the stern windows, remembering the flag lieutenant breaking the news. As if he were personally to blame. He said, "Does every one know about *Medusa?* You did, probably before me."

Jago said only, "There 'ave been a few whispers of late. Naval stores, an' then I 'eard tell of it from a fellow in the rigger's crew." He shrugged. "No secrets last long in this man's navy!"

"Well, Luke, until it's official . . ."

"Aye, aye, Cap'n. Not a word."

Adam turned toward the harbour again. Small wavelets cruising ahead of the breeze, seabirds rising and screeching in protest. The flags on other vessels moored or at anchor were no longer listless, but streaming out to a steady northwesterly. Like an omen. He felt his senses quicken. *Will you ever lose it?* Ready for sea. But when?

He walked back across the cabin, his hand briefly, unconsciously, touching the old chair.

Jago had seen it plenty of times. *Like old mates.* He waited for the moment. "What will become of Cap'n Tyacke?" And when Adam did not answer, he thought he had gone too far.

But Adam faced him eventually. "He is still the flag captain. An important post, ashore or afloat. They must take that into consideration."

He heard the distant chime, almost lost in the murmur of tackle and loose rigging. Eight bells. He straightened his back and said briskly to Jago, "At least it's not Friday!"

Jago heard the door open and close, the stamp of the Royal Marine sentry's boots. A different sentry in the time he had been here: it was now the forenoon watch. He smiled to himself. *Not Friday.* Only Bolitho would remember his coxswain's old superstition.

The skylight was partly open and he heard the pipe being repeated along the deck.

"Hands to quarters! Clean guns!"

He muttered aloud, "You just give the word, Cap'n. We'll scupper 'em!"

Even walking the short distance to the wardroom on the deck immediately beneath his own cabin, Adam was aware of the unusual stillness, the squeak of gun trucks very audible as an eighteen-pounder was manhandled for inspection and cleaning, with only an occasional shouted instruction. But the forenoon was usually the busiest time in a ship of war, especially at anchor. He knew it was largely imagination. But the feeling persisted.

The deck tilted slightly and shuddered. *In for a blow.* He could almost hear Julyan saying it.

A seaman on his knees polishing some brass scrambled to his feet as his captain approached, hesitated, and then ventured, "Mornin', sir."

Adam nodded. "Looks good, Savage." It was an easy name to remember, and the courtesy mattered. Some officers, even captains, never cared, until *they* were in trouble.

He saw Vincent waiting by the wardroom entrance. Perhaps he thought this meeting was a waste of time. He might be right.

The wardroom was unusually crowded. Apart from the officers and senior warrant officers, all the other warrants seemed to be present, the specialists or the "backbone," as Adam had heard his uncle describe them. The bosun and the gunner; Tilley, the sailmaker; and the cooper; and of course Hall, the carpenter, bent almost double because of his height. The tallest man in the ship. Probably anywhere . . . And one midshipman, Hotham, the senior. That had been Vincent's idea.

They were all seated. Adam was the visitor here.

Vincent said, "All present, sir, except the surgeon. He's still ashore."

"I knew that. But thank you." He looked around at the array of faces. "I expect most of you know, or might have suspected, that *Medusa,* our flagship, is being paid off." He saw a few quick, startled glances, but no real surprise. "She will lie in ordinary until her fate is decided."

He noticed Lieutenant Squire shaking his head, perhaps thinking of some particular ship in the past. At the end of the line . . .

Adam continued, "Our patrols will proceed, as ordered. But more and smaller ships will be needed." He paused. "And officers to command them." He saw Devereux, their new Royal Marine, turn as Prior, the clerk, bent to recover a few pages of his carefully written notes, which had fallen to the floor like dried leaves.

Adam had met Devereux only briefly when Vincent had introduced him for what he called "the formalities," and had liked what he saw. Keen, intelligent and open, even if he had been sent to *Onward* under something of a cloud. When he had asked Devereux if he were disturbed by the transfer from a seventy-four to a frigate, he had seemed unable to contain himself.

"On the contrary, sir, I feel *alive* again!"

Vincent had remarked with an odd sarcasm, "Thanks to your predecessor," although minutes earlier he had been making the newcomer welcome.

Adam heard the brief rumble of trucks directly overhead in the great cabin, and could imagine Morgan anxiously watching every move as an eighteen-pounder was checked. At least here in the wardroom, one deck lower, they were spared the presence of guns.

He reached for his hat and said, "We have a fine ship!"

Someone gave a cheer but was drowned out as Harry Drummond, the bosun, lurched to his feet, sending his chair crashing behind him. "An' we've got a fine captain!"

They were all standing now, some taking up the cheer as the door closed behind him. Adam stood quite still, for how long he did not know. The same seaman was nearby, now leaning on a broom. *I should not have insisted on coming. These same men trusted me, and some have paid dearly for it.*

A few minutes later Vincent joined him. It was quiet again. "I was wondering about cordage supplies, sir."

Their eyes met, captain and first lieutenant once more. Adam thought of Vincent's own words. *The ship comes first.* He was wrong.

"What the hell?" Vincent was staring at the ladder. There were muffled shouts and feet thudding on deck: a boat coming alongside, and making heavy weather of it. And here came Walker, their youngest midshipman, almost falling as he slithered to a halt.

"Officer of the guard, sir!" He held out a thick envelope. "For you, sir!"

Adam took it. The familiar buff colour, his own name and rank in perfect script. Walker puffed importantly, "It needs the captain's signature!"

Vincent snapped, "We *know* that."

Adam said, "Thank you, Mr. Walker," and smiled at the boy. "You must take more exercise. *Onward* is too confined for you."

The wardroom door was open, and Prior was waiting patiently with a pen and an ink container. Between his prominent teeth was a paper-knife. Nothing ever seemed to catch him unawares.

Like the burial service at sea or the Articles of War, Adam knew these words by heart. *Being in all respects ready for sea . . .*

Midshipman Walker, still panting, had brought a stool from

somewhere, and was looking on wide-eyed as Adam leaned down with the pen and signed his name.

Vincent said, "I'll give it to the officer of the guard, sir," but it sounded like a question.

Adam blew on the ink to dry it. "Sailing orders." He folded the main section and thrust it inside his coat. "The day after tomorrow, weather permitting." He moved toward the ladder. "I shall give it to him myself."

The wardroom door was still open, but there was not a sound to be heard.

Vincent repeated, "Day after tomorrow, sir?"

Adam wanted to smile. Jago, for one, would not be surprised. It was a Friday.

"We will talk soon." He paused, with one foot on the ladder. "The flag captain will be sailing with us."

Lieutenant James Squire stood by the forecastle in the eyes of the ship and gazed down at the anchor cable. He had done this too many times to remember, but the moment never failed to impress him, standing like this with his back turned on the remainder of the ship, sharing it only with the figurehead and his outthrust trident. Most people, even those who thought they knew him well, might be surprised by the intensity of his emotions.

He could feel the deck stirring under his feet, and the breeze was strong and steady, enough to create little waves beneath the stem as if *Onward* were eager and already under way. He should be used to it, but this time it felt different, and knowing why was no help.

He turned almost reluctantly and looked along the full length of the ship. Men being mustered in readiness for putting to sea. Senior hands checking names, others facing aft toward the quarterdeck. And the capstan, unmanned as yet. Twelve bars like the spokes of a wheel. Twelve men to each bar. He had known times when it had taken more, when wind and sea had joined to fight them before the anchor had broken free.

Squire saw the small knot of people near the big double wheel, Vincent pointing at something, and Julyan, the master, nodding as if in agreement. And along the upper deck and gangways a midshipman standing sturdily here and there, to relay messages or chase up stragglers if an order was not obeyed promptly.

He glanced over at his own two particular "young gentlemen," Napier and Simon Huxley. They had become part of his team in more ways than one, like the seamen around them, who knew exactly how far they could go before Squire had to put an edge to his voice. All in all, a good crew to control, although Squire would never have told them so.

The captain was nowhere in sight: probably still in his cabin, making sure he had forgotten nothing before the flag captain came aboard. A senior officer and the admiral's right hand . . . Squire had come up the hard way, and still nurtured many of the grudges and prejudices of the lower deck.

Onward had swung to her anchor and the flagship was almost hidden by canvas and rigging. Maybe the day of the "liner" had come to an end? The old Jacks scoffed about it, but when *Medusa* was paid off . . .

"Sir!" Midshipman Huxley was gesturing, interrupting the disturbing thoughts. "Boat leaving the flagship, sir!" He was a youth who rarely smiled, but he was a close friend of Napier's, and Squire was oddly proud of them both.

He looked away abruptly and saw the sudden bustle and excitement as the call was piped to muster all hands. The flag captain was cutting it fine, he thought. Sailing time was set for noon.

He had seen Lynch, the cook, leave his galley a while back, his old fiddle half-hidden by his apron, ready to get these feet stamping around the capstan while he still had the taste of rum on his lips to inspire him.

Squire walked deliberately to the opposite side of the deck, knowing from experience that the older hands always watched him at this critical moment in case he revealed any uncertainty. He half smiled. *Panic, rather.* The other anchor was catted, but ready to let go if there was a sudden emergency. None so far, but there was always a first time.

More shouts: the side party at their stations now to receive the flag captain. Even above that he could hear Lieutenant Monteith venting his impatience on someone in the afterguard, and saw two of his own men exchange grimaces. He could hardly blame them.

The wardroom was a small, private world, or should be. But as far as Squire was concerned, Monteith was still a stranger. Maybe Monteith had changed in some way since the landing party. *Or is it me?*

"Attention on deck! Face to starboard!"

Squire could hear the steady beat of oars, double-banked, although the boat was hidden by *Onward*'s side.

The captain would already be there to greet his superior. But it went deeper than that. There was friendship as well as a mutual respect: you could feel it when you saw them together. Bolitho, of course, was much younger than Tyacke, and he had never been a diplomat and found it harder to disguise his true feelings when he was under pressure. Like that moment when he had turned and said simply to Squire, "If I should fall . . ." And Squire remembered his own reply, spoken without hesitation.

He stared aft again, to gauge how much longer . . . But *Onward* had swung slightly at her anchor, and instead of moored harbour craft he could now see two large buildings, one with a long balcony: the Osprey Mission.

Would Claire see *Onward* when she weighed? Would she care? Now, all she wanted was to forget. But life had to be faced again and lived no matter what, and he would only be a painful reminder. Like the scars on her skin and her memory.

He knew that he was biting his lip, a habit he had sworn to conquer, and bellowed, "Stand by, lads!"

He saw Midshipman Napier reach over to touch his friend's arm. It was all still an adventure at their age.

Another voice: Harry Drummond, the bosun. "Man the capstan! Jump to it!" And the squeak of halliards as the Jack was lowered. For good or ill, the waiting was over.

"Heave, me bullies, *heave!*" More men running to throw their weight on the capstan bars, and a few marines piling arms in case their strength, too, would be required.

Squire found himself holding his breath until, after what seemed like an age, he heard the first metallic click from the capstan as the pawls began to move. The cable looked bar-taut, shining like metal as it took the full strain.

Vincent's voice rang out, clear and final. *"Hands aloft! Loose tops'ls!"*

Despite the orderly confusion Squire could hear the cook's fiddle, and his foot stamping time.

> *On Richmond Hill there lives a lass*
> *more bright than Mayday morn . . .*

The sun was behind Squire and he took a moment to look aloft where the topmen were already spacing themselves along the yards, like puppets against the sky. Skill and experience, the true seamen in any man-of-war. But for every one of them there was always a first time, too, and Squire had never forgotten the sight of the deck or the sea sway-ing so far beneath him. And the flick of a starter across his backside if he was slow about it.

The capstan was moving steadily, and he thought maybe a little faster, and *Onward* had swung in response to wind and current. The mission was hidden, the guardboat was pulling away, someone waving from the sternsheets. He heard one of his own men mutter a joke, and laugh as if completely untroubled.

Onward would stir any man's heart when she spread her canvas, and the anchor was catted just a few feet from his vantage point. And Claire might be watching. Remembering . . .

Squire studied the cable again, and the swirling traces of mud and sand in the water.

"Stand by!"

He saw Napier turn toward him and for a moment thought he had spoken her name aloud. He jabbed Napier's shoulder. "Pass the word! Larboard quarter!"

He knew Huxley had been watching the procedure closely. Perhaps imagining himself in his own ship one day. Like his father.

"Up and down, sir! Hove short!"

If the water was clear enough, *Onward*'s great shadow would be visible right now, reaching for her own anchor.

Click click click.

Squire stared aft again and saw the men on deck peering up at the yards, others ready at the braces. Like a familiar pattern but, as always, the captain stood alone.

Slower now. Some of the waiting marines had squeezed themselves into the revolving wheel of seamen. One of the scarlet uniforms was the new officer, Devereux. Squire had met him only briefly. It would take time. He was young.

He smiled. *Of course.* He held up his arm, and saw Vincent's immediate acknowledgment.

"Anchor's aweigh!"

Adam Bolitho listened to the capstan and felt the deck shudder beneath his feet as the anchor broke free of the ground. Two helmsmen were at the wheel, and Donlevy, the quartermaster, was standing by, as he had been since all hands had been piped. Julyan, the master—"Old Jolly" as he was called behind his back—was not far away, one of his mates beside him, slate and pencil poised for anything that might need recording in the log, or on a chart.

The shrouds and stays trembled and rattled as the first canvas broke and filled at the yards, and again the deck quivered as if other hands were trying to control the rudder.

Adam was standing in the shadow of the mizzen, just paces abaft the wheel, and without the sun in his eyes could see the full length of the ship. Squire and his men in the bows watching for the first sign of the anchor-ring, the "Jews-harp" as it was known, breaking the surface, so that it could be catted and made secure. More men being sent to the braces to lend their strength, and heave the great yards further round until each sail was full-bellied and stiff in the wind. A few men slipping in the struggle with wind and sea. To the landsman or casual onlooker, it must appear utter confusion until order was finally restored, topsails set, and the unruly jib trimmed and sharp, like the fin of a shark.

Adam watched the shore moving now as *Onward* gathered way, and the two hills which had become familiar, essential landmarks for this final run to the headland, and beyond to the open sea.

He leaned back now, gazing at the spread of canvas above, the masthead pendant stiff as a lance in the wind. Some topmen were making a lashing secure, or waving to others on the foretop, apparently indifferent to the distance from the deck.

The shudder again: the rudder taking charge.

"Anchor's secured, sir." Vincent was watching critically as the capstan bars were stowed away.

Adam thought he heard Jago's voice above the thud of canvas and the chorus of rigging. He was standing near the boat tier kicking a wedge like a gun-quoin into place, to make them more secure for sea. He seemed to feel Adam's eyes on him and twisted round to give his little gesture, like a private signal. So many times.

"Fall out the anchor party!"

More voices now: the nippers, youngsters who would be joining others stowing the incoming cable after they had scrubbed every fathom of it. Adam beckoned to Midshipman Hotham, who was standing by the flag-locker, a telescope over his shoulder.

Hotham said, "No signal, sir. Only the acknowledgment to mine." He almost blushed. "*Ours,* sir!"

Adam levelled the glass but regretted it: in the short time since they had up-anchored, the bearing and distance had completely changed. The flagship now seemed bows-on, her masts in line and her figurehead unusually bright in the sunlight. Her pendant was still flying, but her ensign was obscured by the high poop. No boats alongside, and nobody on deck as *Onward* had passed. A ship already dead. He thought of the flag lieutenant. *Finished.*

He handed back the telescope and wondered why he had left his own in the great cabin beneath his feet. He glanced at the skylight, covered now by a heavy grating as a precaution while getting under way, in case something should fall from aloft. *Easier than cutting new glass*, he had heard Hall, the carpenter, remark.

But he was thinking of Tyacke. They had scarcely spoken since he had climbed aboard. There had been only a quick, firm handshake and an apology for his abrupt arrival, then he had made a point of going straight below where Morgan would make certain he was not disturbed. If that was possible in any man-of-war preparing for sea.

Adam knew it was why he had left the old telescope there. Tyacke was probably focusing it even now, watching the harbour opening out, headlands sliding aside for their departure.

Or looking astern at *Medusa*?

"Southwest-by-south, sir!" Julyan was by the compass box, his lips pursed in a silent whistle. "Full an' bye!"

Adam looked up at the yards, braced hard round, sails firm but not flapping or losing the wind. The ship was performing well. The topmen or those on the lee gangway could be looking down at their own reflections by now. And unless . . . He felt his mouth soften into a smile. *Unless* was every captain's sheet-anchor.

He thought again of Tyacke, when they had last spoken. The only other sound had been the first clink of the capstan.

"We're going to New Haven." He had paused, regarding Adam searchingly. "You already knew, didn't you?"

Adam had answered, "I guessed."

Tyacke had shaken his head. "There's a hell of a lot of Sir Richard in you, Adam, and I'm bloody glad of it!" He had still been smiling when the cabin door had closed.

But what was Tyacke thinking now, alone with his memories? A born sailor, and an officer of distinction. *The devil with half a face.*

He turned as he heard Monteith's voice, not for the first time since the capstan had been manned: "What d' you mean, you didn't understand? Are you so stupid? Do I have to say everything twice?"

Adam knew Vincent was watching. So much had happened. Men had died and he had blamed himself, but he was proud, too. Of them.

The responsibility is mine.

He looked toward the land again and did not need a glass to see that the two hills were beginning to overlap. Soon now they would alter course, and with the wind in their favour make more sail. A lot of the canvas was still new, untried. He had heard Julyan say, "That'll shake the gum out of 'em!"

He saw the surgeon by one of the guns, pausing to speak with Squire, gesturing at the headland. Different worlds, but they seemed firm friends now.

Three bells rang out from the forecastle as *Onward* altered course. One and a half hours exactly since the anchor had been secured to Squire's satisfaction. Into the deeper, stronger swell of open water, with a temporary stand-easy as a hasty meal was arranged for most of the ship's company, the welcome aroma of rum reaching even the great cabin when Adam quit the quarterdeck for the first time.

After the sun and reflected glare, the cabin seemed almost dark. But the grating had been removed from the skylight and Tyacke was sitting at the table, a folio of papers and an enlarged section of chart pressed under one elbow.

He seemed about to stand but changed his mind as the deck tilted suddenly, in time with the shudder from the rudder. "Getting lively, eh?"

Adam sat opposite him and heard the pantry door creak. Hugh Morgan was on his toes, as always. "I'll get the t'gallants on her when I have more sea-room, sir."

Tyacke made to lift his hand but put it back down immediately as some of his papers began to follow *Onward*'s motion. "No formality, Adam—not here, anyway." His blue eyes moved briefly around the cabin, with an expression Adam could not determine. "I'm only a passenger this time. The admiral's errand boy." He had twisted round in his chair to look at the spray-dappled glass. "Nothing like it, is there?"

Adam noticed that the old telescope was wedged in the bench seat, within reach. He said quietly, "You could have stayed on deck with me," and Tyacke shook his head, laughing.

"Not likely—it's bad enough with one captain at a time. I should know!" He looked up as something fell on the deck overhead, and there was a shout, and the thud of bare feet as men ran to respond.

When he looked back at Adam he seemed calm, even relaxed. "As I'm sure you know, there is no love lost between Rear-Admiral Langley and Sir Duncan Ballantyne at New Haven. Your visit was overshadowed by that bloody business at the mission. But for your action, I don't know how we would have found out the truth."

He touched the papers. "The schooner you discovered and captured gave us a few clues. She was once a privateer, then she was taken by the French almost at the close of the war. Then sold, and bought by a yard in England. She ended up here in Africa. As a slaver."

Adam remembered the hazardous passage in the *Delfim*. The warning maroon. He said, "New Haven is the key. Somebody must know."

Tyacke smiled faintly, so that his scars seemed more livid. "The 'carpet knight'?"

"We have no proof."

Tyacke stretched his arms and some of his papers slid to the deck. "Then we'll find some!" And for a second, Adam saw "the devil with half a face," more feared than any other by the slavers. "Tomorrow, first thing, I want to go over the charts with you, and any one else you care to call. I have some 'instructions' from the admiral for Ballantyne." He broke off just as abruptly, and gave Adam the piercing stare again. "What did you make of our honourable guest, by the way?"

Adam heard more running feet, then silence. Vincent could cope. Was probably enjoying it, in fact.

"I had the impression he had already made up his mind."

Tyacke nodded slowly, his eyes steady. "As I said earlier, so like Sir Richard. And I agree."

The pantry door opened an inch. "May I bring some wine, sir? Or a little something from the cask?"

Tyacke looked at his papers and shook his head. "Not for me. Later, mebbee." He grinned. "If I'm asked, that is." He looked over at Adam. "These are *your* quarters, after all."

"Yours, too." Adam gestured to the high-backed bergère. "I shall be *there* until we're well clear of local craft." He stood up; he had heard footsteps outside the screen door. "But now . . ."

There was a tap on the door.

"Midshipman of the watch, *sir!*"

It was Napier, droplets of spray glittering on his sleeves. "First lieutenant's respects, sir." Their eyes met. "Requests permission to loose t'gallants?"

Adam saw Morgan bringing his hat. Tyacke was quite still, watching them.

He touched the boy's arm. "How are *you*, David?" So formal. Withdrawn. How it had to be. "My compliments to the first lieutenant. I shall come now."

But Napier had already hurried on ahead, having glimpsed something in the flag captain's scarred face, and holding the knowledge to himself like a secret. Understanding and regret, a strange sadness.

And envy.

14 SURVIVAL

THE TWO CAPTAINS STOOD side by side at the chart table while the ship seemed to quieten around them. It was the forenoon watch, their first at sea.

At moments like this Adam felt as though his senses were still on deck, or in some obscure part of *Onward*'s hull where someone or something was related to certain sounds or movements. The morning watchkeepers groping their way below for a hurried meal and stowing their hammocks in the nettings, probably not long before all hands were piped to make or reef more sail. The wind had remained steady and fairly strong, and men working aloft had to be doubly careful. But spirits were high, with the ship alive and responding well to her helm.

He felt the table press into his hip, then withdraw, as if *Onward* were holding her breath before the next plunge. He was conscious of Tyacke's silent concentration, broken only when he scribbled a note on the pad at his elbow, or used a glass to magnify tiny print or some diagram Julyan had already provided.

Tyacke said as if thinking aloud, "It's just as well that you've visited New Haven before," and smiled without looking up. "So have I. Unofficially."

Adam heard Squire's strong voice from the quarterdeck: officer of the watch, doing what he enjoyed most, holding the ship in his hands. For him, it had been a long journey. Vincent would be snatching some breakfast before taking over matters of discipline and routine.

Tyacke was saying, "The admiral wanted Ballantyne to maintain complete records of every vessel, cargo, and owner using the harbour and approaches." He smiled sarcastically. "To save *us* money."

Adam shook his head. "One day, maybe, if New Haven ever becomes another Freetown."

Tyacke said shortly, "Not in our lifetime!"

Julyan interjected, "Will you excuse me, sir? I believe I need my other log," and slipped out, closing the door behind him.

Tyacke seemed to relax visibly. "Now we can talk."

They both knew Julyan had left deliberately.

Tyacke tapped the chart. "There's too much money invested in slavery to expect a few laws and some keen patrols to put a stop to it. I've tried to explain this to our admiral. He won't listen, of course. All he can see is the next step up his personal ladder—and soon, he thinks." He stared around the small chartroom as if he felt trapped by it. "It's all I've heard since he hoisted his flag over *Medusa*. I hope they appreciate it at the bloody Admiralty, or wherever they decide these things!"

He touched Julyan's old octant, which the master liked to keep on display. "To hell with it. I shouldn't let it scupper me like this—in front of you, of all people."

Adam touched his arm. "I'll not forget," and smiled. "Did you manage to get any sleep?"

Surprisingly, the scarred face lightened into a broad grin. "A damn sight better than you, I'll wager. That chair was empty every time I woke up!" Then he glanced toward the door. "He's coming back. Thinks he's given us long enough to trade secrets."

When Julyan entered with a new chart folded beneath his arm, he found both of them joking and very much at ease. As he had intended. One captain was enough.

Lieutenant Mark Vincent sat at one end of the table and flattened out the list reminding him of several outstanding tasks. Not that there were many: he tried to be certain of that wherever possible. He had been on deck in charge of the morning watch, and was still feeling the strain of a first night at sea after a long spell at anchor. Men working in the darkness, falling over their own feet, waiting for the dawn.

He pushed a plate aside, but could hardly remember what the messman had offered him. The wardroom was empty, which was the way he liked it while he was sorting out his tasks and duties. At sea again, but for how long? *Onward* had left England on a mission, and that was completed. So why the delay? Chasing slavers was not work for a fine frigate like this one.

He tried to smother another yawn. The captain wanted the gun crews to exercise action today, either to reassure or impress their senior passenger. And the purser had asked for some stores to be shifted again. The man always seemed to have something stowed in the wrong place, and never made the discovery until after they had weighed anchor.

Vincent thought of the frigate *Zealous*, which they had left riding untroubled at her anchor. Her captain was apparently too new and inexperienced to be entrusted with a passenger like Tyacke, but how else would he gain the necessary confidence? He knew he was being intolerant, unfair to a complete stranger, but after this, what would follow for him?

He swung round in the chair and saw Monteith hovering by the door.

"I was told that you wanted to see me." Monteith's eyes flickered toward the other door, which was swinging half open.

Vincent said curtly, "There's nobody in there," and looked at his watch, which was lying on the table beside his list. "You're with a working party up forrard, aren't you?"

Monteith had his head on one side, an irritating habit Vincent always tried to ignore. "I left them with *full* instructions. It's not the first time I've told them what I expect when I'm needed elsewhere."

Vincent leaned back in his chair and attempted to appear in command. He should be used to Monteith by now, and immune to him. They shared the daily routine, in harbour and in action, and they shared the only escape: this wardroom.

He said, "I know you better than most of the hands you deal with.

Harsh, perhaps unfair treatment of men in front of their messmates can easily rebound on the one in authority, *and* at the wrong time. I don't want to make an issue of it."

Monteith seemed to draw himself up with a cocky indignation. "Has the captain said as much? If so, I'd like—"

Vincent slapped the table. "Between *us!* But the captain isn't deaf, *or* blind, so get a grip on your temper when you're handling the people!"

Monteith retorted, "I hope I know my duty, *Mister* Vincent!"

The door clicked open, and one of the messmen entered with a bucket. Vincent stood abruptly, and snapped, "And so do *I*, Mr. Monteith!"

He realised too late that he was standing with his fist raised, his limbs adjusting independently to the motion of the hull, but it was a moment he would always remember, like those other times: Monteith, mouth half open for another outburst, the messman still holding the bucket, his eyes fixed on the two lieutenants.

Wind and sea, sails and rigging. The sound might have gone unheard.

"Gunfire!" he said.

Perhaps he was mistaken. Then he thought he heard someone shout, a young voice, a midshipman's, but it reminded him of his early days at sea, and the Battle of Lissa. The last major sea-fight of the war. Vincent had never forgotten it, or his captain, William Hoste, who, at the age of twelve, had served under Nelson in his famous *Agamemnon*. Hoste had once complimented Vincent on his "attention to detail."

He snatched up his little list and said, "I'll see *you* on deck!"

On the upper deck the hot wind was almost refreshing after the sealed wardroom. The watchkeepers were at their stations, and working parties, including Monteith's, were going about their various tasks without any visible excitement. Vincent quickened his pace, rebuttoning his coat when he saw Bolitho and the flag captain together near the wheel. Squire was close by, gesturing up at the masthead.

The two captains turned as Vincent joined the group by the wheel, and Tyacke said, "You heard it too, eh?" He stared aloft. "Good lookouts, but nothing reported."

Drummond, the bosun, said quickly, "I've put young Tucker at the fore," and to Tyacke, "One of my mates, sir. Used to be our best topman. Not much escapes *his* eye."

Adam moved away a few paces. "I'm sorry you were disturbed, Mark." He looked along the deck to where Monteith had just reappeared, and was standing with his back to them. A heavier hand might still be required there, but it would not be Vincent's decision.

Tyacke said, "I know of two other patrol vessels on this stretch. *Endeavour* and *Challenger*, both brigantines."

Vincent said automatically, "Commander Mason, *Challenger*. A good man, by all accounts."

Tyacke nodded. "It's only a matter of time."

He did not explain, and Adam had seen how hard it was for him to remain detached from any plan that might have been decided.

Adam unslung his telescope and walked to the side. Despite the steady wind and occasional bursts of spray over the deck, his shoes were sticking to the seams in the heat. He levelled the glass and focused it, but it was the same unending coastline, monotonous, like a solid bank of motionless cloud. The edge of Julyan's "invisible valley." He licked his lips: they tasted like dried leather.

"Excuse me, sir." It was Maddock, the gunner, shading his eyes with his hat to peer up at Squire. "We was supposed to exercise the gun crews this forenoon."

Vincent interrupted, "I'll have it piped when . . ."

He got no further. There were more shots, hurried and in rapid succession. Adam tried to see it in his mind. A brigantine, but no return fire, and the echoes were lost almost immediately in the slap and boom of canvas and the thud of *Onward*'s rudder. "Shaking the trunk," old sailors called it.

Drummond called, "Nothing in sight, sir!"

With the others, Tyacke was staring up at the maintop, and then toward the land. "Everybody's staying well clear today . . . Better maintain our course until—"

He turned to look at Adam and saw the flash reflected in his eyes.

Several seconds seemed to pass before they heard the explosion, like a clap of thunder. Then nothing, not even an echo.

Adam said, "Midshipman Hotham will go aloft and speak with the lookouts." He saw Napier watching. "You, too," and their eyes met. *"Easy does it."*

Tyacke moved to the compass box and glanced up at the mast-head pendant. "I suggest you carry on with your gunnery exercise." He walked to the side. "If it's proof we need, we'll have it soon enough."

David Napier climbed into the shrouds and steadied his feet on the ratlines to get his balance. The tar on the rough cordage, heated by the sun, felt as if it were still fresh. He began to climb, but not before he had seen more figures crowding on deck, some peering at the land, or the empty horizon to starboard. He had also seen his friend Simon Huxley beside the quartermaster on the quarterdeck, ready to pass any new orders along the gangway: a "walking speaking-trumpet," a role all the midshipmen hated.

A ship had been blown up, how or why they must discover.

I am not afraid. The thought reassured him, like a hand on the shoulder.

Squire stood watching the two climbing midshipmen until they were hidden by the curve of the main topsail and those few seamen still working aloft. The wind had remained steady, and the motion seemed easier after the last alteration of course: they were now steering due south.

He walked to the quarterdeck rail and stared along the ship's length, from the visible cathead where he had seen the anchor made fast, to the place where he now stood on watch and in command, unless anything else happened.

The captain had gone below to the chartroom with his senior officer, leaving Squire with just a nod: the words, "Call me," had not needed to be spoken. Unlike some captains he had known, he thought.

He looked toward the land. Hard to believe anything had happened to rouse *Onward* to this state of tension and readiness. A few shots and then the flash, the explosion. It might have been something ashore, but his ears were trained to such things. But where? How?

He saw Vincent by the fore hatch, some seamen gathered nearby, gun captains and quarter gunners, who were each responsible for the responses and efficiency of four of the eighteen-pounders: *Onward*'s teeth. Any moment now and they would exercise action. And this time it would have a stronger significance for all concerned.

Monteith was walking aft, apparently deep in thought. He had been below with Vincent when the first shots had been heard. Squire did not know the reason, but could guess. He closed his mind to it. Despite his age and seniority, he still felt like a stranger in the wardroom.

He walked to the side and gazed at the sea creaming away from the quarter. Except at times like this, when the ship was his.

He blinked as a bird seemed to drop from nowhere, hit the water and rise immediately, a catch in its beak like a sliver of silver.

"He'll be eating that ashore while we're still pounding along out here!"

Murray was so light on his feet Squire had not heard him crossing the deck. The surgeon was in uniform, but carrying one of his familiar smocks over his arm.

Squire said dryly, "Always prepared, aren't you?"

The hawk-like profile was surveying the deck. "They say sound moves faster over water than land." He faced Squire. "I've been wanting to talk with you, James. But I was ashore most of the time before we sailed." He paused. "And I gave my word, you see."

"You saw Claire. I had a feeling about it. Ever since . . ." He waited until a seaman coiling a halliard over his arm passed, without appearing to see them. "I've been thinking about her. Quite a lot."

Murray repeated, "I gave my word." He crossed himself with his free hand and gave a thin smile. "Until we sailed, at least. She didn't want you to concern yourself." Then, with a touch of impatience, "It's for your own good, man. She's still reliving her experiences. That's only too common, in my experience, although in my profession we tend to underestimate the damage to the mind." He fell silent as a bosun's mate walked toward the fore hatch, moistening his silver call with his tongue.

Then he said, "Am I wrong about this, Jamie?"

Squire said, staring at the sea, "I have nothing to offer her," then looked steadily at Murray. "But I've never felt like this about any woman." He shrugged, trying to dismiss it. "I'll probably never see her again, anyway."

Murray gripped his wrist with surprising strength. "*I hope you do.* For both your sakes."

Whatever else he might have said was interrupted by the shrill of the call: "All hands! All hands to exercise action!"

Murray turned to leave the quarterdeck, the white smock streaming from his arm. But he paused long enough to watch the gun crews running to their stations, each man no doubt thinking that the next time would be in deadly earnest.

He had seen too much of it, and there was always the bloody aftermath. He looked aft again but Squire was by the compass box, calling to the two helmsmen. Where he belonged, Murray thought.

Above all of them, David Napier climbed into the foretop and paused to regain his breath. He had already visited the maintop, and had left Midshipman Hotham with another lookout.

Tucker greeted him with a grin and a thumbs-up. "Too much good food, David," and Napier loosened his shirt.

"Not as young as I was, *David!*"

They both laughed.

Napier looked across the larboard bow, balanced and shading his eyes against the fierce glare. It was an exciting sensation, this towering structure of masts, spars and canvas all quivering with power. He could recall when he had been too scared to release his grip, let alone dare to look down at the ship beneath him.

He asked, "Are you settled now?"

Tucker shrugged. "Now an' then I find meself looking up at the t'gallant yards, an' further!"

Napier felt the barricade press into his hip as the mast leaned over again, thinking of Hotham, who had already been appointed acting lieutenant more than once. He would be the next to confront the

Inquisition. And at some time in the future, with luck, it would be his own turn. Once it had seemed impossible: he had not even dared to imagine it. He felt himself smile. Back in those days when Bolitho's cousin Elizabeth had called him his captain's servant.

He realised that Tucker had said something and must have repeated it: he was suddenly tense.

"Could I use your glass?" Tucker pushed some hair from his eyes, and seemed oblivious to the deck and the sea far beneath him.

Napier watched his profile as he adjusted the telescope with strong fingers, pausing only to murmur, "Not a patch on Sir Richard's old glass, eh, Dave?" But he was not smiling.

Tucker handed the telescope back to Napier. "I wasn't sure. It's still too far."

Napier steadied the glass and knew Tucker was waiting for his reaction. He could see nothing but the glare like metal on the water, and the constant change of colour and movement, the swell steep and angry in the steady wind. There was nothing solid, nothing you could describe or recognise. Only flotsam, fragments driven by wind and tide; it might have covered several miles.

But it had once been a living vessel.

"I'll tell him!" He was halfway into the lubber's hole when Tucker called out, "Slow down! We don't want to lose you!"

Napier hesitated, one foot dangling in the air. "I want the captain to know *you* saw it first!"

He knew Tucker was still gazing after him as his feet found the first ratline.

He was not even breathless when he completed his descent and scrambled onto the starboard gangway. The picture in his mind was as vivid as the moment he had seen it.

The gun drill had stopped or been curtailed, but most of the crew were still at their stations. Those on the starboard side looked up as his shadow passed, and their upturned faces were full of questions. Napier knew the first lieutenant was there, but avoided him and kept his eyes on the quarterdeck at the end of the gangway, his pace steady and unhurried. Something he had learned from experience.

They were all there, as if they had not moved in all the time he had been crouched high above them. The captain came to meet him, the others remaining grouped near the compass and wheel.

"D' you need time for a second wind, David?" He said it kindly, turning him a little away from the others. Napier felt a shiver run through his body, although the sun was hot across his shoulders.

He said, "Wreckage, sir," and gestured ahead, and saw some seamen turn to scan the empty horizon. "On either bow, sir. Pieces. No part of ship we could recognise." He faltered, realising that another shadow had joined theirs. It was the flag captain.

He swallowed hard but straightened his back in response as Tyacke smiled and said, "Don't stop, Mr. Napier. I've heard every word so far," and averted his face slightly, as if he knew that the scars were disturbing Napier.

The boy gulped and pressed on. "The lookout, David Tucker, saw it first, sir. Even without a glass. He *knew.*"

Tyacke said, "A good man, I hear."

Napier saw Drummond, the bosun, who was standing with the others, give him a quick nod. *I told you so.*

Napier went on, "A small vessel, sir," and fell silent as Tyacke turned back, and seemed to measure his response.

"Perhaps. We must do more than hope." He gazed at the sea, indifferent to the metallic glare. "The wreckage lies across our course." He looked up at the masthead pendant. "An hour? Two at the most?"

Adam nodded, aware that Vincent had come aft to join them. Even men off watch or excused from deck duty seemed to have gathered, and the cook with one of his assistants was peering out from the galley hatch, probably wondering if it would interrupt his schedule. Lieutenant Devereux was in animated conversation with Sergeant Fairfax, breaking down the inevitable barrier of his predecessor's death. He could sense Tyacke's mind working, his patience perhaps running out.

Adam said, "We shall shorten sail but hold this course, until we can discover more evidence."

It was enough for the moment. They all had plenty to think about. He looked down over the quarterdeck and saw Jago leaning against the boat tier. "We'll need a boat if we find anything." Almost as if Jago had put the thought into his mind.

He turned back as Vincent said, "I should like to take the boat, sir."

"I shall remember that when the time comes, Mark." He glanced up at the taut canvas. "But shorten sail when you've mustered the hands."

Vincent half smiled. "Aye, aye, sir!"

Adam saw Midshipman Huxley leading Napier to the companion; Tyacke must have already slipped away unseen to the great cabin. They had not spoken of it, but Tyacke must be wondering what the admiral would have in store for him when they eventually returned to Freetown. And after that?

It was as if the whole ship had been waiting for the word. Drummond did not need to use his call.

"Hands aloft! Move yourselves, there!"

Squire stood beside the wheel and listened to the squeal of tackles as the gig was lowered from the quarter davits. It was never an easy task with the ship at sea, after first manhandling it from the tier below the quarterdeck, and he could hear one of the helmsmen's heavy breathing as he fought to hold the helm steady and the compass under control. Under reefed topsails and jib *Onward* was a different creature, her performance sluggish, at the mercy of the wind instead of commanding it. Jago looked up, waiting, as Vincent judged the right moment before clambering down to join him.

Someone called, "Hope they got strong arms, Luke! It'll be a hard pull!"

Julyan was standing by, and Squire heard him mutter, "Hope they have strong stomachs, more likely."

Squire stared from bow to bow, feeling the deck shudder to the surge and plunge of the rudder. The gig was moving away, clear of the quarter, oars already lowered and motionless like wings. It was not a light boat but it seemed to move like a leaf on a mill-race, and yet Jago remained on his feet, his hand on the tiller. Vincent was squatting in the stern-sheets, hatless, and shielding his eyes from the spray now being thrown up by the blades.

A few strokes while the gig pulled clear, and there were already fragments of wood, badly charred, being carried between them. Further away there were larger pieces which must have been blown from the hull by the explosion. A hatch cover, a few broken gratings, and farther still, a piece of spar. A small vessel then, maybe a cutter or schooner.

He tensed as something gleamed through the swell and vanished. A shark. Vincent might have seen it. He would not need reminding of the last time, when he had boarded the sinking, abandoned *Moonstone*. Jago had been with him then, and Napier also. Like a pattern for the events that followed.

He heard the captain's voice, clear and unhurried. "Tell Mr. Monteith to put more men larboard side forrard!" A pause. "You do it, Sinden."

Someone shouted from the gangway nearby. Squire knew it was Midshipman Walker, their youngest, and no stranger to action or to danger. But his cry was like that of a girl.

Men were already running to the side, one carrying a grapnel and line. It was a corpse, but someone must have secured him alive to the hatch cover after the explosion, where the shark had reached him. A terrible death.

Squire heard the captain cross to the opposite side of the quarter-deck and thought he heard Julyan's voice. Perhaps asking a question.

And the reply. "No, we'll alter course when I'm satisfied. Not before."

It seemed an eternity, the sea was almost empty again. It was only one man's decision. *Suppose it was mine?* He thought of Vincent, the expression on his face when he had volunteered for the boat party. He would never admit defeat . . .

He turned as a shout rang through the chorus of sounds from loose canvas and shrouds.

"Deck there!" It was Midshipman Hotham, still in the maintop with his big signals telescope.

The sun had shifted, or was hidden by a partly reefed sail. Adam stared up at the arm pointing from the top and trained his own glass on the same bearing. A mistake, perhaps? Or Vincent signalling to admit failure and request support for his exhausted oarsmen?

Adam tried again, waiting for the gig to reappear. The swell was deep enough to hide it completely. He held his breath and watched the one upright figure.

Then he lowered the telescope and said quietly, "They've found somebody. Alive."

"Give way, together!" Jago lurched against the tiller bar, keeping his balance as the oars brought the gig under control. It took all their skill and strength to do it, with the sea rising and sliding away on either beam as if to swallow them.

The gig carried two extra men, standing in the bows with boathooks to fend off any floating debris that might impede the stroke or damage the hull. They had both struggled aft to help haul the survivor inboard, and now he was lying in the sternsheets, his shoulders propped against Vincent; the first lieutenant's breeches were soaked with blood. He was gulping air unsteadily, sometimes rasping and shuddering as if losing the fight.

The stroke oarsman gasped, "Don't give up, matey!" and Jago glared at him.

"Save yer breath, or you'll be the next!" Jago stared at the man they had found clinging face down to a piece of framework, the sort used to separate cargo in a small vessel's hold. It had been intact, not even scorched.

He watched Vincent unfastening the sodden coat. It was green, like the uniforms of the "private army," as he had heard one of the marines call it, which he had seen during their visit to New Haven. He scowled. Who the hell had given it a name like that? He recalled the brief gunfire and later, that one God-awful explosion. Nothing made sense.

Someone said, "Pity our doc ain't with us!"

Vincent did not look up, but snapped, "So pull harder. He could do no better out here!"

Jago would have smiled at any other time. *Bloody officers.* But he reached down from the tiller-bar and gripped the hand which had suddenly returned to life. Weak at first, as if unable or unwilling to find hope, and ice-cold, although the thwarts and bottom boards were bone-dry in the sun.

The eyes were suddenly wide open, unblinking, and Jago tightened his grip.

"Steady as she goes, matey. Just a bit longer!"

He had seen a lot of men fighting for life in all the years he had served at sea. And had watched plenty of them give up. The eyes were still on his. Not fear. It was disbelief.

Vincent dragged his hand into the sunlight. Some dried blood, but nothing much. He spoke softly, his voice almost drowned by the creak and thud of oars.

"Broken ribs. The explosion." He glanced at the oars, slowing now. The breathing was louder. "As soon as we get him aboard . . ." He did not finish, knowing the man was trying to turn his head to look at his face, or perhaps the uniform.

Vincent leaned over him. There was more blood on his own white breeches. "We're taking you to safety. Try to rest. You're among friends now."

Jago eased the tiller yet again and watched *Onward* as she appeared to lengthen across the gig's stem. There would be many helping hands once he had managed to work his way alongside, without much of a lurch. He thought of Vincent. Strict but fair, not a hard-horse like some. He tried to smile. *Like most.* But the smile did not come.

He eyed the masts, the poop, the big ensign streaming from the gaff above. Closer now, men on the gangway, some running, tackle being hoisted as a further guide, where the surgeon would be waiting.

"Bows!" *Onward* was reaching out to receive them, with extra ladders and rope fenders to cushion the impact as he guided the final few strokes of the sweating oarsmen. *Onward* was rolling, reefed sails still holding the wind, showing her copper one minute and then the reflection of her gunports as she dipped toward him. Jago shut everything else

from his mind, conscious of the man's grip on his ankle as he was trying to keep his balance and fix the moment. Nothing else could interfere.

Vincent was calming the survivor, and he was suddenly silent, as if he thought he had imagined the ship so close.

Jago shouted, "Oars!" and as the blades lifted and steadied, showering spray over the men beneath, he was unsettled by the silence. A heaving line snaked out of nowhere and was seized by one of the bowmen.

Vincent must have stumbled or been taken unawares by the motion. The rescued man had dragged himself on to his knees and was staring up at Jago as he eased the tiller for the impact.

His voice was cracked, strangled, but as the stroke oarsman came to Jago's aid he began shouting at the top of his voice. It was garbled, meaningless. Then he stared directly into Jago's eyes again. As if he was judging the moment, holding him: Jago could not look away.

A voice not much different from his own. Loud and very distinct, but only one word.

"Mutiny!"

His eyes were still wide open. But he was dead.

It was not dark in the cabin, but it seemed almost gloomy after the activity on deck.

Adam stood by the stern windows, his hand on the bench, feeling the motion, the regular thud of the rudder. The sea was streaked with gold, the last sunlight, and there seemed no horizon. Behind him Tyacke was sitting at the little desk, his shoeless feet protruding into a slanting patch of coppery light. Someone was hammering overhead, but otherwise the ship noises seemed very subdued.

Tyacke said suddenly, "Tomorrow, then?" and Adam nodded.

"At this rate, some time in the afternoon. Maybe later if the wind drops inshore." He could picture the chart in his mind. He glanced at the bergère and dismissed the idea. If he gave in now, it would take another explosion to wake him.

He had been on deck again a moment ago. Almost deserted but for the watchkeepers, and a few anonymous figures sitting by the guns or looking at the sea alongside. And the canvas-wrapped body beside one of the eighteen-pounders, not for burial this time.

Tyacke had remarked, "They'll want to know. To be sure." It was curt, but it made sense.

He had struggled to his feet now and was looking for his shoes. "Your cox'n, Jago—he did well today. I told him so."

Adam heard the pantry door open perhaps an inch. He recalled Jago's face as Tyacke had spoken to him. And something else. Vincent had said nothing to him. He could imagine Jago's voice. *Bloody officers!*

And the surgeon, who had been waiting to examine the dead man when he was hoisted aboard. When Murray had made his report, his hands red from scrubbing, he had said simply, "I don't know how he managed to stay alive."

Tyacke had replied only, "But now we know *why!*"

He was looking toward the pantry door now, and raised his voice a little. "A lifetime ago somebody suggested that a drink, maybe two, might be forthcoming!"

Morgan padded softly to the table and put two glasses within reach, frowning and tutting as the deck tilted and the rudder groaned in protest. They each took a glass, and Morgan filled them without spilling a drop, murmuring, "Your health, gentlemen."

Tyacke drank deeply and gestured to Morgan to refill his glass, and said almost wistfully, "Like old times."

Sir Richard Bolitho's flag captain would never forget.

15 SEEK AND DESTROY

ADAM BOLITHO PAUSED near the top of the companion ladder to prepare himself. He felt the air on his face, cool and refreshing, stirring the folds of his clean shirt. The coolness would be brief. The morning watch was only an hour old, the ship almost quiet except for sounds which, like his own breathing, were too familiar to notice.

It had been a moonless night, so that the stars had seemed exceptionally bright, paving the sky from horizon to horizon. He thought he had slept reasonably well in the bergère with his feet propped on a stool which Morgan must have put there, but he had heard Tyacke cry out during the night. Somebody's name: a woman's. But the sleeping cabin door had remained closed, and he had heard nothing more.

He braced his shoulders and mounted the last of the steps. It was always like this at the end of a passage. You could *feel* the nearness of land, even imagine you could smell it. And there was always the doubt. The uncertainty. He touched his chin and smiled ruefully. He had shaved himself, not as well as Jago would have, but if anybody needed rest now it was his coxswain.

Figures were already turning toward him as he stepped on to the quarterdeck. His white shirt would have been like a beacon in the dimness before dawn, and he had always hated stealth, unlike a few officers he could have named.

Vincent had the watch and was standing by the compass box, its tiny flame reflecting in his eyes. He said, "Wind's eased a bit, sir. But I thought I'd wait for some light before sending the hands aloft to spread more sail. Besides . . ."

"It's better to see than be seen. I agree." Adam looked at the spread of canvas which seemed to contain their world. The sea on either beam was still black.

Vincent hesitated. "Can we expect trouble when we make a land-fall, sir?"

Adam rested both hands on the quarterdeck rail and looked toward the forecastle. Beyond the pale stretch of deck, there was little to see: the vague shadows of hatches and the regular black shapes which were the breeches of the guns, and now an occasional spectre of spray rising, then fading, above a gangway. His brain was shaking off any lingering desire for sleep.

He faced Vincent and said, "I think we always have to expect trouble, Mark. Especially after what you discovered." He saw him glance in the direction of the guns, where the canvas-wrapped body was stowed. "As soon as we call hands and it's safe enough, I want top-chains hoisted and rigged at the yards."

Vincent showed his teeth. "Thought you might, sir. If we're called on to fight, there could be casualties enough without falling spars adding to the bill."

Adam almost smiled. No doubt the admiral would describe them as "unsightly."

Vincent gestured toward the sea. "Surely they'd never dare fire on a King's ship?"

Somebody called out and another hurried to obey. But Adam was reminded of Tyacke's comment when they had been alone together. *Our flag flies in many lands, but not always by invitation. To most of them, we're still the invaders.*

There was a sudden metallic clatter forward, followed by a familiar bout of coughing. The cook was already up and about, and no matter what might lie ahead, for him the galley came first.

Vincent said, "He was on deck when I took over the watch. Who needs the sand-glass?"

Lynch had spent most of his life at sea in one kind of ship or another. At the first hint of danger the galley fires would be doused to avoid any accident, but Lynch liked to have enough food prepared and ready for the return of what he called "kinder times."

Vincent turned away to watch a seaman running across the deck, but he was lost in the predawn shadows.

"When the flag captain visits the governor . . ." He paused. "If he does, will he be taking the gig?"

Adam said only, "You are ahead of me, Mark," and thought Vincent might have shrugged.

"A cutter might be a better choice, sir."

"Good thinking. A cutter can mount a swivel if need be. Better safe than swamped!" They both laughed, and a seaman who was taking a mouthful of water from the ready-use cask looked up and muttered, "Not a care in th' bloody world!"

Adam walked slowly aft, past the men at the wheel and Tozer, the master's mate, who had been with him in *Delfim*'s prize crew. Here it was deserted, only a small part of the ship, the sea astern still in darkness. In another hour or so all hands would be piped, and the land would lie ahead like a barrier.

He slipped his hand inside his shirt and gripped the ribbon. A little worn now, and fraying, but hers.

A precious moment.

"*Captain, sir!*"

It was over.

Harry Drummond paused by the boat tier and stooped to pick up a piece of codline before tucking it into his belt. It would probably not be needed, but as *Onward*'s bosun, and even long before, he had learned to make use of almost everything. The miles of standing and running rigging, the massive cables now stowed and drying below deck, were *his* responsibility. He smiled to himself and felt his mouth crack. Next to the first lieutenant, of course.

He stood in the shade beneath the braced canvas and stared

disapprovingly at the top-chains on the upper yards: necessary maybe, but unseamanlike. They had rigged them just in time, too. The ship had altered course again and the yards were hard-braced; to a landsman she would appear to be almost fore-and-aft. But every sail was firm and filled. A few seamen were still working aloft, bodies half-naked in the sun. Some might be sorry afterwards: it was going to be one of the hottest days yet.

Drummond looked at the land again, but there had been no change. It reached from bow to bow in an endless green barrier, without shape or identity. Otherwise the sea was empty. No local craft hugging the coast for convenience, nor blackbirder making a run for it with rumours of a man-of-war in the area.

Drummond thought of the drifting wreckage and the human remains, followed always by those accursed sharks, and his eyes rested briefly on the canvas-wrapped corpse near one of the guns. Who would know or care? Better to have put him over the side like the others.

He looked at the land again. Unless the wind picked up they'd be lucky to anchor much before dusk. He had seen the captain with Julyan, the master, comparing notes on the quarterdeck. And the flag captain had shown himself a couple of times, too. A fine-looking man . . . or had been.

He saw Luke Jago climb from the fore hatch, his old cutlass beneath his arm.

"Taking no chances, eh, Luke?" It was somehow reassuring to see him like this, apparently unmoved by his experience amidst that grisly flotsam, but who could tell? Jago gave nothing away.

He was peering up at the taut canvas. "Pity we can't make more sail," and Drummond nodded sagely.

"They don't want any one to sight us too soon, I reckon."

They turned as several loud clangs seemed to shake the deck beneath their feet.

Jago said, "They'll bloody well 'ear us before that!"

There were shouts and the din stopped. It was one of the gunner's armourers hammering something on the anvil. The watch below had yelled their protests, eating what might be their last meal before they were called to quarters, with a tot for good measure.

Drummond said, "Not many captains would care that much, Luke." He could share things like that with the burly coxswain, inscrutable though Jago often was. They had little in common except the ship and their friendship, which had only begun when Drummond had joined *Onward* to replace the dead bosun, but the navy was like that. Sometimes there was no reason to consider a man a good mate, but it was a fact.

Then he added hastily, "I'll shove off now. One of your young gentlemen's approaching." It was Napier.

Unexpectedly Jago said, "Stay, will you?"

Drummond shrugged. "You got the tiller, Luke."

Napier slowed down and halted by the stand of boarding pikes at the foot of the mainmast. He had already recognized the old cutlass, despite its scabbard. The same one which had saved his life aboard the sinking *Moonstone*.

He was saying rather shyly, "I wanted to see you, when you have a moment. Maybe later—" when a voice echoed along the deck.

"Bosun!" Pause. *"Bo-sun!"*

Drummond raised his fist and bellowed, "Comin', sir!" and added quietly, "I'd better go. Mister bloody Monteith *needs* me!"

He grinned defiantly at Napier and strode away.

Jago saw the boy's eyes on his hand as he closed it gently around his forearm.

"I've been wanting . . ." The grip tightened very slightly.

"I think I knows what you want to say. One day when you're a cap'n, with your own ship an' all the men to fetch an' carry for you, you'll remember the bad old days with us. Eh, *sir?*"

"Well, that'll keep *him* quiet for a bit!" Drummond was back, and somehow he knew they were both glad of the interruption.

Adam Bolitho walked into the great cabin and closed the screen door behind him. This sanctuary was always the same, and yet he never took it for granted. More spacious, even bare without those familiar articles which had already been safely stowed away.

Hugh Morgan gestured to the chair and the sword lying across it. "I've given it a proper polish, sir."

Adam nodded, but he was looking at the sleeping cabin door. "I just wanted a moment with him."

Morgan lowered his voice. "Captain Tyacke is almost done, sir. Then I'll clear the space. As usual."

Adam continued on his way aft and gazed at the sea, the changing colour almost gentle after the pitiless glare on deck.

He touched the chair, alone now and facing astern. Even the little desk had been taken away, with his most recent letter half-finished in one of the drawers.

Morgan murmured, "If you would care for something before—"

"Later, maybe."

He listened to the rudder and the regular clatter of rigging. The motion was uneven, erratic, and had been since the change of tack.

Tyacke's leather satchel was lying on the bench seat beneath the stern windows. Where he must have used the old telescope to look back at his flagship—perhaps for the last time if the breaker's men were waiting in the wings. The thought made him look away from the sea and around the dim cabin again. Suppose it was *Onward?*

"Ah, there you are, Adam. I was just coming to have a few words."

Adam had been half expecting it, but it still came as a surprise. Tyacke was in full uniform, even to the tarnished gold aiguillette fastened across his breast.

He said, "No more signs of trouble, then? Good." He had not waited for an answer. Adam watched him walk to the bench seat and lean on it while he peered down into the water below the counter.

"I'll have the cutter lowered when we're more in the lee of the land."

"A good boat's crew?" But he said it as if his mind were elsewhere. "Something I wanted to ask you." The scarred face turned, the sea's light reflecting across it. "I'd like one of your experienced midshipmen to go with me. He can take care of the admiral's instructions." One

hand moved dismissively. "Not your signals middy—he's acting lieutenant, if you need one. I thought young Napier would fill the bill, after
what I've seen of him." He looked up as a call shrilled somewhere and
feet responded across the deck. "With your consent, of course."

In the seconds before Adam could answer, Tyacke had walked over
to the bergère, and was gazing down at the sword as if he wanted to
touch it.

He said only, "Equality Dick," and the blue eyes came up steadily
and held Adam's.

Adam said, "I'll do all I can."

Morgan interjected sharply, "I think you are wanted on deck, sir."

He was for the most part a warm-hearted person, but as Adam
strode past him on his way to the door he saw Morgan regarding Tyacke
with something like hatred.

Vincent was waiting by the companionway. "I thought you should
know, sir." He glanced past him as if he expected to see Tyacke close
on his heels. "Masthead reported another sail, same course as ours. But
small, hard to identify. May be one of those brigantines the flag captain
mentioned."

Adam opened his telescope and climbed into the nettings. There
was mist nearer the coast, and the vessel was directly stern-on, all sails
set but scarcely visible, overwhelmed by the solid mass of land reaching
out on either bow as if waiting to ensnare them.

"You may be right, Mark, but she's well ahead of us. Warn the lookouts to report any change of bearing." He knew the others near and
around the wheel were trying to hear what was being said.

He jumped down to the deck and saw that the second cutter had
already been moved to the quarter-davits, ready for lowering. "We'll
lower the cutter when we clear the point. Closer for the oarsmen, but
room enough for *us*, if we need to change tack in a hurry."

Vincent said, "I'm told that Midshipman Napier is going with the
flag captain, sir?" He hurried on. "He's young, but I daresay experienced
enough. He should be safe enough in the same boat as Captain Tyacke!"

He turned away as Julyan appeared on the quarterdeck. "The master is about to rig a dog-vane, sir. Close inshore it can detect any change of wind quicker than anything. He swears by them."

But Adam was looking at the empty cutter, and Vincent tried to imagine what he was thinking.

It was the right decision. But would I have made it?

Lieutenant James Squire leaned over the quarterdeck bulwark, observing the cutter's slow progress down *Onward*'s side. Always an anxious time in the open sea, in case something vital was left behind or forgotten. He had hoisted and lowered boats countless times during his years at sea. But there was always the possibility of some potentially fatal oversight.

He watched for the cutter's shadow as it rose and fell beneath the keel.

"Handsomely does it!"

Too soon, and the boat might overturn when it hit the water. Too late, and . . .

"Avast lowering!"

Squire looked up briefly at the outthrust spur of land, saw some tiny white-painted hut or beacon perched at the seaward end. Closer now, but it would still be a strong pull for the cutter's crew, double-banked or not. He had done it a few times himself.

"Pass me the glass!" He had to repeat it. Midshipman Huxley was paying more attention to the cutter, no doubt too busy thinking about his friend Napier going ashore with Captain Tyacke.

A few more turns and the cutter was pitching and plunging alongside, some of her crew already securing equipment while trying to keep their balance, Fitzgerald, her coxswain, peering critically across the span of open water to the unmoving layer of mist, above which was a tiny patch of colour. The Union Jack.

Squire turned as someone muttered a warning, "Heads up!"

Captain James Tyacke walked to the quarterdeck rail and stood in silence, studying the land. Squire was aware of the effect of the uniform, and saw it in the faces of the seamen around him. Perhaps, by that gesture, the day had suddenly acquired new meaning and purpose in their eyes.

He heard Vincent call, "I'll have the cutter brought to the entry port, sir!" and saw Tyacke shake his head.

"Take too long." He might have smiled, but there was another emotion in his eyes.

"Man the boat!" Fitzgerald touched his hat, and ran to the ladder which had been lowered soon after all hands had been called. Tyacke waited until the cutter was fully manned, two seamen to each thwart, and a swivel gun at the stem. Only then did he turn and extend his hand to Adam Bolitho.

Vincent was watching the masthead pendant and the rebellious flapping of canvas, impatient to bring the ship under command again once the cutter had pulled clear.

Adam returned the handshake. Strong and uncompromising, like the man. There was no more time. Adam said only, "Signal, if you need us."

Tyacke gazed up at the ensign curling easily against the clear sky, his blue eyes almost colourless in the fierce light. "I *hope . . .*" He released his grip. "Until we meet again, Adam."

He turned abruptly and climbed down into the cutter, and seconds later, or so it seemed, it appeared well clear of *Onward*'s side, unhurriedly, all oars pulling as one.

Adam remained by the rail and watched their progress as the ship came alive around and above him, her canvas filling, and resumed her course. Then he walked slowly across the deck with the wind in his face. Julyan's dog-vane was fluttering from a half-pike mounted in the weather shrouds: his own battle ensign, perhaps.

He heard Vincent call to one of his leadsmen, already stationed in the chains for the approach, their landmark that tiny, distant flag, heard the splash, and the leadsman's chant.

"No bottom, sir!"

They were ready.

He looked again, but the cutter had disappeared.

. . .

"Steady, lads. Easy does it!" Fitzgerald was half crouched, half standing at the cutter's tiller, staring over the twin banks of oarsmen at the out-thrust spur of land.

It was just for something to say, and he knew it was because of his passenger. His crew were all skilled seamen; they would not be here otherwise. Even the midshipman with the satchel wedged between his knees was not one of those *I-know-best* types he had met in the past. God help poor Jack when *they* walked their own quarterdecks . . .

He felt spray on his mouth as the stroke-oar leaned away from him again. The cutter was answering well, despite carrying a few extra bodies: two marines in the bows as well as a man with a boat's lead-and-line, although it was not needed yet. You could see the bottom through the clear water, even dark patches of weed, coming alive with the current as the oars dug deep on either beam.

They were all armed, cutlasses stacked beneath the thwarts, and the marines, already sweating heavily in their scarlet uniforms, were in charge of the swivel gun, which was concealed by a canvas hood.

Fitzgerald eased the tiller again and fixed his eyes on the far-off flag: the Union Jack, the same flag they saw hoisted or lowered every day of their lives. But out here it seemed alien, out of place.

Deeper water now, steadier in some way. David Napier felt the salt spray splashing over the gunwale and soaking his legs. He tried not to look into the faces of the oarsmen as they lay back on their looms, fol-lowing the stroke-oar, measuring every breath. He had seen their eyes, staring astern after they had cast off from the frigate's side, and was glad his back was turned. He had never found leaving the comparative safety of the ship an easy moment.

And Captain Tyacke had scarcely spoken since his agile climb down into the boat, apart from exchanging a few words with the coxswain and with one of the marines, a corporal who had just been transferred from the flagship. The corporal had apparently once served with Captain Bolitho.

Napier felt himself frowning, and not merely because of the brutal sunlight, trying to remember everything he had been told concerning his duty with the flag captain.

There had been a few slaps on the back from the others, sly comments of, "Another step up the ladder!" and a handshake from Simon Huxley, but no words. And he had heard the captain say, "Watch yourselves, lads." But Napier knew Bolitho had been speaking to *him*.

Tyacke half turned suddenly, almost startling him, and said, "There's a pier and a smaller jetty. We'll be directed to one or the other." His face was slightly averted, the disfigurement hidden, and Napier imagined he could feel his own injury. The limp, which he had beaten. He pressed his leg hard against the satchel.

"*Oars!*"

Another heave, then the blades paused, dripping like wings, as Fitzgerald said, "Easy now, lads," and then, "I heard shots, sor!"

The corporal confirmed it. "Muskets, sir!"

Tyacke said fiercely, "*Carry on!* May be up-river or further inland. We don't have time to hang fire at this stage!"

The oars picked up the stroke and the cutter gathered way once more. Napier watched the land falling away to reveal the entrance to a natural harbour: the anchorage beyond was still half hidden by the headland. No place to venture after dark.

There were two small boats, fishing craft, moored to a ramshackle trestle, and a few birds, which took off as the cutter turned slightly to starboard, where the outgoing current confronted and contested an ocean.

Napier thought of Jago, and his efforts to talk to him. Always a barrier, and yet . . .

"There's the pier, sir!"

Tyacke straightened his back and said sardonically, "What, no red carpet laid out for us?" and grinned as if it reminded him of someone.

Fitzgerald leaned closer, murmuring, "Lucky we didn't bring the corpse with us!"

Tyacke said, "Pull to the next part," and looked down at the satchel. "I'm not waiting for—"

They all ducked instinctively as the air quivered to a drawn-out explosion.

He shouted, "Next jetty!" He stared across the looms and braced shoulders. "Stand by with the swivel!"

But the ginger-haired corporal had already removed the hood and was training the muzzle beyond the pier.

Napier slung the satchel across his shoulder, ears still throbbing from the explosion, smoke and grit between his teeth.

He heard Tyacke calling out to the cutter's crew, "Stand by, lads!" but very calmly, one hand resting on his sword hilt.

A grapnel had been thrown on to the low jetty, and a few men almost fell as they came alongside, metal clattering as they seized their cutlasses. A couple of them dragged muskets from beneath the thwarts.

"Clear the boat!"

But Napier hung back, as if he were unable to move.

He felt Tyacke's hand lightly on his arm, was conscious of his voice, quiet and compelling. Almost matter-of-fact. "Ready, David?"

And his own answer. "Aye, ready, sir!"

They were ashore. But the Union Jack had vanished.

Aboard *Onward*, the musket shots had passed almost unheard except by a few men on watch in the tops, and even then they were nearly lost in the usual chorus of shipboard noises. One man raised the alarm, then the full impact of the explosion rolled against the hull, given extra power by the echo reverberating from the backdrop of high ground.

Adam stood by the rail, gazing the full length of his command, seeing men off watch coming up from their messes, some still chewing the remains of a hurried meal. Others, working on or above the decks, had fallen silent, looking aft toward the quarterdeck.

Only Midshipman Hotham spoke. His signals telescope was still trained on the shore. "They've lowered the Jack, sir."

Adam watched the great arrowhead of blue water, and the overlapping humps of land that guarded the harbour entrance. He sensed Vincent and Squire standing somewhere behind him, and others near the wheel. Waiting. Perhaps dreading.

Jago's shadow merged with his own across the deck, and he heard the steady breathing. Then he lifted his arms and felt the coxswain clip the old sword into place.

It was like a signal.

"Beat to quarters and clear for action!"

16 No Quarter

Vincent faced aft and touched his hat. "*Onward* cleared for action, sir!"

Adam returned his salute and stood looking along the length of the upper deck. Vincent's formal use of the ship's name seemed to make it more personal. Immediate.

He had already seen Maddock, the gunner, on his way to the semi-darkness of the magazine, his felt slippers gripped in one hand, appearing to glance briefly at the guns with a word or a nod to each crew. His head was, as usual, cocked to one side in case the deafness caused him to miss something, which in Maddock's case was unlikely.

These were his men. Every day of their lives they carried out countless tasks to keep the ship alive and running. But in the end, this was their purpose. To work and fight these guns; if necessary to die doing it. They often discussed it, even joked about it, on messdecks and in wardroom alike. But now the ship was quiet. Waiting.

Vincent said, "They knocked two minutes off the time, sir." It was meant to break the tension but his face remained drawn, and Adam thought he was in need of a good sleep.

Adam looked up as the topsails flapped untidily before filling once more. The land still seemed a long way away, but it was having its effect, like a giant barrier. He touched the telescope he had borrowed, but changed his mind.

"Load when you're ready. As planned. Not a race." Vincent was already gesturing to a bosun's mate. "But don't run out!"

He moved nearer to the wheel where Tobias Julyan was comparing notes with Tozer, his mate. Julyan peered up at the masthead pendant and pursed his lips.

"We'll be losing a knot or two when we change tack next time, sir."

Tozer ventured, "The *last* time afore we enter harbour, sir."

Adam turned and saw the leadsman in the chains hauling in his line, his mouth soundlessly forming the soundings. Then he shouted, *"By the mark, ten!"*

Julyan grinned. "No wonder it's a long haul!" Ten fathoms. Sixty feet. *Onward* drew three fathoms.

The second leadsman was already leaning against his apron, and lowering his own lead in readiness.

They were feeling their way, like a blind man tapping along an unfamiliar street.

Adam said, "Part of your 'valley'?"

Julyan nodded, feeling the pocket where he kept his bulky notebook. "Don't want to scrape off her barnacles just yet, sir."

"Deep nine!"

Julyan licked his lips. "I think I'll keep my mouth shut!"

Surprisingly, one of the helmsmen laughed.

The rest was drowned by the rumble of gun trucks as breechings were cast off, and the eighteen-pounders were manhandled inboard and loaded under the watchful eye of every senior hand. Adam saw the fists raised as each crew finished. But the guns were not run out.

He looked up at the tops where Royal Marines, stripped of their bright coats, were already lying or crouching with muskets or manning the swivel guns. They would be feeling the full heat of the sun up there.

Adam walked to the side of the quarterdeck and touched one of the blunt carronades as he passed. Hot, as if it had just been fired, and already loaded, each round packed with cast-iron balls in tiers, and deadly metal disks. At short range, they could transform a crowded deck into a slaughterhouse.

He unslung the telescope and trained it abeam, and felt the metal sear his fingers. Towards and across the harbour entrance. Like the impression on the chart, "hacked out of the African coastline," as Julyan had described it.

He imagined the governor's building. The line of cannon, and the flag. Not a lot of room to manoeuvre, but compared with Portsmouth Harbour, where ships of the line were expected to enter and depart at the drop of a signal, New Haven seemed spacious.

And quiet.

Vincent said, "Shall I shorten sail, sir?" He had moved to join him, perhaps so the others would not be concerned by any apparent last-minute hesitation. *And so they might.*

Adam looked briefly at the feathered wind-vane. "We're going in."

"And the boats? Cast them adrift?"

Adam glanced down at the boat tier. If boats were kept aboard during a fight, their flying splinters caused more casualties. He had seen it often enough, even as a midshipman. Like David . . . He shut his mind to it.

"Hold your course, Mark. Be ready to run out." Their eyes met. "Then fire when I give the word!"

"By th' mark, seven!"

Captain James Tyacke paused at the top of a steep slope and leaned against a pile of freshly cut timber. He sensed that the cutter's crew had also stopped, and were watching him or peering up and around at the bare headland. There was not only timber, but piles of bricks, either to extend the pier or the gun emplacements, most of which faced the harbour entrance or the open sea. The musket fire and the single explosion had demonstrated more clearly than anything that the threat was coming from the opposite direction.

He tugged at his coat and drew a long, slow breath; he was sweating strongly. The uniform had been a gesture. He was paying for it now.

He could see the flagstaff clearly against the sky, and some of the buildings also; he could even see that the flag halliard was lifting and trailing slightly in the hot wind, which Fitzgerald had already noted with his keen and younger eyes. Not lowered. It had been cut.

Perhaps the governor, Ballantyne, had already sighted *Onward* and was attempting to warn her?

Fitzgerald said, "Heads down, lads, but keep your eyes open!" Calmly enough, but there was an edge to his words. He was looking down toward the jetty and pier, and the sea beyond. A sailor's instinct.

Napier was squatting on a slab of rock, the satchel between his feet. He looked up and found Tyacke's eyes on him and smiled.

It was time to move. Their arrival must have been seen. Tyacke fought the desire to turn and stare back at the sea. Suppose something had made Adam change his mind? Who would dispute it, or blame him?

Fitzgerald stood up and eased his shoulders. "I was thinkin', sor . . ." There was a faint click and he froze, and another voice murmured, *"Still! Someone's comin'!"*

Tyacke groped for his sword hilt, but let his hand fall. If he had led them into a trap, it was already too late. He called, "Stand fast!" and gestured to Napier. "You, with me!"

He stared past the others at the litter of building gear and beyond, like a skeleton against the hillside, a partly demolished barn with a rusting horseshoe nailed on a post.

"An unavoidable delay, Captain Tyacke, but you are *welcome*, beyond words!" It was a deep, authoritative voice, and for a moment seemed to come from nowhere, or the ground itself.

Tyacke had on two occasions seen, but never met, Sir Duncan Ballantyne, but he was as he remembered, and as Adam Bolitho had described. *A face from the Armada.* Even to the neatly trimmed beard, showing grey now against darkly tanned skin.

He strode toward them, frowning with a faint disapproval as one of the seamen released the hammer of his musket. He said calmly, "My own men were watching you as well."

Two or three heads appeared as he spoke, and Tyacke saw the gleam of weapons. He took the proferred hand. Strong, but the palm was smooth. A gentleman.

Tyacke said, controlling the urge to touch his scars, "How did you know my name?"

Ballantyne smiled diplomatically.

"I know of only *one* flag captain." His dark eyes rested on Napier. "A younger blood, too. I am honoured!" He gestured toward the building with its empty flag mast. "Come."

He was coatless, but Tyacke noted the finely made shirt and white breeches, obviously expensive, as were the black riding boots, their polish gleaming beneath the inevitable coating of dust. About sixty years of age, according to Flags' notebook. Without the beard, he would seem younger.

Guilty, he thought. *You're as guilty as hell. And one day I'll prove it.*

Ballantyne had stopped and was pointing back at the water. "I see that you were taking no chances, either!" He laughed.

The corporal was standing bareheaded behind his swivel gun, his hair in the sunlight blazing almost as brightly as his uniform.

Tyacke found that he had fallen into step beside Ballantyne. Corporal Price would have known that, at this range and bearing, the swivel gun would have been an indiscriminate killer.

"Your men can rest a while." Ballantyne waved toward the nearest building. "I can offer you something to quench your thirst." Again the quick, quizzical glance. "But we are under siege at present! *Here*—I will show you something." He halted again. "Your ship is under sail? Then who commands her?"

"Captain Adam Bolitho. I understood that you had already met him."

The tanned hand was on Tyacke's sleeve. "*Bolitho?* Must be God's will!" He repeated the name, as if his mind was elsewhere. "A fine young man. But a certain sadness in him too, I felt."

They had reached the gateway to a circular courtyard, cobbled, and probably built by slaves. Common enough in New Haven, or whatever it had originally been called. But Tyacke noticed none of it. Across the courtyard before him was the mast, the severed halliard still catching the breeze from the sea.

A man lay dead at the foot of the mast, but one hand was still moving, firmly grasping the halliard. The same green uniform, but with a piece of scarlet bunting which Tyacke had at first taken for blood wrapped around his neck like a scarf.

Ballantyne kicked a loose stone across the yard until it rolled against the corpse.

He said, "So that *they* can tell the difference!" He turned back toward Tyacke, his eyes filling his face. "Mutineers, rebels, call them what you will. They are still *traitors!*"

He walked on, and although Tyacke was a tall man he had to quicken his pace to keep up with him. He thought he had seen some human shadows through a colonnade, as if there were others watching, perhaps waiting to remove the dead intruder.

Now they were on another side of the building, on a terrace overlooking the next stretch of anchorage. There were a few small vessels, obviously derelict or abandoned, and beyond, the full panorama of hills.

Tyacke kept walking toward the low wall but stopped when Ballantyne touched his sleeve.

"No further, Captain. We are possibly out of range here, but why take the risk?"

As if in response there was a dull bang, probably a musket, but no hint of any fall of shot.

Ballantyne said calmly, "*We* are the ones under siege. We can withstand any frontal attack by those scum, but we are cut off from our supply routes." His hand indicated the terrace. "This place was built to defend others!"

He had taken Tyacke's arm again. "Look yonder, Captain. Perhaps the fight is already lost!"

Tyacke shaded his eyes with his hat to gaze across the glittering breadth of New Haven. There was wreckage clinging to a long sandbar, and smaller fragments still breaking away beneath a layer of fine smoke, like mist. Tyacke recognised the shape of the vessel's hull, and the gleam of blue paint, which he knew had only recently been applied. Now a total wreck, mastless and abandoned, if any one had lived long enough to escape.

He said quietly, "*Endeavour*. One of my patrols."

There were more shots, no closer, even haphazard. As if they were being held in check. Then he said, "We picked up one of your men. That was how we knew about the mutiny." He dragged out a crumpled piece of paper and flattened it on a bench, away from the wall. It was badly stained with smoke and dried blood.

Ballantyne stared at it and nodded slowly, several times. "John Staples. Acting bosun. A good man. I should have seen it coming." He swung round and exclaimed, "I'll not go under without a fight, damn their bloody eyes!" It was strange to see him suddenly defeated.

Tyacke felt someone beside him. It was David Napier, holding a telescope which must have been concealed in the satchel.

"I didn't know you had that with you."

"The captain told me to bring it. In case we might need it." Napier's chin lifted, and he sounded very young. "*Do* we, sir?"

Like a hand on the shoulder. Tyacke swung toward the harbour entrance, his mind suddenly ice-clear. *A single shot.* One of the deaf gunner's "specials." The signal. *Onward* was on the way. No matter what.

He took the old telescope with its finely engraved inscription, and opened it carefully, almost reverently. Bolitho's telescope. *Like those other times.*

Napier watched him, conscious of the sudden silence around them. "What can *I* do, sir?"

Tyacke answered without hesitation, "Fetch our flag from the cutter. Tell Fitzgerald to run it up to the masthead."

He broke off, his mind too full to continue. He did not even hear Napier say, "I'll do it myself!"

Tyacke was watching the picture in the powerful lens acquire shape and significance. Like seashells caught in the reflected glare. *Onward*'s topsails.

He hardly recognised his own voice. "Sir Duncan, you're not alone any more."

·   ·   ·

Adam Bolitho stood at the quarterdeck rail, one hand resting lightly on the smooth wood, which seemed to burn beneath the sun. It helped him to remain in the same place, where he could see and be seen, when every urge and instinct dictated that he should be on the move.

It was quiet, the shipboard noises muffled, perhaps by their slow progress. The most persistent sound came from an almost constant alteration of helm, the creak of the big double wheel, or a sharp correction from quartermaster or helmsman.

A glance aloft, and the loosely flapping topsails and listless pendant told their own story: the nearness of land. Without moving, Adam had watched the rugged coastline creeping out on either bow, as if *Onward* were intent on running ashore.

He could sense the readiness among the men around him. Extra hands now at braces and halliards, a few wearing bandages. Even those from the sick quarters were not spared. And the men at the guns, some peering at the land, visible now on both sides, or looking aft. Waiting was the worst part.

"By the mark, seven!"

Adam watched the leadsman hauling in his line, his bare shoulders wet with spray. He tried to recall the chart and Julyan's crude but accurate copy. *Holding steady.* He glanced at the tiny white shape on the nearest elbow of land. Soon after this, more soundings would be necessary.

A splash and a brief flurry of smoke: the last of the galley fire.

He saw a seaman climbing aloft, carrying a container of water and watched by the nearest gun crews. All their mouths were as dry as dust, but the plight of the marines, the marksmen sprawled in the tops, must be far worse.

He saw Lieutenant Devereux talking to two of his men by the fore hatch, in full uniform, sword gleaming at his side. The duelling sword, Adam wondered? Devereux was smiling, and so were his men.

He heard Vincent speak to the quartermaster before joining him at the rail.

"Good thing we didn't lower the boats after all, sir. We don't need another anchor!" He seemed calm enough, but his voice was edged with the usual impatience. *A first lieutenant's lot*. Adam had not forgotten what it was like.

Vincent looked sharply along the deck as somebody gave a wild cheer. "What the *hell!*"

But others had joined in, gun crews peering or climbing on to their gangways, even individuals calling from yards or shrouds.

Luke Jago shouted up from the boat tier, "They've run up the flag, Cap'n!"

Adam reached instinctively for his telescope, then remembered. *Our flag*. He saw a seaman turn toward him, grinning. Perhaps he had spoken aloud. He walked to the side and lifted his hat to the shore.

Someone called out, "Wreckage, larboard bow, sir!"

Vincent said, "I'll be up forrard, sir."

"And I shall be *here*, Mark."

The cheering had stopped. There were more shots, but it was impossible to judge the bearing or distance. Like the wind, it was playing tricks. Adam stared at the headland again: the ensign was very clear now, a twin of the one above the poop.

Midshipman Hotham offered him the big signals telescope. "They're on the wall, sir."

Adam trained it carefully and waited for the criss-cross of rigging to dissolve away. There were faces on the first stretch of the battery wall, and somebody was waving, perhaps cheering as *Onward* came past. Well-sited guns were a ship's worst enemy, apart from fire. He moved the glass again and saw Vincent's face pass, blurred and barely recognisable. Squire would be on his way aft to relieve him. Both good officers, but any newcomer might think they scarcely knew each other.

The telescope steadied, finding the range. A few boats huddled together, a shed and part of a slipway, then a cluster of ragged trees. Adam tensed. Someone running.

He heard Squire's heavy breathing beside him, but did not lower the telescope.

"What do you make of it, James?"

Squire wiped the sweat from his cheek with the back of his hand. "I think the attackers must be on this side, sir. A few marksmen maybe, but until they can—" A jagged ridge of spray rose and fell, interrupting him. "Maybe only one gun. But properly laid and trained, all it would take to slow or disable them while stronger forces were summoned."

Adam said, *"Run out!"*

He did not even hear the pipe, only the chorus of gunports being hoisted open. *Showing her teeth.*

"Ready, sir!"

Onward was heeling slightly, her topsails clutching and holding the offshore wind. But still no target. He could hear a few curses, and thumps from the gun deck as quoins were forced beneath the breeches to depress some of the guns still further.

Someone yelled from forward as a boat under oars pulled strongly from a tiny cove, which had been concealed by rushes or tall grass.

Adam steadied the glass again, and felt himself flinch as several flashes spurted from the boat's gunwale. *"As you bear!"* He saw the nearest gun captain crouching over his breech, one hand raised, ready to jump clear.

"Fire!"

Only four guns could be brought to bear at this range. One would have been enough. The boat had taken a direct hit amidships, shattered as if by a giant's axe. Eventually it settled and was already drifting abeam, planking, broken oars and a bare mast. And bodies.

Musket shots, but only a few, until Sergeant Fairfax's powerful voice brought another fusillade.

"*Gone soft, have you?* What d' you think they'd do to *you?*"

The firing began again.

Green uniforms, with scarlet scarves. Life or death.

The guns had hardly finished reloading when lookouts sighted more wreckage. The remains of a small vessel, probably one of Tyacke's brigantines, aground on a sandbar. She had been hit at point-blank range.

Adam stared at the other shore, but the battery wall was now out of sight. Only part of the nearby settlement was still in view, and it looked deserted. Abandoned. Waiting to accept the victors, perhaps? It must have seen many over the centuries.

Squire said heavily, "The brigantine was ahead of us, sir. It took more than a few shots to do that to her."

Adam strode to the compass and wheel, but ignored both, looking at the masthead pendant and then at the master's dog-vane. It was holding up well in spite of its frail cluster of cork and feathers.

He saw Julyan watching him through the receding gunsmoke. He might even have smiled.

He said, almost to himself, "While *we* are here, they're trapped. There's only one way to escape."

Another gun, but further away. No fall of shot.

Sea against land. He thought suddenly of the Battle of Algiers, some three years ago, when Pellew, now Lord Exmouth, had won a resounding victory over combined land and sea forces. He could remember his own surprise and pride when he had read the admiral's comment in the aftermath of his victory. He had described Adam Bolitho as *a born frigate captain*. From England's greatest, it was praise indeed.

A cry from the forecastle: "More wreckage—ahead, sir!"

Julyan murmured, "Soon now, I think . . ." He did not finish.

This was as far as a vessel of any size could reach and retain room to tack or come about. Any one else could come overland, or up-stream, as had happened during the attack on the mssion.

Adam looked along the deck, at the gun crews baking in the sun, lookouts cupping hands around their eyes, midshipmen sweating and watching the land. Everything.

And the leadsman's chant. *"Deep six!"*

He thought of Vincent, up there in the eyes of the ship where their figurehead, the boy with his trident and riding a dolphin, was pointing the way.

The ship comes first.

If *Onward* dropped anchor to avoid running aground, she would become a sitting target, to be destroyed by guns from the shore or by waterborne explosives. He saw more pieces of wreckage drifting past, part of a topmast lifting above the rest like a charred crucifix.

"Stand by to come about! Warn all hands!"

Men running, answering the shrill of calls, some already perched on the yards high above the guns and their motionless crews. Adam saw that even the cooks and messmen were adding their weight to the braces. He thought with a sudden, strange apprehension of Tyacke and Napier. Where were they now? He looked again for the flag, even though he knew it was out of sight.

Julyan lowered his eyes, watering from staring at the sun's path. Like tears. "Give the word, sir!"

"*Belay that!*" It was Squire, his head thrown back to stare up at the braced topsails even as Adam came striding toward the compass. "*Foretop*, sir!"

Midshipman Hotham had also heard the lookout's cry, and although he felt a little lost without the signals telescope he could see this in his mind. Like a signal.

Enemy in sight!

Adam lowered the telescope and felt someone take it from him. The image was imprinted on his brain. The ship, almost bows-on, sails fully braced. A big schooner, three-masted, he thought, even larger than the slaver they had taken as a prize. He watched closely. They would meet and pass in half an hour at this rate. Less. The stranger would be armed, but no match for a frigate.

"The other one will try to slip past us!"

Adam looked away from the pyramid of pale canvas. It was another midshipman, Simon Huxley, waiting to act as a "walking speaking-trumpet." His eyes were fixed on the approaching schooner.

"Ready, sir!" Julyan, anxious, fretting over the delay.

Adam shook his head. "Maintain course!" And to the quarterdeck at large, "Hold your fire!"

He had the telescope again but did not recall having taken it from Hotham. *Suppose I am mistaken?* On the larboard bow. About half a mile, and looking as if she were sailing on dry land. An easy error of judgment at this range, and across the hard glare of the anchorage. A trick to lead *Onward* into the shallows. Julyan had warned him, but he did not need it.

The smaller vessel, another schooner, was *not* trying to slip past while the others faced and fought.

His shirt was clinging to his body, but it felt cold. Like the dead.

"Steady!" From the corner of his eye he saw faces peering up at him from the nearest eighteen-pounder. He stared through the shrouds and ratlines, keeping his eyes on the schooner. As if she were snared in a net.

There should be uncertainty, doubt, even a consciousness of failure. There was none.

More shots, closer now, and he heard, even felt the deck shake as some found their mark. Marksmen in the tops were firing too, although at this range it would have little effect. He thought he heard Jago's voice calling to some of the afterguard: "You'll soon know, so watch yer front!"

Somebody was questioning why *Onward* was turning away from a challenge, and allowing an enemy to escape.

Julyan called, "Ready when you give the word, sir!" He was calm enough. He had no choice.

Adam gripped the rail with both hands and watched the smaller schooner's masts begin to turn, in line, her canvas in confusion for the first time. From habit he reached for the telescope; he had lost count of the times, but this time he did not need it. Those same sails were all aback now, the hull heeling slightly, without purpose.

He knew Squire was beside him. Sharing it in his own fashion. He spoke for him. "They've got boats in the water! Abandoning ship!"

Adam laid his sword flat along the rail. He did not remember having drawn it. He said, "The schooner. *Open fire!*"

Someone shouted, "What about the boats, sir?"

Adam did not look up at the masthead pendant. There was no time left. He thought he heard Vincent directing the forward guns. He lifted his sword and knew each gun captain was watching, staring aft, eyes fixed on the blade. The sword flashed down; every gun on the larboard quarter must have fired simultaneously. Even as their recoil was halted, the half-naked crews were already sponging out and ramming home the next charge, selecting another ball from the nearest shot-garland.

As the thunder of the broadside rolled away the gun captains were yelling to each other, some coughing as the gunsmoke streamed through the open ports.

Adam heard Monteith, almost shrill above the noise, calling someone's name. Then a seaman running, perhaps in answer. Another rattle of musket fire, closer now, shots hitting the hull or slapping through the canvas overhead.

The running man swung round as if taken by surprise. Then he fell, a few paces from the nearest gun crew.

Adam forced himself to look away, to turn his eyes toward the approaching ship. Nothing else must distract or concern him. The masthead lookouts and Vincent, up forward, would have an unbroken view. Two ships, *Onward*'s bowsprit pointing directly at her enemy's jib. The shooting was almost continuous now, and the Royal Marines were firing with regular precision, as if on a range.

At any moment *Onward*'s bow-chasers would come to bear, then her carronades.

He tore his eyes away to look for the abandoned schooner. That, too, had been a ruse, without regard for their own lives. The schooner was heeling over toward him, her deck splintered. Another splash through the clinging smoke, and she was mastless.

Somebody cried out, near or far: he was beyond understanding. As if all the air had been forced, punched out of his lungs, or his ears were covered by unseen hands. How long? Maybe only a split second, and then came the explosion. He felt spray across his face as fragments hit the sea almost alongside. Something striking the deck with a shower of sparks. As his hearing returned he became aware of the shouts, and the clank of pumps, spilling water over the sun-dried planking.

The smaller schooner had vanished. Some of her remains were coming to the surface. They had misjudged *Onward*'s change of direction. Even the schooner's crew had not escaped.

Vincent was waving, perhaps shouting to confirm his readiness. A drop of the hand, and a nine-pounder responded from the forecastle. The smoke was fanning away as one of the carronades shook the hull.

Julyan was shouting now, and Adam saw him gesture toward the big schooner. "They're cutting it fine, sir!" He stared down at his own arm, which was smeared with blood, then seemed to shrug casually. Adam had seen the gesture so often, in the chartroom when dealing with a problem which he usually managed to solve.

The big schooner had altered course again. If she drew closer to the other shore, she still might reach the open sea. They were still firing, and her upper deck seemed to be full of uniforms. The schooner was the transport. They were the main force, so far. And mutiny was a contagious disease. It could soon spread.

He winced as the second carronade fired its deadly charge across the other vessel's forecastle. He did not need a telescope to see the splinters flying, men scattering like rags under a full charge of grape.

"Helm, hard over!" Adam saw Squire turn from the compass box and nod. He was biting his lip.

But *Onward* was answering slowly. There was an extra helmsman at the wheel. One already lay dead near Squire's feet.

Squire saw Midshipman Huxley duck by the bulwark as more shots hammered into the deck. He caught his attention and called, *"Keep on the move!"* then swore under his breath as a splinter sprang from the deck within inches of his own foot.

Adam watched the great arrowhead of water between the two ships. In a few minutes they would be carried further apart. He picked up his sword, and heard some of the seamen calling out to one another. He felt a shot hit and ricochet from one of the eighteen-pounders. One of the crew, leaning on his rammer, did not move. He was still gazing aft at his captain.

More shouts, this time from the foremast. The upper yard, the royal, had been damaged or dislodged by the explosion, and some men were up there in the thick of it. The top-chains were holding, but even as he watched one of the tiny figures threw up his hands and fell.

Adam raised his sword and looked again toward the big schooner.

There was a lull in the gunfire, and many voices suddenly merging. There must be hundreds on board, outnumbering *Onward*'s company at least two to one. Fists were raised, and he thought he saw the lens of a telescope flash in the smoky sunlight, either watching the sword or taking aim.

He shouted, "Full broadside! Together!" The sword was at his side, but he was gripping it with all his strength.

A moment later, *Onward*'s entire broadside fired as one. Fourteen eighteen-pounders, *and anything else that can strike a match,* as the old gunners used to say. Like thunder, but no longer at any distance.

"First lieutenant wants you! *Now!*"

It was a call for the "speaking-trumpet," and Adam saw young Huxley come to life and call out to a bosun's mate before running toward the larboard gangway.

A smoke-grimed face peered up from the deck. "Don't ye spoil that fine uniform, *sir!*"

Huxley glanced down and might have smiled, then he collapsed. Before any one could reach him, he was dead.

Midshipman Hotham saw him fall, but he was needed elsewhere. But still he hesitated, one hand in his pocket, feeling for the little crucifix he always kept there, which nobody else knew about. "Dear God, please receive the soul of Simon Huxley." Now he was reunited with his father.

"Ready, sir!"

The next broadside was slowly, more patiently aimed.

For another moment, Adam thought that they were overhauling their enemy. Her foremast was down and, with its broken shrouds and rigging, was pointing toward them like a bridge. Hardly any part of her side seemed to have escaped cannon or small arms fire, and even without a glass the carnage on deck was terrible to see. Adam unclenched his fists. Even the scuppers were trailing patterns of blood. As if the schooner herself was bleeding to death.

And the angle of the remaining masts had changed.

Julyan exclaimed, "She's hard aground!" and then, looking over at

Adam, "As soon as we can, sir." He fell silent as the bosun crossed the quarterdeck, picking his way past the dead and the injured.

Drummond cleared his throat. He had been shouting and running from one emergency to another for what seemed hours, and there was a gash in his sleeve, a wound he could not remember receiving; another inch and he would have been dead.

He had Adam's attention now.

"They've run up a white flag, sir."

"I'll need a boarding party. Then we will anchor." And he saw Julyan nod, satisfied.

Jago was nearby, and Adam felt his lips crack when he tried to smile at him. This was no victory to be proud of. But few were.

Jago said only, "You'll be needin' the gig, Cap'n."

"The governor must be informed."

Jago peered around for some of his crew, if they were still alive.

Adam stood a moment, his hand resting on a jagged splinter. The anger returned and swept through him, and he welcomed the strength it gave him. "But first, I will go around *our ship*."

Vincent had come aft, eyes red-rimmed from smoke and strain, as two seamen were dragging the dead helmsman away from the wheel. "What if they renege on the truce, sir?"

Adam walked past him, touching his arm briefly as he did so. He could see Huxley's body, which had been moved to clear the gangway for the passage of messages. He knew Vincent was blaming himself, and that was why his question was doubly important.

He said quietly, "Then, every gun. *No quarter*."

Midshipman David Napier sat in the cutter's sternsheets and tried not to listen to the regular creak of oars as they pulled away from the land. He could not recall when he had last been able to sleep, but he knew if he was offered the finest bed in the world right now, it would still be denied him.

The journey from shore to ship was much less in distance than when they had set off to meet the governor, but already it seemed very long.

Tyacke was sitting beside him, and the same stroke oarsman faced him, eyes barely moving as he lay back on his loom for every stroke.

Napier could see *Onward*'s masts and loosely furled sails directly ahead, and the flag, so vivid in the pale light. It was dawn. He glanced down at his hands, clenched so tightly that the knuckles were white beneath the tanned skin. This would pass. It had to.

It was seeing the flag that brought it all back to him. As if it had just happened. Stark and brutal.

He had hoisted the ensign on the flagmast where he had seen the dead mutineer when *Onward* had made her appearance and engaged a small vessel which had proved to be the decoy. He had climbed on to the roof of a low outbuilding to watch the frigate pass the main anchorage.

Something had made him turn, some sound or sense of warning. Even as he had turned there had been two shots, so close they could have been a single blast. He had lost his balance and fallen, but not before he had seen the sprawled body of the governor's servant, a black youth around his own age. He had tried to warn him but had been unable to shout, because he had no tongue. He had been killed by the ball intended for Napier. The second shot had cut down the attacker, whose scarlet scarf spoke for itself.

The governor had been there almost immediately. On his knees, holding the boy's hands in his, calling him "Trusty."

Napier shifted on the hard thwart and kept his eyes on the frigate. He could see some of the damage now, the scars and the gaps in the rigging. Men were already working aloft, fresh canvas overlapping, flapping in the offshore breeze. He had heard the hammering and other sounds during the night, his mind flooding with images of the faces he knew.

He had twisted his leg when he fell. It had saved his life. But he was already struggling to overcome it, as he had before. Like the moment when he had been about to climb into the cutter and the ginger-haired Corporal Price, still hatless, had tried to assist him.

He had done enough, but when Adam had tried to make Price climb aboard ahead of Napier he had declined.

"You know what they say about us Royals, sir? The first to land . . ."

Napier had finished it for him. "And the last to leave!" Somehow, they had both managed to laugh.

Tyacke was shading his eyes and looking toward the ship, although there was no fierce sunlight at this hour. He said, "When we get back to Freetown, I'll soon have her looking as smart as paint again."

Napier watched the masts rising above them, faces on the gangway, and peering down from the yards as the cutter came alongside. He recognised most of them, even at a distance. But he did not see the one he expected, and somehow, he must have known.

Tyacke was patting his pockets. "I'll be sending *Onward* home after this. Not before time!"

David Napier straightened his hat and watched the oars being tossed, side-boys already waiting to receive the cutter alongside. The captain was at the entry port, his hand raised.

Napier stood up carefully, and waited for the flag captain to leave the boat ahead of him.

Going home. Now it had a new and precious meaning.

Epilogue

It was around noon when H.M. Schooner *Druid* entered Falmouth and finally moored alongside, after her short passage from Plymouth.

A few hours, but to Adam Bolitho it had seemed endless. He had hoped to hire a carriage, if only to lessen the formality after leaving *Onward* in the dockyard, as he had on his previous return. But he had been warned that the roads might be treacherous, even impassable, as there was snow in the West Country. *Snow.* After the long haul from Freetown, it seemed unbelievable.

The schooner's master had told him more than once that his command, one of the fleet's hard-worked couriers, covered more sea-miles per year than any proud ship of the line. Especially, he added, *these days*.

Adam dismissed it, stepping ashore. The frozen ground seemed to move beneath his feet, and every impression seemed blurred and dreamlike. At least in a vehicle he could have slept. Or would he?

So many memories.

Freetown. But before that, the sea burials. Voices, faces he had come to know. And they him. "The bill," as Vincent termed it. Twelve killed, most by musket fire. Two more had died later, despite Murray's unfailing attention. Most of the other casualties should recover. But they would not soon forget that brief ferocity, or their escape from their intended fate.

Small, stark images had stayed with him, even aboard the little

Druid with her talkative master and her own sounds and busy routine. In Freetown when some extra hands had come aboard to help remove or replace damaged rigging and had been gazing around at the damage, he had heard Monteith exclaim, "We showed them!"

Midshipman Hotham had turned his back, in contempt or disgust. At any other time Monteith would have reacted very differently, but he had hurried below without a word.

And *Onward* was once again in the hands of the dockyard. There had been no serious damage to her hull, and most of the standing and running rigging had been put to rights at Freetown.

He stood breathing the cold air, his mind lingering on the one moment, above all, that he would never forget. Neither would Captain James Tyacke. The flag lieutenant had hardly been able to contain his excitement and delight when he had announced to both of them that Rear-Admiral Langley had sailed for England, having been suddenly recalled. Adam remembered Ballantyne's terse summing-up at their first meeting. *Promotion or oblivion.*

Tyacke's expression had become one of utter disbelief when the lieutenant had pointed to the rear-admiral's flag. It was now Tyacke's own.

Adam halted and looked back along the jetty. The schooner's crew were already taking on stores, and perhaps new passengers. Napier was looking eagerly toward the town, but caught his eye and gave him a smile. Recovering. Still recalling the last moments, the handshakes, embarrassed grins, or blunt relief at being alive.

Each time, it was always different. For the survivors.

He turned back and saw her standing near the carriage he had known would be here. She was wearing a full-length cloak, her head covered by a fleecy hood, which fell back as she ran toward him.

Young Matthew turned away to calm the horses, and was able to yawn hugely without showing it. They had been waiting here since dawn, or so it felt, and his feet were frozen, but this made it all worthwhile.

Adam held her tightly, but felt her flinch as something shrieked from the harbour. Had he turned, he would have seen clouds of vapour rising like smoke from one of the new and experimental paddle-steamers.

Lowenna pressed her cold cheek against his and murmured, "A new navy, Adam?"

He knew David Napier was looking across the harbour, his face alight with interest.

"*His*, not mine."

She said, "Take us home," and saw Young Matthew open the carriage door. "*If ever . . .*"

But she stopped, and said nothing more. That was yesterday.

BB
F
Kent

2011